The Love Game

Other Five Star Titles
by Kay Gregory:

Marry Me Stranger

The Love Game

Kay Gregory

Five Star • Waterville, Maine

Five Star First Edition Romance Series.

Published in 2001 in conjunction with Kay Gregory.

Cover photograph by Robert Gregory.

Set in 11 pt. Plantin by Minnie B. Raven.

Printed in the United States on permanent paper.

Library of Congress Cataloging-in-Publication Data

Gregory, Kay.
    The love game / by Kay Gregory.
       p.   cm.—(Five Star first edition romance series)
    ISBN 0-7862-3036-3 (hc : alk. paper)
    I. Title.   II. Series.
  PR9199.3G7598 L68 2001
   813'.54—dc21   00-049485

To Lorraine Kaczor,
Who always has time to listen
when I need a friendly ear.
With love and thanks.

Prologue

The instant the bell rang, mobs of shouting, shoving children surged to their feet and stampeded for the doors.

School was over for another year. Summer stretched ahead, a time of sunshine and laughter and freedom from study and alarm clocks. Or so it seemed to the eager boys and girls who, in this moment of release, forgot about boredom and rain and the endless holiday complaint, "But, Mom, there's nothing to *do*."

In the crowded hallway, a small girl with mousy brown hair and freckles across her nose missed her footing and stumbled against a lanky blond child who came strolling unhurriedly out of one of the classrooms.

"Sorry, Dolores." Tamsin, the mousy one, steadied herself against an olive green wall smeared with the prints of hundreds of dirt-smudged fingers. "I didn't see you."

"It's all right." Dolores hesitated, perhaps waiting for a break in the noisy throng streaming down the hall. "Have a nice summer, Tammy—in case I don't see you again."

Tamsin, swinging a fat brown school bag by its strap, said, "Thanks. You too." After a moment she added in a low voice, as if she knew the answer but had to ask anyway, "Do you *have* to go away to Nashville?"

Dolores nodded and let out a small sigh. "I told you I did."

"I know, but I didn't want to believe it. I wish you weren't leaving Clamshell Bay just when we were starting to be friends."

7

Dolores's smile was resigned, even a little bitter. "You'd get used to losing friends if you had parents like mine."

"I suppose so." Tamsin was doubtful. She knew the other girl's parents were country western singers, and she couldn't help wishing her own parents were as glamorous. There was nothing very exciting about a father who was a small-town bookkeeper and a mother who stayed home and kept house.

She let her school bag thump to the floor and grasped her companion by the elbow. "All that touring around, though—it must be so . . . so not dull. You are lucky—"

"I don't feel lucky." Dolores interrupted her. She leaned her head against the doorjamb. "I'd much rather stay on Vancouver Island than go to Nashville. I've only been here three months."

Tamsin's sudden enthusiasm shriveled, and she dropped her arm to her side. "It seems way shorter, doesn't it? Isn't there *any* chance? Maybe your parents will let you come back."

"I doubt it." Dolores shook her head. "They never leave me any one place for long. Last year I was in Minot, North Dakota. The year before that it was Butte, Montana. They usually dump me on some aunt or other while they go on tour. I've got a lot of aunts."

"I know. You told me. That's why I hoped this time—"

"No point hoping." Dolores brushed impatiently at a trailing length of blond hair. "Look, we probably won't see each other again, so let's say good-bye right now." She held out her hand.

Tamsin took it, though she wasn't quite sure what to do with it, then quickly let it go.

Unexpectedly Dolores leaned forward and gave her a warm hug. "It's been great knowing you," she said, and turned away without waiting for an answer.

Tamsin bent down to pick up her bag. "Yes," she murmured. "It's been great. . . ."

She watched the other girl drift languidly down the hall through the scrum of pushing, shouting students. Although Dolores looked neither to the right nor to the left, all the boys watched her progress with interest. The girls pointedly ignored her. When she reached the end of the hall, she turned and waved.

Tamsin waved back. Oh, it *was* too bad Dolores was leaving.

They hadn't really been friends, of course, but, given time, they might have been. Dolores had been in a different class—she was thirteen and Tamsin only eleven—so they hadn't talked to each other until a couple of weeks ago when a gang of boys had started teasing Tamsin about her freckles. Dolores had sauntered over to the group, arched a disdainful eyebrow and remarked that freckles were a lot cuter than the spots sported by most of Tamsin's tormentors—and wasn't it too bad they didn't have anything better to do than pick on a girl?

To Tamsin's astonishment, after a moment's gaping silence, followed by a few resentful mutterings, the jeering gang had shuffled away. In that instant she would have become Dolores's slave if the older girl had asked her.

As it was, they had struck up a conversation and discovered that they were both outsiders at school, though in different ways—Dolores because she was new, Tamsin because she was so studious and quiet. In the space of a few weeks, and in spite of the difference in their ages, the tenuous ties of friendship began to form.

Tamsin swung her bag against the wall with a dull *thunk*. She could no longer see Dolores.

It would have been nice to have a friend.

Chapter One

All right, where had it got to? The Barraby-Fines portfolio? He'd had it in his hands only yesterday.

"Tamsin!" shouted Nick Malahide, owner and chief mover and shaker of Malahide's Custom Design Furniture. "Tamsin? What's happened to the Barraby portfolio?"

Silence. He waited, but heard only the buzzing of a fly against the window and the drone of noonday traffic along South Granville Street.

"Tamsin!" Nick shouted again. "Are you out there?"

Still no answer. That meant Tamsin Brown, his trusty assistant, wasn't in her office on the other side of the door attending to his business as she was meant to be. Damn. Tamsin was always there. He glanced at his watch. Twelve-thirty. Lunchtime. But Tamsin never left the office for lunch. She always ate a sandwich discreetly at her desk. Which was exactly where he wanted her.

He waited five minutes, in case she had gone to powder her nose or whatever it was women did when they disappeared for ridiculous lengths of time to perform functions that would take men less than a minute. When she didn't come back, he swore and began opening and closing file cabinets, slamming drawers and conducting a futile and increasingly irritable search for the missing portfolio.

By the time Tamsin appeared in his office doorway at one o'clock on the nose, Nick was out for blood. Anybody's blood. Preferably the blood of whomever had his paws on that portfolio.

"Ah. Tamsin," he said, placing two fists on the kidney-shaped desk that had belonged to his father before him, and leaning on it with the kind of smile he generally saved for trainee carpenters who didn't know a rabbet from a bevel. "Good of you to spare us a moment of your valuable time."

When Tamsin—skinny, inconspicuous, compliant little Tamsin with her short, mousy brown hair and soft gray eyes—merely blinked and returned calmly to the outer office to place her ugly beige handbag in her desk drawer, Nick decided the time had come to bring her back into line.

"Ms. Brown," he said, striding up to her desk just as she sat down. "I wasn't speaking to you for the pleasure of hearing my own voice. I want an explanation for your absence."

"Sorry." Tamsin turned to study the data on her computer screen. "I didn't think to tell you I'd be out. My lunch hour *is* actually from twelve to one."

Nick drew in a breath, held it, then released it very slowly. He reminded himself that his ability to control his latent Neanderthal instincts was one of the reasons for Malahide's success.

Yes, no doubt he had given Tamsin some such schedule when she'd started as his assistant five years ago. But that didn't mean she had his permission to vanish without notice.

"You never take a lunch hour," he pointed out, narrowing his eyes to inspect her more closely. "And what have you done to your hair? It looks . . . brighter."

"I had it lightened. I've been to the hairdresser's."

"What on earth for?"

"So it would look brighter," she replied, favoring him with just the glimmer of a smile.

Nick conquered an urge to wipe it off her face. "All

11

right," he said. "I can't deny your right to take a lunch break, but I can insist you tell me when you're leaving."

"Of course. I'll remember that next time." Her smile disappeared.

Nick nodded, only partially satisfied. He didn't like the sound of that "next time." Putting his hands in his pockets, he stared down at her with the calculated concentration he usually reserved for Malahide's weightier financial affairs.

Something was different about his predictable assistant today. It wasn't her clothes. Her linen dress with matching linen jacket, both in her ubiquitous springtime beige, were eminently suitable for Vancouver in May. In December it would be brown wool skirts with matching brown wool jackets. He'd never seen her wear any other colors. But if it wasn't her clothes, what the devil had she done to herself? It wasn't just the hair. And she still had that dusting of freckles on her nose, so it wasn't makeup either.

"What's happened to you?" he asked. No point in speculating when a direct question was more likely to yield an answer. "You look different." He didn't add *Like a woman,* but he thought it.

"Nothing." Tamsin's smile was brief and demure. "I expect it's my hair. What can I do for you, Mr. Malahide?"

Nick knew a brick wall when he encountered one. Funny, he'd never thought of Tamsin as a wall. More like a useful beige sponge. She absorbed whatever instructions or information he threw her way, stored it, and released it again on demand. And she never got in the way as walls could.

He felt a further flicker of irritation. As a sponge, Tamsin suited him perfectly, and he didn't like disruptions to his office routine. With Tamsin efficiently handling the day-to-day details, he was free to deal with the actual business of running the company he had inherited from his father.

"Mr. Malahide?" Her soft voice interrupted his train of thought. "You wanted something?"

"The Barraby-Fines portfolio," he snapped. "Where is it?"

"In your desk drawer, Mr. Malahide. You put it there yourself."

He shook his head. "Think again, Ms. Brown. I've already looked in my desk."

Tamsin stood up, walked into his office and opened the bottom drawer of the kidney-shaped desk. When she straightened, she was holding a thin blue binder in her hand.

"Is this what you're looking for?" She handed it to him without batting a single pale eyelash and without saying "I told you so" which, Nick had to concede, she had good reason to do.

"Yes," he said. "It is. Thank you."

Instead of leaving, she stood there for a moment watching him, again with that annoying glimmer of a smile. He waved a hand in dismissal. "I said thank you. You can get on with whatever you were doing."

Tamsin went back to her desk. When the door behind her slammed shut, her smile expanded into an outright grin.

Mr. Malahide had actually noticed her absence. Maybe she should absent herself more often.

He was, of course, a genius when it came to attracting business. In the five years she'd been with the firm, she had seen Malahide's grow from a small, moderately successful enterprise catering to the tastes of the moderately affluent, to an up-market establishment patronized almost exclusively by the very rich and discriminating. But his brilliance didn't extend to dealing with the endless office trivia that kept his business running smoothly. When it came to mundane matters such as locating files or remembering to return important calls, Nick Malahide was your typical incompetent male. Maybe even a couple of notches below typical. At times she wondered if he'd remember to breathe if she wasn't there to remind him.

He would certainly miss a lot of appointments.

His carelessness was arrogance mostly, she'd realized long ago. Not the jumped-up arrogance of the newly rich or famous but the natural assurance that came with a consciousness of rightful authority, of knowing his status in a world of less confident mortals.

The commotion over the Barraby file was a case in point. He regarded keeping track of files as *her* job.

Tamsin was still smiling as she typed up an estimate on her computer. It wasn't taking much to make her smile today. Last night Paul had been kind and admiring and attentive, and they had got along so well that he'd asked her out. On a date. A proper date. Tonight. Just the two of them, without Dolores or any of her noisy, boisterous crowd.

To think she had almost refused to go when Dolores had pressured her into joining her group of friends at the Red Mustard Club.

"Oh, don't be such a *mole*, Tammy!" her roommate had exclaimed. "You're twenty-three years old. You can't sit home by yourself *every* night."

"I don't see why not. Susie and I often did."

"Yes, but Susie's not your roommate any longer. *I* am, and *I* like going out and having fun."

Yes, Tamsin had noticed that. It would have been hard not to after sharing the apartment with her quiet cousin,

Susie. She and Susie had grown up together in the small Vancouver Island town of Clamshell Bay, and as roommates they had suited each other well. Then, just over a month ago, Susie had announced that she'd had enough of city life. Almost overnight she had packed her bags and returned home. Dolores, courtesy of the classified pages of *The Vancouver Sun,* had replaced her.

Tamsin still found it hard to believe—not that Susie was gone but that the leggy blond who responded to her advertisement had turned out to be Dolores.

"We've met before, haven't we?" she'd asked, only minutes after taking her prospective roommate up the creaking staircase that led to her second floor apartment. "I'm sure I know you from somewhere."

Dolores, perched casually on the arm of the faded rose sofa, had allowed the sandal dangling off the end of her toes to thump onto the greenish-gray carpet. "I don't think so," she began.

"We have. I'm sure of it."

"Maybe, but I don't—"

"Got it!" Tamsin interrupted triumphantly. "Of course. Dolores Rowan. You went away to Nashville."

Dolores gave her a puzzled frown. "What? Where . . . ? I mean, yes, I've been to Nashville a couple of times. My parents—"

"Are country singers. I know. You told me."

"I did?" Dolores blinked, and Tamsin knew that her schoolmate from long ago had no recollection of those magical weeks when they had started to be friends.

"On the Island." Tamsin persisted, willing the other woman to remember. "You went to school in Clamshell Bay. I hoped—that is, I thought we might have become friends if we'd had the chance."

15

"Friends? You wanted to be friends. With me?"

Tamsin nodded with a hint of defensiveness. "Yes. I didn't have any real friends, except my cousin, Susie. And you didn't seem to have anyone either."

"You're right about that." Dolores tossed back her hair and laughed as if it didn't matter. "Girls never liked me much, and besides, I was hardly ever anywhere long enough to make friends."

"You still don't remember, do you?" Tamsin knew it was foolish to mind, but she did.

And all at once Dolores *had* remembered.

"Tammy!" she cried, jumping up to drag Tamsin out of her chair and into an exuberant bear hug. "I *do* remember you! Of course I do. But you've changed so much in twelve years! You had freckles, and gray eyes bigger than your face. And you wanted me to stay, and I wished I could." She stopped, and her arms dropped abruptly to her sides. "I meant to write, I think, but I never did. There didn't seem much point."

"No, not much." Tamsin laughed, giddy with an unexpected relief. She had never quite forgotten Dolores. It was good to be remembered too.

"I still have the freckles," she said, sitting down again. "I used to hate them."

Dolores sank back onto the sofa. "I can't believe it!" she exclaimed. "Oh, Tammy, it *is* good to see you again."

Tamsin hoped her beaming smile was answer enough. She was too choked up to reply.

After that there had been no question of Dolores living anywhere else, although Tamsin had soon found out that her new roommate was nothing like sweet, chunky Susie. A golden-haired beauty with a coterie of fun-loving companions, Dolores had a seemingly limitless supply of slavering suitors. And she had refused to take no for an answer when Tamsin insisted she wasn't the nightclub type.

"How would you know? You've never been to one," Dolores had accurately pointed out.

In the end Tamsin had given in. And, oh, she *was* glad she had. Paul was so handsome in a smooth, Latin sort of way, so—"

"Tamsin? Didn't you hear the intercom?"

She looked up. Mr. Malahide, his arms crossed, was standing in the doorway between their offices glowering. Oh, dear. He did look formidable. Yet, such was her mood today, she was willing to concede that he wasn't altogether unattractive—if you happened to like tall men with irregular features, longish bronze hair, hazel-green eyes, and lips one of his more besotted girlfriends had once told her were "to die for." They *were* unusual. Full, not terribly wide, curving at the corners with a sensuality not common in men's lips. But Tamsin didn't think she'd want to die for them. Not when they had already been sampled by so many others— none of whom seemed to last longer than a month or two.

When she had first set eyes on her boss, she'd felt a faint fluttering in the region of her stomach but had doused it at once with a liberal dose of practical common sense. Men like Nick Malahide didn't fall for women like her, and that was that.

Since then her stomach had given her surprisingly little trouble.

"What are you staring at, Tamsin? Have I grown scales? Or turned green?"

She started as his deep voice cut into her thoughts. "No, of course not, Mr. Malahide. Sorry. Um, no, I didn't hear the intercom." She had, but it hadn't really registered. "Did you want something?"

"Yes. I want you to give your full attention to your job. Do you think you can manage that?"

Ouch. He was right. She had been daydreaming.

"Yes, of course," she replied, summoning her coolest smile.

"Good. Then take these drawings down to the workshop for me, will you?" He handed her a folder. "And when you've done that, you can show Mr. Barraby and Mr. Fines into the boardroom. They should be here shortly."

"You remembered!" she exclaimed.

He laid his palms flat on her desk and nailed her with a critical green gaze. "One of us had to."

"Yes, of course." She shifted uneasily in her chair. Whatever had possessed her to call attention to his habit of relying on her to remind him of appointments? That, after all, was presumably one of the reasons he had hired her.

Eventually, taking his time about it, her boss straightened, gave her a final stringent inspection and strolled back into his office.

Tamsin watched him go. He looked good from the back. Maybe her senses were extra-heightened today because of Paul.

Mmm. Nice firm backside, ditto thighs, shoulders not *too* muscle-bound, and he had the walk of a man who knew he owned the world. She wondered how old he was. Thirty-three? Thirty-four? Not that it made a difference. From what she'd seen, he'd be past a hundred before it occurred to him that women were made for anything besides bed.

He swung around just before he closed the door, and when their eyes met, she rather wished they hadn't. Although he didn't speak, it had never been hard to tell when Mr. Malahide was displeased.

Tamsin jumped up and hurried down to the workroom with the folder.

Nick had a headache. A general bodyache, too. Now that the night was over, he wondered if the effort involved had been worth it.

Gloria, as usual, had been great. So why did he have the feeling their relationship had become a sterile waste of time? He ran a thumb along the edge of his desk. The wood wasn't as smooth as it had once been. Perhaps he should consider refinishing it soon.

How long had he been going out with Gloria? Or, more often, in? Almost three months, he supposed. Maybe it was time for a change. Yet when he first met her, he'd been convinced that at last he had found his ideal woman—a woman who wanted nothing from him beyond bed and the occasional breakfast. She had said so as forthrightly as any man, with none of the flirtatious hopefulness he had come to expect from the opposite sex. Gloria wasn't interested in marriage—a view with which he heartily concurred.

He had never been able to see why a man would willingly tie himself down with a wife and family. His father had married once—by mistake, he'd said—and had chosen not to repeat the experiment after his wife deserted him for a Hollywood stunt man, leaving him sole custodian of two energetic and bewildered little boys. The elder Nick Malahide had brought his sons up to believe women were useful for two reasons only, neither one of which was marriage.

Nick hadn't been hard to convince. He'd missed his mother, resented her leaving and on her infrequent visits did his best to ignore her. His younger brother, Dennis, was more forgiving.

Even so, in the end their mother had stopped coming to

visit. Until her death a year ago, she had sent cards on birthdays and a photocopied letter at Christmas. That had been the extent of her contact with her sons.

The hammer in Nick's head smashed down with redoubled intensity. He rubbed his temples and swore under his breath.

"Would you like an aspirin?" a solicitous voice inquired.

He switched his gaze from glowering contemplation of a particularly flashy pen given to him by a grateful female customer, to find Tamsin standing on the other side of his desk. She was still all beige, but she had even more of a glow about her this morning than she had yesterday.

Nick wasn't in the mood for glows. "Why should I want an aspirin?" he growled.

"You look tired. And kind of stiff."

Tamsin smiled so sweetly that his suspicions were instantly aroused. Why the devil couldn't she go back to being the unobtrusive, efficient office widget she had been for the past five years? Dammit, members of his staff weren't supposed to glow. And they sure as hell weren't supposed to comment on his health. Why couldn't people, especially female people, do what they had been designed to do? Gloria at least knew what she was best at. So had Tamsin—until recently.

"I am not tired. Or stiff," he added, massaging the back of his neck. "Don't you have anything to do?"

"Oh, yes, lots," she said with a cheerfulness that made him grit his teeth. "I just thought I'd ask."

As she left the room, the scent of violets wafted up his nose.

Good grief. Ms. Brown was wearing *perfume*. Nick shuddered and closed his eyes.

To his growing consternation, Tamsin continued to glow

all week. The transformation was not one of which he approved, especially when two of his male customers, on separate occasions, commented that his taste in assistants was as distinctive as his taste in furniture. When a third customer, cruder than the others, asked, "How is she in the sack?" Nick was tempted to punch him on the nose. He began to wonder if it wasn't time he hired a new assistant. Preferably one with bowlegs and buck teeth. Trouble was, he'd have to train her if he let Tamsin go.

Alternatively, he could make an attempt to get to the bottom of the assistant he already had. He smoothed a hand over his jaw. Not the most fortunate way of putting it, he supposed—but perhaps appropriate.

Tamsin was replacing the cartridge in her printer when she became aware that Nick Malahide was breathing down her neck. More or less literally. He was standing right behind her, and she knew it was him because she could smell the rich, piney scent of his aftershave. She stifled a giggle. How often had she read a line like that in a book, almost invariably followed by a longwinded description of a kiss? She turned to face her boss and had to clamp a hand over her mouth to stop herself from laughing out loud. Imagine even *thinking* of kissing Mr. Malahide.

"Is something funny, Tamsin?" he enquired.

She shook her head, speechless.

"Then unless you're planning to be sick over my shoes, I'd be obliged if you'd remove your hand from your mouth."

Tamsin swallowed hard and complied.

"Good," he said. "Now what was that all about?"

"Uh—nothing. I just, um, forgot something. And then I remembered."

"I see." He leaned down to stare into her face. "Tamsin?"

"Yes, Mr. Malahide?"

"Is there some reason you've never called me Nick?"

She returned his stare with blank disbelief. "But—Mr. Malahide, you've never asked me to."

"Hmm." He straightened, and she found herself staring at a neat gold tie stud embossed with the figure of a griffin.

"I suppose I haven't," he admitted. "You seemed comfortable with Mr. Malahide, and it didn't occur to me that . . ." He paused. "Look at me, Tamsin."

Tamsin raised her eyes to the bridge of his nose.

"That it's normal these days for staff to call their employers by their first names. Malahide's isn't some huge, faceless corporation."

"Oh, no," Tamsin agreed quickly. "It's never been like that. I'll call you Nick if you prefer it, Mr. Malahide."

Nick groaned. "I do prefer it," he said.

She nodded. "Okay. Is that all you wanted, Mr.—Nick?"

"Not necessarily."

"Oh." *Now* what was the matter with Mr. Malahide? He'd been kind of odd and broody all week. Which was irritating, because *she* felt on top of the world. She was going out with Paul again tonight. He'd taken her out three times since that first night, and although he hadn't yet kissed her properly—only a quick peck on the cheek—she was certain he meant to do it right this evening.

"I said not necessarily," Nick repeated.

"Oh. Yes. What else would you like, Mr.—Nick?"

"Your company," he said. "You've been working quite hard lately. How about I take you out to lunch?"

The cartridge Tamsin was still holding slipped and almost landed on the floor. She laid it carefully on top of the printer. When she turned back to her boss he was looking at her with that smile his women friends called sexy. Personally, she refused to acknowledge it as anything but predatory.

"I always work hard," she said. "And it's very kind of you to ask, but I'm getting my hair done again on my lunch hour."

"Why? It looks fine as it is."

"Yes, but I'm going out with my . . . my boyfriend." She used the word for the first time with shy pride. "I want it to look special."

"Hmm. Heavy date then?"

She sucked in her breath. "I don't think that's your business, Mr. Malahide."

He stared at her, his features expressionless, yet she could tell he was mildly put out. Women didn't usually turn down the chance to have lunch with him. But, of course, Nick Malahide didn't think of *her* as a woman. Not in that sense. In his well-ordered mind he had her neatly labelled *Office Only*.

"You're quite right," he said briskly. "It isn't my business. Have a good time at the hairdresser's."

Tamsin glanced at him doubtfully and went back to replacing the cartridge.

When Nick came in to work on Monday morning, he hadn't been in the office ten minutes before he noticed, with considerable relief, that his assistant's personality had returned to sponge. Not so much as a glimmer of a glow. Thank God for that.

The day passed smoothly. No files went missing, all his calls were returned, and when he wanted information about a customer's line of credit over the lunch hour, Tamsin was right there to provide it.

By five o'clock he was satisfied that his assistant had recovered from her lapse into the inconvenient world of dating and was prepared to resume her appointed role as his competent handmaiden.

His satisfaction lasted only until he stepped into Tamsin's office to tell her he was leaving to pick up Gloria, who was inclined to complain if he was late. As he paused in the doorway, he heard a sound. Not a hiccup exactly, and not a croak. More of a cross between a muted howl and a groan.

Was Tamsin entertaining a zoo on his premises? He glanced at the polished wooden floor, then past the functional line-up of filing cabinets, fax machine and printer. His eye came to rest on her square, box-like desk. For a business that specialized in imaginative furniture, he had to admit his assistant's office wasn't much of an advertisement. No plants or flowers to lighten its stark efficiency, no personal ornaments—and no zoo. No Tamsin either.

So what *was* that extraordinary noise?

"Tamsin?" he called. "Is that you?"

No answer. He approached the door to the landing. "Tamsin?"

Still no response. He moved to the top of the carpeted stairs leading down to the showroom with its careful groupings of fine furniture. The sound was louder here, but he didn't think it came from below.

A slight movement drew his gaze along the landing to a pair of cream-colored velvet curtains that concealed a window seat set into an alcove above the street. What on earth?

Ah. If he wasn't mistaken, that was the toe of a sensible beige shoe he spied in the gap between the curtains and the thick gold pile of the carpet.

Wasting no further time, Nick strode to the curtains and whipped them back.

The small beige figure crouched on the window seat gasped, and he found himself looking down into soft gray eyes that brimmed with unshed tears.

Hell! Stunned into immobility, he watched the first one break loose to forge a silvery path down his assistant's pale cheek.

After that the dam burst, and the croaking hiccups he had heard earlier turned into noisy, gut-wrenching sobs.

Nick stifled an expletive and sat down beside her to stem the flood.

Chapter Two

Tamsin drew in half a dozen long, gasping breaths, gave a last shuddering moan and fell silent.

"Better?" Mr. Malahide's voice enquired from somewhere close to her ear.

He sounded quite calm, as if he was used to women howling on his shoulder. Which he probably was, considering how quickly they came and went in his life. But—oh, dear heaven! It really *was* Mr. Malahide's expensively suited shoulder beneath her cheek, his muscular arm she was clutching and his big hand patting her back. Yet when she had first looked up and seen him standing over her gripping a handful of curtain, he'd been appalled. She knew he had. It was the look of masculine horror on his face that had somehow released all the pent-up misery and hurt she'd been struggling so hard to hold back—until the strain of remaining efficient and unflappable had become too much for her.

The window seat, with its thick, concealing curtains, had seemed an adequate temporary refuge.

Bad choice, she conceded now, as the reassuring warmth of man and muscle began to quicken her senses in a most alarming way. She was practically sitting in Mr. Malahide's lap, and her face was pressed into the smooth, quality fabric of his charcoal-gray pinstripe.

When he said "Better?" again, she raised her head a fraction and saw that the fabric in question was dark and sodden with her tears.

She nodded mutely and dabbed at the damp patch with a tissue she fished from her sleeve.

"Never mind," he said, catching her wrist. "It'll be just fine if you let it alone."

Tamsin pushed the tissue back into her sleeve and tried to lower her head, but he put a finger under her chin and tilted it up.

"Good grief," he said. "I thought women were supposed to look beautiful when they cried."

"You must know better than that." She jerked her head away and continued to study the stain her tears had left on his shoulder. The pressure of his masculine thigh against her leg was disturbingly sensual.

"Why must I?" He sounded genuinely puzzled.

"All those women you're always loving and leaving—don't they ever cry?"

"Ah. I take it you don't approve of my social life."

Did he think his free-and-easy lifestyle was funny? "No, I certainly don't," she assured him with feeling.

"Hmm. And what makes you think I'm always the one who does the leaving?"

"Aren't you?" Surprised, Tamsin looked up. He was smiling, but it was a cool smile, and she realized that, after all, he *wasn't* particularly amused.

"Sometimes. But there *have* been occasions when the lady left me, having come to the entirely accurate conclusion that I'm lousy marriage material."

"Oh. And they didn't cry?"

"A couple did. But just so you know, I don't enjoy making women cry."

"Don't you?"

"No. And if it makes you feel any better, I grew up in an all male world where tears were definitely a rarity."

"You mean they make you uncomfortable?"

"You could put it that way."

"Oh, dear."

Nick glanced at his watch, and Tamsin remembered he had an assignation with one of those women he didn't want to marry. It was in his appointment book. She must pull herself together at once.

"I'm fine now," she said, attempting to convince him with a smile.

Nick ignored her. "So," he said, taking a clean white handkerchief from his pocket and drying her face with surprising efficiency, "are you going to tell me what this is all about? The boyfriend, I suppose."

Was it that obvious? Yes, of course it was. "I do apologize," she said. "I didn't mean to bring my personal problems to work."

Nick took another look at his watch, which Tamsin suspected was even more expensive than his suit. "It's after five. You're on your own time," he pointed out. "Just remember to leave the problems at home tomorrow."

Was he angry? He didn't sound it. Merely businesslike and a little impatient.

"Of course," she said, trying to match his tone. "It won't happen again, Mr. Malahide."

"I told you to call me Nick. Look on it as a new office procedure, and follow instructions as you normally would." He patted her rear as if to emphasize his point, then seemed to realize what he was doing and abruptly moved his hand to the small of her back.

"Yes, Nick. Of course." She didn't dare look at him in case she was blushing.

"Good. Now, are you going to tell me what's the matter?"

Tamsin sniffed. He was an unlikely father confessor, and she didn't much want to tell him, although he seemed to expect it. "I'd rather not," she said. "Why do you want to know?"

"If your personal problems are likely to affect the smooth running of my office, then I want to know so that I can take whatever steps are necessary to solve them."

"But *you* can't solve them," Tamsin objected.

Nick leaned back against the wall, drawing her with him, and once more she became horribly conscious of who he was and of the fact that she was practically draped across his hip in what, under other circumstances, would have been regarded as a compromising position.

She wriggled out of his grasp and slid to the far end of the seat.

"They say it helps to talk," he said resignedly, and not as if he particularly believed it.

"It's all right. I won't do it again."

"For heaven's sake, you sound like a little girl who's been caught feeding her vegetables to the cat."

Tamsin felt her hackles rise—which was a whole lot better than feeling guilty and embarrassed. "We never had a cat," she said, purposely misunderstanding. "My mother's allergic. And, anyway, I don't think cats eat vegetables."

"Hmm." Nick said nothing for a few seconds; then his eyebrows drew together as if he'd had a thought he didn't like. "You're not going to get pregnant on me, are you?"

"Pregnant!" Tamsin swallowed an astonishing urge to laugh. Which was ridiculous, because the suggestion was offensive as well as ludicrous, and only an hour ago she had been certain she would never laugh again. "No. Pregnancy isn't in my job description," she replied, folding her hands sedately in her lap.

"What?" Nick's greenish eyes narrowed, but eventually a small, speculative smile lightened the serious contours of his face. "Very funny," he said. "Ms. Brown, you are full of surprises."

Tamsin's momentary amusement faded. She thought of what she'd lost—or actually never had. That, of course, was what hurt more than anything. And now Mr. Nick smart-ass Malahide knew exactly what a fool she had been.

She turned away to stare gloomily out at the traffic crawling bumper to bumper along South Granville. As she watched, a girl in a white dress came out of a shop across the street and was met by a young man wearing overalls covered in grease. He swung her up into his arms, and when he set her down again, her dress was covered with black spots, like the back of a dalmation. But the girl only laughed.

Tamsin felt her eyes fill with tears.

"Not again," muttered Nick, noticing. "Now see here, Ms. Brown—"

"I'm not going to cry," she said quickly.

"No," he agreed, "you're not. You're going to come with me to the boardroom, put yourself on the outside of a damned good glass of brandy, and talk."

"But you'll be bored."

He stood up and held out his hand. "Come on."

"Oh." Tamsin took it doubtfully. It felt big and warm and—oh damn—comforting. But Nick Malahide wasn't supposed to be comforting. He was supposed to be her clever, abrasive lady-killer of a boss.

She tried to pull away, but Nick firmly retained custody of her hand as he towed her into the conference room and directed her to a padded white chair with rosewood arms. A dozen such chairs circled a stately rosewood table in the center of the plushly-carpeted floor. Turning his back on

30

her, Nick went to a cabinet set into the wall and started clinking about with glasses and bottles.

"Here," he said, handing her a healthy snifter of brandy. "Drink. And sit tight for a minute. I have to make a phone call."

In less than three minutes he was back. The lines around his mouth seemed sharper than they had been, and when he sat down across from her and began to drum his fingers on the table, Tamsin guessed that someone was in for trouble. She hoped that someone wasn't her.

"Okay," he said. "Shoot."

Perhaps because of the intimidating surroundings and his boss-like behavior, it didn't occur to her not to do as he said.

"There's not much to 'shoot' about," she said, sipping her brandy and enjoying the warm feel of it sliding down her throat. "I got dumped, that's all. Happens to everyone. At least that's what Dolores—she's my roommate—says. Except nobody ever dumped her."

"She's right," Nick said. "It does happen to just about everyone. But everyone doesn't hide behind a curtain and cry until her face looks like a turnip."

"It's always a turnip," Tamsin said morosely.

"Feeling sorry for yourself, Brown? On a good day, which this isn't, there's nothing wrong with your face." He got up and poured himself a small amount of brandy. "So why did he dump you? Not because you heard non-existent wedding bells, I hope."

Tamsin adjusted the neck of her jacket and squared her shoulders. Did he think that she, plain Tamsin-the-Turnip Brown, had no business to be thinking about marriage?

"No," she said. "Why would I? I'd only known him a week."

Nick sat down again and leaned across the table so that

his face was only a foot or so from hers. "Are you telling me all this commotion is over some fellow you've known for a week? One lousy week?"

She nodded. "Yes. I know it sounds crazy—and I swear it's never going to happen again."

"It had better not. I've never heard such cr—idiocy, in my life."

"Mr. Malahide—"

"Nick."

"*Nick*. I didn't ask for your opinion. Or your sympathy. You're the one who insisted I should talk." She swallowed the rest of her drink in one gulp, choked, sneezed and stood up. "Thank you for the brandy. And now I think it's time I went home."

He didn't react at first but sat looking at her with blank hazel eyes. Then he, too, rose to his feet. "I'll drive you," he said.

"Oh no, there's no need for that. I'll take the bus as I always do."

"Where do you live?"

He didn't know? She'd been working for him for nearly five years, and she knew where *he* lived. In a big house on a hillside in West Vancouver from which he probably had a perfect view of Burrard Inlet.

"On West Sixteenth," she said. "But I can take the bus. Really, I always do."

He ignored that. "You don't have a car?"

"No. I've no use for one. I'm only a short ride from work and I take the bus whenever I go to the Island to see my parents."

"I see. What an eventful life you must lead. Come along then. I *don't* take the bus, and my car is parked in the company lot."

"There's really no need—"

"I know there's no need. Do you have a coat?"

"No. It's warm out."

"So it is." He took her arm as she turned toward the front stairs and reversed her in the opposite direction. "This way."

Tamsin gave up. She was tired, she was embarrassed, she was depressed, and she didn't really want to get on the bus wearing what Dolores called her leftover-fish face. Nor did she feel like arguing with Nick Malahide, who, sometime during the course of the day, seemed to have turned from her detached, impersonal employer into a bulldozer.

"This is it?" Nick asked, as his silver Lincoln slid smoothly to the curb in front of a two-story house built around the turn of the century.

Looking at it from a visitor's point of view, as Tamsin rarely did anymore, she saw chipped, gunmetal-gray paint, a glassed-in porch piled high with battered wicker furniture, and a front door that might once have been white but was now the color of mold.

"Yes." She was defensive. "This is it. It's not bad once you get upstairs, which is where we live."

"I'm sure it's not. Doesn't anyone live downstairs?"

"Oh, yes. Mrs. Sawchuk, her son, Barry, and their cat. Their entrance is around the side." That was all he needed to know about the Sawchuks, though by now it wouldn't be all Mrs. Sawchuk knew about him. Tamsin could see her bony face, cigarette attached to its lower lip, peering through the white net curtains covering the downstairs front window.

"I see," Nick said.

Before Tamsin could ask him what he saw, he was out of

the car and holding open her door.

Oh, she did wish he would just leave. It was going to be hard enough to live down this awful day without the added knowledge that her urbane, elegant boss had seen her home and found it wanting.

Instead of leaving, Nick followed her up the path to the porch.

"Thank you," she said, turning reluctantly to face him. "You've been very kind. I'm afraid I can't ask you in because . . ." Help! Why couldn't she? "Because Dolores may be entertaining a boyfriend," she finished. It was the first excuse that came to mind, but it proved an unfortunate choice.

"Really?" Nick's eyebrows went up. "I had no idea you lived in such a den of depravity."

"I don't. Don't be ridiculous." Tamsin turned to put her key in the lock so she wouldn't have to face the mockery lurking in his eyes.

"Then what's the problem? I'd prefer to make sure you're all right. Besides, I seem to be at loose ends this evening."

"No, you're not." She swung around automatically, quite forgetting that she didn't want to look at him. "You're meeting Ms. Van Gelder at six."

"And it's now six-thirty. Gloria took it rather badly when I called to tell her I'd be late. In fact, she hung up on me."

Oh, dear. So that was why he'd come back into the boardroom looking like the Inquisition in search of a handy heretic. And it was all her fault. "Didn't you call her back?" she asked.

"Of course not. I don't take kindly to being hung up on. So you see, I *am* at loose ends."

"Yes, but I'm sure if you took her flowers or something she—"

34

"I have no intention of taking Gloria flowers. So, are you going to ask me in or not?"

"Not," Tamsin said. "I'd be terrible company. Though I am sorry about Ms. Van Gelder."

"I'm not. It was great while it lasted, but now it's time to move on."

"Oh." How cold and hard-boiled he sounded. Poor Ms. Van Gelder was probably in tears. Well, no, on second thought she was probably sticking pins in voodoo dolls resembling Nick Malahide. Even so. . . .

"I *am* grateful," Tamsin said. "But—"

"But you want to be on your own. Okay. As long as you're sure you're all right."

Tamsin was about to ask him what difference it made, but she changed her mind when he smiled. Maybe he did care a little.

"I'll be fine," she said. "If you don't mind, I *would* like to be alone—well, except for Dolores. But that doesn't mean I don't appreciate—"

"Of course not. I'll see you tomorrow then. By the way, do me a favor and do something about those red eyes. They don't go well with beige."

Tamsin, who had been about to thank him yet again, flashed him a smoldering look and shut the door in his face.

Smart-mouthed bastard. Who did he think he was? She stomped up the musty-smelling stairs and into the apartment with her lower lip stuck out at such an angle that Dolores asked if she'd been stung by a bee.

"No." Tamsin slung her jacket over the back of a faded, chintz-covered rocker. "I've been stung by Mr. Malahide, who caught me crying and said I'm to call him Nick. And by Paul, and—oh, Doro, I don't know what to do."

"Wash your face," Dolores suggested. "Then pour yourself a glass of wine and eat your supper."

"You made dinner?" Tamsin shuddered. One of Dolores's tofu concoctions would be altogether too much on top of the day she'd just had.

"Don't look so scared." Her roommate waved a willowy arm at the fridge. "I only threw together a big salad. I didn't think you'd feel like cooking tonight."

"Oh. Thanks, Doro."

"You're welcome. So tell me what happened."

Tamsin told her.

"Men!" her roommate exclaimed sympathetically when she'd finished. "Even when they're trying to help they drive you crazy."

"I know." Tamsin sighed. "Listen, do you mind if I lie down for a bit. I've got a pounding headache."

"Sure." Dolores dropped gracefully onto the faded rose sofa. "You go off and brood. I'm going out with Richard, so you'll have the place to yourself. You can always eat later. I've had my share of salad."

"Thanks." Tamsin picked up her jacket and trailed into her bedroom, closing the door behind her with one foot.

The moment she was alone, she kicked her shoes into a corner, her purse into another, and slumped onto the bed with the blue chenille bedspread she'd brought from home.

She didn't care that her beige skirt rode up and crumpled around her hips, didn't care about anything much. She wasn't even sure what it was that depressed her the most. Paul's defection or the humiliation of being found in tears behind a curtain by her boss.

When she had phoned Paul on Saturday night to ask why he hadn't picked her up for their date, his roommate had told her he'd rushed off to deal with a family emergency. On Sunday, after she'd spent all morning and afternoon worrying, Paul had finally called, but only to tell her not to phone again.

"What?" She'd been stunned, certain she must have heard wrong. "What do you mean?"

"I mean don't call again. We're through, Tammy."

"Through? But, Paul, *why?*"

He didn't answer directly. "Did you know Dolores dumped me for some guy she met in a mall?"

"Richard. Yes. Actually, she met him years ago. He was one of her clients. But, Paul, she's *pleased* you're going out with me. I thought—"

"You thought wrong, Tammy. Not that I care what Dolores thinks. I don't need her any more than she needs me."

"Paul, she doesn't *care*—"

"I know."

Tamsin stared at an arrow-shaped mark where someone had scratched a pen down the wall next to the phone. "Are you telling me you only took me out to get back at her?"

"I suppose so. Mostly," Paul admitted. "But. . . ."

"But when she didn't care, you figured you'd get back at her by hurting me. Is that what you're saying?"

"Listen, I'm sorry." Belatedly Paul attempted to soften the blow. "You're okay, Tammy. But we weren't built to last, see, and—"

"And you've met someone else, I suppose? Good-bye, Paul."

She had been so dazed and disoriented in that moment that she'd hung up the phone on her first love with barely a pang.

It wasn't until somewhere in the small hours of the morning that her protective insulation fell away and the full force of Paul's betrayal hit her.

He had only been using her until someone more interesting came along. So much for thinking that quiet Tamsin Brown had at last overcome her natural reserve and turned into the kind of woman who could attract a handsome male animal like Paul. Well, now she knew. She wouldn't fall so fast or far again.

This morning she had felt empty, with nothing to look forward to. Before her recent venture into dating, she'd been used to that, so she went to work as usual, determined to put Paul out of her mind.

Throughout most of the day she had succeeded, mainly by keeping herself frantically busy. By late afternoon there wasn't a document left to be filed, a letter to be answered or a single phone call to be returned. She had even completed a stack of numerical filing for Sally, the receptionist who presided downstairs. After that there had been nothing for her to do except go home and cook something for dinner before settling in to read or watch TV. This was the dreary prospect that had finally sent her flying for cover behind the cream-colored curtains.

If only Nick hadn't found her.

Tamsin flung herself onto her back. How was she going to face her boss tomorrow? He'd been kind on the whole, but behind his kindness she'd sensed a certain speculation, as if he found it intriguing that his quiet, efficient assistant actually had feelings.

She plucked at the chenille beneath her fingers, and three tufts promptly came loose. All right, so there was nothing to be gained by lying here destroying her bedspread. She might more usefully put her mind to the knotty problem of how to face Mr. Malahide in the morning.

Tamsin closed her eyes, the better to concentrate, but in the end the problem proved so knotty, she fell asleep.

★ ★ ★ ★ ★

Dolores, fidgeting around the living room while she waited for Richard to arrive, heard her roommate's restless movements subside, and shook her head.

Poor Tammy. Yet it was past time her friend learned the three principles of dealing with the opposite sex. Never allow a relationship to get serious. Never let it last. Always be the one to break it off. That way the man stayed interested and didn't get the chance to break your heart.

She had absorbed that lesson herself as a teenager, when any inclination to cling had invariably been nipped in the bud by her parents' departure to wherever their next gig was booked. Sometimes they took her with them. Other times, especially once she started school, they dispatched her to live with whichever one of their multitude of relatives had not yet refused to take her in.

She crossed to the window and discovered the Sawchuks' black cat sitting on the roof of the porch contemplating an hors d'oeuvre of baby bird.

She hadn't been a difficult child, and the aunts and uncles had been sympathetic in their way, but most of them weren't wealthy, and they had grown tired of clothing and feeding the little girl their footloose siblings had so carelessly produced. As a result, Dolores had learned early not to let love or friendship assume too much importance in her life. Except for Andrew. She banged on the window to distract the cat, who twitched his tail and jumped down.

She'd been nearly eighteen when Andrew came along. In the grip of her first, and last, grand passion, she had naively believed he loved her and, on the eve of yet another move, had willingly surrendered her virginity. But when she phoned him a few days later, his mother told her he was out with Elaine, who had almost but not quite been her friend.

Tammy, though. . . . Dolores ran her thumb over a pear-shaped smudge on the glass. Tammy was different. She had come to care about her gentle, unsophisticated roommate with the dry sense of humor and sweet smile. Fortunately, Tammy's ad in the paper had appeared just when her previous roommate, a solid young man who had assured her he was gay, suddenly turned amorous. As the apartment was his, she'd had little choice but to look for other lodgings.

Enter quiet, undemanding Tamsin Brown, the first real friend she'd had. The others—the noisy, party-going crowd—were really more acquaintances than friends.

She had known the moment she recognized Tammy as the girl from Clamshell Bay that she had found the new home she was seeking.

Dolores slanted a wry glance at the closed door to Tamsin's bedroom and headed into the bathroom to apply the face that was sure to knock Richard Kerrigan dead. Well, not dead exactly—she had plans for that long, lean body of his—but at least temporarily stunned.

When she'd finished with her face, she gave the rest of herself a quick once-over in the long mirror hanging behind the door.

Not bad. Not bad at all. The clinging white dress flattered her slim figure. The rhinestone necklace and earrings might be a bit flashy, but growing up around show people had given her a taste for glitter. If Richard didn't like it—she wrinkled her nose at her reflection—well, that was just too bad.

Dolores put a hand to her throat as the imperious peal of the front doorbell announced that her latest not-quite-conquest had arrived. After a moment's pause she pushed a strap of her dress enticingly down one shoulder, flipped back her waving blond hair and sauntered down the stairs.

Never appear too anxious, that was her motto.

Richard didn't appear to be remotely anxious either. He had his back to her when she opened the door and was standing with his hands thrust casually into the pockets of gray slacks. His crown of gold hair that was almost as fair as her own lifted attractively in the breeze.

"Hi," she said in the low drawl experience had taught her men liked. "Are you coming in?"

Richard took his time about turning around. "That depends on whether or not you're ready. I'm not waiting on the step if you're planning to take half an hour to fluff your hair or add another layer of warpaint to your face."

Dolores tried not to frown, and raised her heavily mascaraed eyelashes to give him the full benefit of her cornflower blue glare. "Why did you ask me out if you dislike the way I look?"

To her confusion, Richard's aquiline features softened, and his lips, which should have been too thin but somehow weren't, curved in what appeared to be an apologetic smile. "I don't dislike the way you look," he said. "At least not the way you look under all that face paint. You see, I remember you the way you were when we first met."

"Oh." Dolores was only slightly mollified. "I don't wear makeup to work."

"I know. So why wear it now?"

"Because I like it."

Richard shook his head. "You look better without it."

Dolores felt her cheeks begin to burn beneath the makeup. "And you're extremely rude," she told him. When he made an effort to look contrite, she added grudgingly, "You'd better come in. There is something I need to do before we leave."

He shrugged and followed her up the stairs. When they

reached the top, he put a hand on her shoulder and asked coaxingly, "Am I forgiven?"

She pushed him away. "Forgiven?"

"For my extreme rudeness."

She was almost sure he was laughing at her, but just in case he wasn't, she said, "I haven't decided," and waved him to the sofa. "Have a seat, and don't make too much noise. I think Tammy's sleeping."

Richard raised a finely arched eyebrow. "I wasn't about to start yodeling. What's the matter with your roommate? Is she sick?"

Dolores didn't feel like discussing Tamsin's lovelife. Without answering, she waved a hand vaguely and disappeared into the bathroom to inspect the artistry Richard had criticized.

So much for knocking him dead. Obviously he was a man who preferred the beauty of the lily ungilded. Tamsin, too, had told her, much more tactfully, that she had a tendency to overdo what Richard had called "warpaint."

Dolores studied the silver glitter on her eyelids. She liked it. It made her feel exotic. Having parents on the stage had accustomed her to surface sparkle, and to her, overstatement was natural. The only reason she never wore makeup to work was that it was too much trouble to put on in the mornings.

She picked up a washcloth then put it down again. She was *not* going to change her appearance to suit a man. And yet, she *had* been ridiculously pleased that Richard Kerrigan remembered those weeks, over two years ago now, when he had come to her for treatment of a back injured in a para-gliding accident.

Her stomach had done a cartwheel the moment he walked stiffly into the premises she and her partners rented in downtown Vancouver.

"My doctor suggested massage therapy," he'd said, pronouncing the last two words as if he resented the very idea. "Can you see me?"

Oh, yes, she could see him all right. He wasn't the sort of man one easily missed—unless you were immune to long, tall Vikings with slate-gray eyes. Thoughtless, arrogant Vikings, she'd amended. Hadn't he ever heard of an appointment?

"I can see you this afternoon at four," she replied, remaining coolly professional with an effort.

"Haven't you anything earlier?"

"I'll see if one of the other therapists is free." She checked the appointment book for Anya and Yoko's schedules with a peculiar reluctance, then announced with feigned regret, "No, I'm sorry. The earliest I can fit you in is at four, and that's only because we had a cancellation." She had added that so he wouldn't think he could wander in any old time he pleased and expect a massage the same day.

"All right," he said grudgingly. "I'll take it."

Dolores refrained from telling him he wouldn't actually be doing her a favor, because, in a way, he would.

He came back at four o'clock, and again the next day, and after that every few days for the next three weeks. Each time she massaged and soothed his beautiful, tortured back until, in the end, the muscles relaxed and he was well on his way to regaining the strength and flexibility she guessed he had taken as a matter of course before the accident.

Richard didn't talk much while she worked on him. Once he even fell asleep. At the end of his treatment she knew only that he was an accountant with a taste for risky sports. As well as para-gliding, he enjoyed skindiving and white-water rafting. When she remarked that he was an odd sort of accountant, he said that not all accountants wore glasses and spent their weekends perusing the latest boring releases from the tax department.

Dolores hadn't seen him again until a week and a half ago, when she had spotted his unforgettable back in a charcoal gray suit in the mall at Pacific Centre. Without pausing to think what she was doing, she had run after him and caught him by the arm.

"Richard! Mr. Kerrigan," she corrected herself when he turned to look down at her with his eyebrows at an angle that made her feel like an ant being eyeballed by an eagle.

"Yes?" he said. "Do I know you?"

"Dolores Rowan. I was your massage therapist. About two years ago. I was wondering if—if you've fully recovered from your accident."

The eyebrows lowered marginally, and he nodded. "Yes, of course. Sorry, I didn't recognize you at first. And yes, I'm quite recovered. Thanks to you in part."

Dolores beamed. "I'm glad."

When he didn't reply but seemed to be waiting for something, she realized she was still gripping his arm. She dropped it at once and inadvertently brushed her knuckles across the backside of a passing teenager in black, who immediately stopped to look her up and down. She thought he was about to say something crude, but when he caught sight of Richard, he appeared to change his mind.

Dolores, annoyed, felt her cheeks begin to flush.

"I do believe the young man imagines I have a prior claim to your services," Richard remarked.

"Services?" She swallowed and fingered the top button of her red blouse. "How would he know what I do for a living?"

44

"He wouldn't, but looks can be misleading. Your skirt *is* . . . let's say on the short side."

"Oh! You don't mean—"

"It's very seductive," he assured her with a flicker of a smile. "Look, I have to go out of town tomorrow. One of my sisters is getting married. What are you doing a week from Monday?"

"I . . ." Dolores gulped. Did he think—no, he couldn't. He knew she wasn't that sort of woman. He also knew what she did for a living. "I don't know," she finished lamely.

"Good. Now you do. I'll pick you up around eight. What's your address?"

To her total befuddlement, Dolores found herself handing him her business card with her home address scrawled across the back. He took it, nodded and moments later had disappeared into a nearby shoe store, leaving her gaping after him in the middle of the busy subterranean mall.

What had happened to her just then? She was always the one in control when it came to men. But the whole episode had happened so suddenly.

And yet, in an odd way, it had seemed as inevitable as her reunion with Tamsin.

Dolores applied a further light dusting of powder to her face and changed her lipstick from plum to fuschia. If Richard thought she was about to let a man dictate her appearance, he was mistaken.

Even if he might be right about the "warpaint."

When she returned to the living room, he had taken off his shoes and was lying on the sofa with his eyes closed.

Quietly, Dolores opened the door to Tamsin's bedroom. Her roommate also had her eyes closed. Good, maybe sleep would help. She shut the door again and stood staring down at Richard's recumbent form. He didn't stir.

"Right," she muttered, and, bending down, put a hand on his shoulder and shook him briskly.

"Hmm?" he murmured, opening an eye.

"I'm ready," she announced.

Richard turned on his side and subjected her to a leisurely appraisal. When his gaze reached her face, he closed his eyes again.

Dolores put her hands on her hips. "So, where are we going?" she demanded.

To her relief, Richard at once swung his feet to the floor. "Wherever you like," he said. "I'm told you're a girl who likes dancing. Is that right?"

"Yes. Yes, it is. How did you know?"

"A couple of my diving friends said they used to go out with you. That's how I found your clinic in the first place."

Dolores frowned. "They couldn't have been my clients. I don't date clients."

He gave her a very masculine version of a Mona Lisa smile. "Maybe not. But they said you had nice hands."

"Oh." She had no intention of giving him an opportunity to take that one any further. "Do *you* like dancing?" she asked.

"It depends on my partner." He grinned. "In your case, I expect I'd like it very much. How about Bentley's? I hear they have a good band. The kind you can sometimes hear yourself think over."

Dolores wasn't sure she wanted to think. Not with Richard looking at her in that funny, speculative way that made her dream of tumbled sheets and warm bodies and long limbs lazily entwined.

"Bentley's will be fine," she said.

Richard stood up and, taking her hand, led her down the narrow stairs and out into the soft May evening.

The rhododendron bushes in the garden across the road nodded their crimson heads in the breeze.

Mrs. Sawchuk, peering through the window behind them, remarked to her teenage son that that blond floozy from upstairs was on her way out with another man.

Barry Sawchuk grunted, waited for his mother to turn her back and helped himself to three of her cigarettes.

Chapter Three

The breeze had died down by the time Richard and Dolores reached Bentley's. The air had turned clammy, and the clouds gathering above the mountains hovered darkly against a backdrop of sickly yellow sky.

"Hmm. Smells like thunder," Richard said as he hustled Dolores inside.

"I love thunderstorms. All that electricity, I suppose. It makes me feel so alive."

It would, Richard thought. Ms. Dolores Rowan had a talent for generating her own brand of electricity. It didn't surprise him that she was drawn to the more elemental kind.

He studied the top of her pale gold head as they sat nursing their drinks in a corner of the rainbow-painted, flamboyantly modern nightclub attached to one of Vancouver's older and better hotels. The four-man, one-woman band was blasting out a song he'd never heard before, and he wasn't sorry when they finished with a rousing rumble of drums and ambled off for their break.

Dolores sat pensively stirring her spritzer. She was an unusual creature. Beautiful, certainly, but beauty alone had never impressed him much. He liked intelligence and personality as well, which this woman had in abundance, although her taste in makeup and clothes left something to be desired. Richard stroked a hand across his mouth to erase a smile.

He had been intrigued two years ago when her skillful

fingers had prodded and massaged his battered body back to health. But he'd been with Elizabeth then, and he wasn't a man who believed in changing partners along with the seasons—or playing musical beds, as Elizabeth had called it.

The memory of Elizabeth came unexpectedly, with a rush of regret that made him restless.

"Want to dance?" he asked when the band returned to work.

Dolores looked up from her spritzer. "Sure. That's what we came for, isn't it?"

"I suppose it is." Richard wasn't entirely sure why he'd suggested Bentley's, or even why he'd asked Dolores out. He stood and held out his hand. "Coming?"

She nodded and touched her fingertips to his, following him onto a dance floor that was scarcely bigger than his kitchen.

Richard breathed in the scent of sandalwood. Thank heaven Dolores's preference in perfume was more subtle than her makeup.

His thankfulness didn't last long. As the two of them moved slowly beneath the flickering orange lights, without warning Dolores swayed forward and wrapped her arms around his neck. Heat stirred in his groin as she pressed herself against him. Slinky silk shimmied across his abdomen.

"You don't suffer many inhibitions, do you?" he said in a voice that wasn't as steady as he would have liked.

Dolores tipped her head back and laughed into his face. "No. If I want something, I go after it. I don't see the point in hanging back."

The beat of the music intensified, mingling with the distant sound of thunder, winding itself around his senses like a drug. Dolores continued to move her voluptuous body in an unmistakable dance of seduction until, in desperation, he detached her arms from his neck and held her firmly away.

Evidently she hadn't been kidding when she said she went after what she wanted. But that didn't mean he was about to give it to her as if he were no more than some likely stud she'd picked up in the mall.

"Cut it out," he said. "I told you I liked dancing with the right partner, not making love in public with all my clothes on."

Dolores giggled. "Now there's an intriguing thought."

Richard didn't think so. Turning her around, he put a hand on the small of her back and guided her back to their corner table through a maze of dark red chairs, fake mahogany tables and plaster columns ringed with colored lights.

"I wanted to dance," Dolores protested.

Richard could tell from the sparkle in her eyes that her pretty pout was mostly for show.

"No, you didn't," he said. "Not really."

She laughed. "You're right. I don't mind either way. What do *you* want to do then? Shall we go to your place?"

"No!" Without meaning to, he had raised his voice, causing the entwined couple at the next table to break out of a cloud of sweet-scented smoke to stare at them with blank-eyed concentration.

"Okay, okay," Dolores said. "I was only asking. Do you live with your parents or something?"

"Good grief, no. I promise you I'm old enough to be let out on my own. My parents retired to Santa Barbara five years ago. I have an apartment in West Vancouver just across the Lions Gate Bridge."

The couple at the next table lost interest and after sharing a couple of long puffs, returned to their former tangled clinch. The band began a new set, slower and more sensuous than before. Another rumble of thunder, closer this time, got caught up in the sultry beat of the drum.

"Then why can't we go there?" Dolores asked. He noticed a slight sheen of moisture on her lips.

"Because I'd rather get to know you here." He had a feeling he already knew more than he wanted to. Yet something about this engaging, uninhibited woman inspired fantasies he'd never dreamed of with Elizabeth.

Dolores sighed with overplayed resignation, twisted sideways in her chair and crossed her legs. "All right. What can I tell you? You already know what I do for a living."

"So I do." He hid a smile as she played with her glass and her hair, the picture of bored acquiescence. "What I don't know is why you chose that particular line of work. Massage therapy doesn't seem like every young girl's dream."

Dolores shrugged. "I had to do something when I finished high school. Then I met this man I wanted to know better who happened to be studying massage. It sounded interesting, and I liked the idea of doing something to help people feel good." She opened her white beaded purse, took out a tissue and dabbed her lips. "Around the same time, the only uncle I'd never actually stayed with died and left me some money, so I decided to put it to good use. I took a two-year course, moved in with a couple of other students and that was it. End of story."

It wasn't, but it was part of it, Richard supposed. He knew about her unsettled childhood—she'd mentioned it casually while working on his back. Perhaps, in a way, her choice of career did make some kind of sense, even though the man she had wanted to know better was apparently no longer around.

"You like helping people, but you don't want to bring their problems home with you. Is that it?" Richard asked.

Dolores stopped fidgeting. "How did you know?"

"Just a guess." As smoke drifted their way from the next table, he asked offhandedly, "You have no problem working with partners then? Or getting along with your roommate?"

"What gives you the idea I'm hard to get along with?" Dolores wriggled her shoulders unobtrusively until both white straps slid down. She followed that maneuver with a smile of pure, unapologetic seduction.

Before Richard could respond, another clap of thunder shook the building. A woman screamed, and a man's voice growled, "Ah, shuddup, Lily. It's only noise."

Richard leaned forward to push the white straps back into place. "Not hard to get along with," he said. "Just hard to hang on to."

"Not necessarily. My two partners and I have been together for over four years. We met at massage school."

"And you're good friends?"

"Good partners anyway. They're both engaged, so we don't see much of each other outside working hours."

Yes, that was exactly what he'd thought. She was a woman who made acquaintances more easily than friends. "What about your roommate?" he asked. "Is she strictly business too?"

Dolores picked up her glass, took a minuscule sip and put it down again. "Tammy? No. She . . . she's more than that."

Why the hesitation? It was almost as if she was afraid to own up to having a friend. He felt a stirring of unexpected compassion. "I suppose you could rent an apartment of your own if you wanted to," he said.

She grimaced. "Not easily. Our practice doesn't exactly earn us a fortune. Anyway, I'm used to having people around. I've moved a lot, but I haven't actually been alone much."

Just lonely, Richard guessed with another stab of understanding. Yet why should he feel sorry for this outgoing, fun-loving hedonist whose project-of-the-month he suspected he was about to become? And how long would he last if he let her have her way?

Just then Dolores recrossed her legs, in the process hitching up her skirt and drawing his gaze to their endless length. The mild amusement he'd been feeling turned into a most explicit ache.

At least dancing would give him an excuse to move. "Will you behave yourself if I ask you to dance again?" he asked.

Dolores grinned. "I doubt it. But you won't find out if you *don't* ask me."

"You have a point," he agreed drily, and stood up.

He held out a hand to pull her up beside him, but before she could move, thunder crashed directly overhead, and the air reverberated with a sound like a thousand cannons going off at once.

Seconds later all the lights went out.

The band screeched to a halt, and a cacophony of screams and moans broke out. In the sudden darkness, Dolores suppressed a gasp that was more excitement than fear. It was blacker than night in the windowless club, making it impossible for her to distinguish Richard's tall figure from all the other shadowy moving shapes.

"Don't worry," his voice murmured close to her ear. "They'll have everything fixed up in no time."

Dolores wasn't worried, but she took advantage of the opportunity to reach for his hand—and found herself clutching his knee. Even better. She slid her palm slowly up his thigh.

Richard grunted, and then his hands were gripping her waist, lifting her out of her chair, holding her briefly suspended in the air, then thumping her down into his lap. At least she hoped it was *his* lap. He'd been standing when the lights went out.

"How do you know it's me?" she asked.

"I don't." A firm male palm explored the contours of her back and came to rest at the bottom of her spine. "But you'll do."

"Oh! How—" Her words were snapped off as someone crashed into a nearby table, shoving it so hard that it caught the back of the chair they were sitting in and sent them sprawling onto the floor.

A man swore. There was another crash, more swearing and the sound of someone hitting a wall.

Dolores lay still as what was probably the remains of her spritzer trickled down her back.

From somewhere in the darkness an authoritative voice shouted, "No cause for panic, people! Please remain in your seats. We'll have the problem under control very shortly."

"Not the problem I'm under," Richard muttered as Dolores, who was sprawled on top of him, gave a little wriggle to avoid the dripping spritzer. "If you don't cut that out," he snapped, "you're going to find yourself in a very embarrassing position once the lights come back on."

"Good," she said, sliding a hand down his hip. "Mmm. You smell nice. That mixture of whiskey and pine is my favorite."

Richard growled something unintelligible. At the same

moment light flared briefly as someone struck a match and the voice of authority announced with confidence, "Just a few more minutes, ladies and gentlemen. Thank you for your patience."

Another light flashed across the wall behind their heads and stayed on, casting a sepulchral glow over silhouettes of tables, chairs and indistinct human figures. Security had arrived with an emergency lantern.

Dolores found herself being rolled unceremoniously onto her back, then Richard was standing over her. "Get up," he said in a voice that didn't brook argument.

She got up.

Immediately her hand was seized in a grip that not even a hopeless optimist could call lover-like. She was an optimist but not a hopeless one.

"Let's get out of here," he said.

"But we're supposed to stay seated."

"Yes. And when have you ever done what you're told?"

"Most of my life," Dolores said, aggrieved. "I didn't have much choice."

"You haven't much choice now," Richard assured her. "Come on, we're leaving. I've had enough of this."

She wondered if that meant he'd had enough of her.

As he led her in the direction of the exit, dimly visible in the soft glow of the lantern, a rustling and murmuring and scraping of chairs started up. By the time they reached the doorway, half the people in the club were on their feet.

"Please remain seated," the now familiar voice pleaded, albeit with less authority than before. "Everything will soon—"

At that moment the lights came on.

"—be under control," the voice finished triumphantly as another peal of thunder shook the building.

"I wouldn't count on it," Richard muttered, towing Dolores around a table under which a shaking couple crouched in each other's arms, and into a long corridor with floor-to-ceiling windows along one wall. Outside, lightning forked across the sky, illuminating the way to the main doors.

"Want to wait for the storm to pass?" Richard asked. "Or shall we make a run for it?"

"Let's run for it. It'll start to rain in a minute."

She was right. Just as they gained the shelter of Richard's gleaming white Corvette, the heavens opened to release the deluge the thunder had preceded. Within seconds the parking lot had become a sea, and the rain streaming down the windows in relentless silver sheets made it impossible to see what lay beyond.

"I guess we sit this one out," Richard said, resting an arm along the back of her seat. "I'll take you home as soon as it's over."

"But it's early yet."

"Yes. I'm sorry."

"Did I do something wrong?"

"Tell me," he said, not answering her directly, "do you always fall into bed with a guy on the first date?"

Oh, dear. This was worse than she'd thought. Though, in fact, she *hadn't* really thought. Instinct had beckoned, and she'd followed. "That's not fair," she said. "We haven't fallen into bed."

"No." He wrapped the fingers of his right hand around the steering wheel. "But I got the distinct impression that's what you had in mind. Didn't you say something about going after what you wanted and getting it?"

"Yes, but I didn't mean. . . ." She stopped. Richard wasn't looking at her but at the rain swimming down the windows. His profile reminded her of a hawk on the lookout for prey. "I suppose I *did* mean," she admitted. "But of *course* I don't always. The truth is, I thought you were only playing hard to get. Most men like it when I make the first move."

"I'm no different from most men," he replied, still without looking at her. "But I don't much like the idea that I'm nothing more than the flavor of the week. One in a long line of flavors."

"I see." Dolores opened her purse, pulled out a tissue and blew her nose. "Look, there have been a few, but not a long line. I only do it with men I really like."

"And I only do it with women I more than like. Ones I mean to keep."

Thunder rumbled gently in the distance, and the assault of the rain slackened to an unrelenting drizzle.

Dolores crumpled the tissue in her fist. "But you haven't kept . . . I mean you're not married, are you?"

"No, I'm not. Why? Do you draw the line at married men?"

She twisted in her seat to face him. "Of course I do. What do you take me for?"

"A very beautiful woman with the morals of an alley cat, who is desperately afraid of getting hurt."

"Why don't you look me in the eye and say that?" Dolores demanded. "And what makes you think I'm afraid of getting hurt?" She shoved the tissue back into her purse and closed it with a snap. Who the hell did this man think he was? And what gave him the right to judge her morals?

"Aren't you?" he asked, turning to face her at last and dropping a casual hand onto her shoulder. "Afraid?"

"No. I'm not afraid. But I learned early on that it's best not to rely too much on other people."

"Haven't you ever met a man—or woman—you could

57

trust not to let you down?" He wound a lock of her hair around his thumb, his nail lightly grazing her neck.

"I don't know. My cousin, Harry, I guess. I lived with his family for a year. And Tammy, perhaps."

"But no men outside of family? You never gave them a chance, did you?"

Dolores pushed at his hand and turned her head away. The drizzle was at last tapering off. "What makes you think you know so much about me?"

"You forget, I knew two of your discards. Apart from that, our backgrounds are alike in a way, except that I have a brother and three sisters. I was an army brat. Like yours, my people never stayed long in one place."

"But at least you *had* a family."

"So did you."

"Yes, but they kept pushing me off onto relatives. Oh, I don't mean they didn't love me." She swung to face him and saw him frown. "They did, of course. It's just that their own needs always came first. Still do, as far as that goes." A car door banged shut somewhere in the parking lot. When it was quiet again, she went on in a softer voice, "I haven't seen my parents for over a year. Your family wasn't like that, was it?"

"No. We were always close. Moving about as often as we did, we had to be able to count on one another, especially when Dad wasn't there."

"Didn't your mother mind his being away?"

"Of course she minded. Just as you minded being left. It wasn't easy for her. That's what made me decide I wasn't going anywhere near the army when the time came to choose a career. I picked something sensible and settled that would keep me in one place."

"Like being an accountant who para-glides and crashes

58

into mountains?" As one who often dealt with the consequences of risk-taking, Dolores hadn't much patience with people who deliberately courted injury.

Richard laughed, the tips of his fingers gently caressing her neck. "I suppose that's where my father's adventurous streak came out. My brother climbs rocks for recreation."

"The rain's almost stopped," Dolores said.

Richard nodded. "I know. Want me to take you home?"

"I suppose so. You don't like me much, do you? *I'm* not one of those women you want to keep."

The beginnings of a smile lifted the edges of his long mouth. "Now you're making me sound like Bluebeard."

"And you're not answering my question."

"That's because I don't know the answer. I asked you out because I found you interesting. I didn't expect to find myself fending you off."

As there didn't seem anything to say to that, Dolores asked, "How come you *haven't* actually kept anyone, Bluebeard? Wouldn't they have you?"

He didn't answer at once, and when she saw a muscle pulling tight along the line of his jaw, she suspected she had stepped on forbidden ground. But eventually he said, "There haven't been that many. A couple of cases of puppy love that ran their course, a girl I thought I wanted to marry but who married someone else. . . ." He paused. "And Elizabeth. She and I were together for over two years. We would have married eventually. But she died."

"Oh! Oh, I am so sorry." Richard's pain, in spite of his determination not to show it, was appallingly evident, if only from the harsh timbre of his voice.

"It's not your fault. She felt ill one night, and in the morning she was dead. No warning. No one knew she had a heart problem."

He gripped the wheel so hard, Dolores was afraid his knuckles would crack. "Oh, Richard." Instinctively she touched his hand, wanting to comfort him. "How terrible for you. I—I wouldn't have asked if I'd known."

"No?" He sounded vaguely surprised. "No, I guess you wouldn't."

What an odd thing to say. He *guessed* she wouldn't. In the dimness his profile gave little away. Had he really thought she went around asking questions calculated to hurt? She folded her hands in her white silk lap and concentrated on the droplets of water shimmering on the windshield.

They were silent for a while, then Richard said, "We can go now."

"Yes." Dolores nodded as he switched on the engine and pulled out of the parking lot with water shooting out from under the tires.

The moment they reached the house on West Sixteenth, Dolores jumped onto the sidewalk, leaving Richard no time to open her door. Her shoes at once filled with water. Even so, she was at the top of the porch steps before he caught up with her.

"It smells nice out," she said inanely, scrabbling to fit her key into the lock. "Fresh."

Richard ignored that. "Why won't you look at me, Dolores?"

When he spoke to her in that soft, sexy velvet voice, it didn't occur to her not to do as he asked.

"Don't run away from me," he said. "You took me by surprise, that's all."

"Surprise?"

"With your questions. And in other ways too. But I didn't mean to hurt your feelings."

"You didn't." She spoke quickly. Too quickly. "I don't

allow my feelings to be hurt."

"Lucky you. Nevertheless, I apologize. Will you at least allow me to say good night?"

"All right," she said cautiously. "Good night."

"No, I meant like this."

She offered no resistance when he tipped up her face and kissed her very gently on the lips.

Nor did she respond.

She was afraid that if she did, she would cry. Which was ridiculous because she never cried.

As usual, the stairs creaked as Dolores made her way up to the apartment. Tamsin, only fitfully asleep, heard her come in and sat up.

"Doro? Is that you?" she called.

"Of course it is."

Tamsin watched her bedroom door open to reveal her roommate, disheveled, breathing much too fast, her blue eyes unnaturally bright.

"Who did you want it to be?" Dolores asked. "Loverboy from the office?"

"Don't be silly. Nick isn't interested in me."

"More fool him." Dolores crossed the room and perched on the end of Tamsin's bed. "Oh, Tammy, I think I've blown it. We're quite a pair, aren't we?"

"I suppose so." Tamsin was doubtful. She had never thought of herself as remotely on a par with the glamorous Dolores. "What's the matter then? What did you do?"

"I put Richard off. And I really like him."

"You did? How? You never put men off. That's my job."

"Now who's being silly?"

Tamsin didn't believe she was being silly. Just realistic. "So what actually happened?" she asked, swinging her legs over the side of the bed and pulling down her hopelessly wrinkled skirt.

Dolores tugged absently at a strap of her dress. "I scared him away, I think. He . . . he asked me if I always fall into bed with a man on the first date."

Tamsin forced herself to ignore the sudden stab of envy pricking her normally sympathetic heart. *She* had never had the opportunity to fall into bed on *any* date. "Did you?" she asked. "Sleep with him?"

"No, but I would have. Funny, I've never wanted to that badly before. I mean, it's never desperately *mattered*." Dolores abandoned the strap and put her hands in her lap. "We went to Bentley's, and all the lights went out in the storm."

"Storm?"

"Tammy! Don't tell me you slept through it. You're supposed to be too grief-stricken to sleep."

"Then I must be getting better." Tamsin spoke more tartly than she'd intended. "Go on. What happened then?"

"We—that is, the chair we were sitting in—got knocked to the floor. It was pitch black and kind of scary in a way, but I felt safe with Richard, as though nothing bad could happen as long as he was there. And I felt sexy, so I—"

"Did what comes naturally," Tamsin finished drily. "At least I suppose it does."

"It does. But, no, I didn't. I tried to, but Richard wouldn't let me. And then the lights came on."

Dolores looked so woebegone that Tamsin might have laughed if she hadn't felt so sorry for her friend, who was used to having things her own way when it came to men. Her simple refusal to acknowledge any obstacle that made the mistake of crossing her path had generally made such obstacles disappear. Apparently not this time. For once the two of them *were* in the same boat.

Tamsin knew that her roommate's distress shouldn't make her feel better about Paul and the events that had followed his betrayal, but somehow it did help to know that even Dolores could be vulnerable.

"Are you sure it's hopeless?" she asked, anxious now to see her friend's natural optimism restored. "I mean, he'll probably call you tomorrow. And, anyway, you've always said there's no point getting too serious about a man, that it's best to walk away before that happens."

"Yes." Dolores smiled ruefully. "Only this time I didn't get a chance to walk away." She sighed. "It's probably good for my character, but I have to say I don't like it."

"No," Tamsin agreed. "It hurts. Are you sure it's over? You could always call him." She thought of her own abortive phone call to Paul and added, "Though perhaps that's not a good idea."

"It's not," Dolores said gloomily. "He'd be even more convinced I'm one of those Greek thingies that lure sailors onto rocks."

"Sirens," Tamsin said.

"Whatever. Anyway, that's what he thinks."

Privately, Tamsin thought Richard sounded as though he had a lot more sense than most of Dolores's boyfriends, but she didn't want her friend to be unhappy. Her roommate's exuberant good spirits always lifted her up when she was down, and although she felt a bit of a traitor to Susie, she had to admit Dolores's cheery presence in the apartment had brightened the atmosphere a lot.

"Sleep on it," she suggested. "You'll probably feel better in the morning. Or you'll think of some way to fix it."

"Did *you* feel better when you woke up this morning? You didn't look it." Dolores, untypically, seemed determined to remain pessimistic.

"No," Tamsin admitted, "but I will tomorrow. Paul's gone, and I really don't want him back. As for Nick Malahide, he doesn't like changes to office routine. I expect he'll behave as if the whole awkward business never happened."

Dolores nodded agreement and left for her bedroom, leaving Tamsin to remove her clothes, pull on her cotton nightgown and crawl back into bed.

Of course Nick would want to forget this evening's scene as much as she did. She needn't worry. Everything would go on as it had before.

This comforting conclusion kept Tamsin going nicely until shortly after ten the next morning, when Nick arrived at the office bearing roses and his usual distant smile.

"Good morning, Mr.—Nick." Tamsin kept her features expressionless.

"Good morning. Here, these are for you." He dumped the roses, long-stemmed yellow ones, onto her desk on his way through her office.

Tamsin's mouth fell open, and she started to rise from her seat. Then, pulling herself together, she remembered her resolve to remain cool and businesslike at all times. No more tears, no more hastily suppressed giggles and definitely no more noticing Nick's looks. No more even *thinking* about his looks. Paul had been a bad enough mistake.

"For me?" she asked in what came out as a very unbusinesslike squeak.

Nick stopped halfway across the room. "I said they were for you. Why are you squeaking at me?"

"I'm not squeaking. I'm surprised, that's all. Thank you very much. It was thoughtful of you." Tamsin sank back into her chair, determined to maintain her dignity.

Nick shrugged, not troubling to turn around. He had a sexy shrug. She watched the muscles tighten beneath his jacket.

Stop it Tamsin. Just stop it! Removing her gaze forcibly from the arresting line of her boss's shoulders, she made herself concentrate on a potential customer's preferences in hand-carved patio furniture.

"It was, wasn't it?" she heard Nick say behind her. "Thoughtful of me. Your office needed brightening up and I decided you were a much more deserving cause than Gloria."

"Thank you," Tamsin muttered again, perplexed.

His door closed with a soft thud, and she wondered why she felt as if she'd just missed a backhand at tennis, a game she hadn't played since her school days.

Abandoning the request for hand-carved furniture, she made her way down to the showroom to pick up a vase for the roses. By the time she returned after stopping to talk to Sally, almost fifteen minutes had passed.

Nick was waiting for her. He had made himself at home on a corner of her desk and was swinging an elegant leg back and forth in a manner that raised goose bumps on her arms. It had never occurred to her before that legs could be intimidating.

"Well?" he asked. "Feeling better today?"

"I'm fine." Tamsin put down a white pottery vase without looking at him.

"Good." He leaned forward until his eyes were on a level with hers. "Ah, yes. Excellent. I much prefer gray eyes to red."

Tamsin waved at the vase and said, "Excuse me. I have to fetch some water."

"Of course." His smile sent her scurrying out the door so fast, she almost forgot the vase. Did he honestly think she *cared* what color eyes he favored?

She peered into the mirror above the sink in the ladies' room. Yes, her eyes were gray, ordinary gray, with sandy eyebrows. Nothing special but definitely not red. She fidgeted with the vase, filled it, decided it was too full, emptied it and started again. Maybe if he got tired of waiting, her impossible boss would go back into his office and stay there.

He didn't.

When she could delay her return no longer, Tamsin found him sitting exactly where she had left him, still swinging his leg and looking as if he had no plans to move before Christmas.

She came to a halt in the doorway.

Nick nodded at the roses. "Finish what you're doing," he said.

"Thank you," Tamsin replied, then wished she hadn't. Of course she was going to finish what she was doing.

Placing the vase on the edge of her desk, she picked up the roses carefully so as not to prick herself and pushed the stems one by one into the water.

"You filled it too full," Nick remarked as a puddle began to spread around the base of the vase.

"Oh, is *that* the problem?" Tamsin grabbed a handful of tissues from a box in her drawer and began to dab at the puddle.

Nick picked up the vase and held it while she dried underneath. "Sarcasm, Tamsin? How unlike you."

He was right. It *was* unlike her to be sarcastic. Oh, if only things could go back to being the way they had been. Before Paul. Before yesterday.

"Is there something I can get you?" she asked when Nick showed no signs of leaving.

"Not at the moment."

"Oh. Well, thank you again for the roses." Maybe he was

66

the kind of man who expected effusive gratitude. "They're beautiful."

"Are they? I wouldn't know. Women seem to like them."

"Don't you?"

He shrugged. "I've no opinion on the matter. We didn't have flowers around the place when I was growing up."

If that was her cue to ask him about that all-male boyhood he'd mentioned, she wasn't going to. It would seem too intimate. "What a shame," she said, moving the roses to the windowsill and taking a moment to listen to a flock of starlings holding a convention on the roof across the road.

"You think so? Are you a gardener then, Tamsin?"

She turned to face him reluctantly. "No, I'm your assistant. And I do have work to do, so. . . ."

"So you'd like me to get off your desk."

"If you don't mind."

"And if I do mind?"

Tamsin sighed. "I'd still like to get on with my work."

"What a very dedicated employee you are. But I suppose I shouldn't complain, since that's the reason I hired you."

"I've always done my best." Tamsin was offended without quite knowing why.

"So you have." He stood up, and at once she seized the opportunity to repossess her desk and start punching keys on her computer. Any keys.

When she heard his door swing shut, she dropped her hands into her lap and let out a sigh of relief.

Right. Nick Malahide had had his morning's entertainment. Perhaps now they could return to the distant but amicable relationship that had served them well for five uneventful years.

The following morning her hopes in that regard were dashed the moment Nick walked into the office. He was carrying a small flowerpot containing something green, prickly, misshapen and, in Tamsin's view, faintly obscene.

"For you," he said, presenting it to her with a flourish.

"Why?" Tamsin asked before she could stop herself. "I mean—"

"You mean, 'Thank you, Nick. How kind of you.' Am I right?"

"Of course," Tamsin said woodenly.

"Tell me something." He parked himself on her desk again before she had a chance to stand up. "What does it take to make you smile? I tried roses, I tried cactus, which, in the circumstances, I thought might be more appropriate, and—"

"I've never found plant life especially funny," she interrupted. "But I'll smile if you'll let me get on with these estimates."

"No," Nick said. "No, I don't believe it. Science hasn't perfected an office robot yet. Or are you part of some top-secret experiment?"

"Nick," Tamsin said desperately, "you were perfectly satisfied with my work until—well, until I made a fool of myself the other day. And you never made personal remarks. Please, can't we go back to where we were?"

"But we weren't anywhere," Nick pointed out.

There was a funny glint in his eye she didn't trust. "Right," she agreed. "We *weren't* anywhere. And you weren't sitting on my desk."

"Ah." Nick nodded. "So that's the problem. All right, point taken. I'll leave you to guard your territory in peace." He stood up, put his hands in his pockets and strolled unhurriedly out of her line of vision.

Tamsin picked up a black felt pen and drew a picture of a dagger on her blotter.

Chapter Four

Richard hung up the phone and swung his chair around to face his partner. "Now I know why you passed Lee and Lee on to me," he said. "It had nothing to do with the fact that you're off on your honeymoon next week. Admit it."

Mark Fletcher, a small man with a red mustache and deceptively innocent eyes, smiled gently and admitted it. "Messrs. Lee and Lee haven't grasped the necessity of keeping accurate records," he explained. "They believe that if a sale isn't recorded, they can't be expected to pay tax on it—which might even work if they'd agree to accept payments in cash. But they won't."

"So I've noticed. So have the government auditors." Richard extracted his legs from beneath his desk, and wandered over to the windows of Kerrigan and Fletcher's offices on the sixteenth floor of a modern, downtown highrise. "Why, Mark? You're just as capable of handling this mess as I am."

"Yes, but the auditors are women." Mark pretended absorption in the fat black file on his desk. "You're better at women than I am."

"That's a hell of an excuse from a man who's about to be married."

"Carla's different." Mark spoke with finality. "She's not susceptible to the kind of charm you have in spades—whether you're aware of it or not."

Richard watched two freighters chug slowly past each other in the gray waters of Burrard Inlet far below. "Nice try," he said, then added with a bland smile, "Is that why Carla's marrying *you?*"

"You'd better ask her." Mark's chair scraped back, and Richard turned from abstracted contemplation of passing shipping to discover that his partner was headed out the door.

"Hold it!" he said. "What about Lee and Lee? I need more information."

"There isn't any." Mark waved cheerfully. "See you later. I'm meeting Carla for lunch."

The door slammed, and a moment later Richard heard the whine of the elevator descending.

He swore, briskly and unsatisfactorily, and for at least the hundredth time wondered what had possessed him to go into partnership with a man he'd met at a poker game. As usual, he came to the conclusion it was probably the same impulse that had led him to take up para-gliding, diving and white-water rafting as hobbies. He enjoyed taking risks.

With Mark around life had no chance of becoming dull. His partner was a competent accountant who had flashes of occasional brilliance, but he also had a habit of acquiring accounts that turned out to be more work than their business was worth. Inevitably, sooner or later, those accounts ended up on Richard's desk.

He'd have to have a talk with Mark when his partner came back from what would undoubtedly be a long and leisurely lunch.

Better at women, my eye! Richard raked a hand through his hair. He ought to introduce Mark to Dolores.

Damn the woman. There she was again, popping into his mind like a mosquito that wouldn't go away.

He slammed the heel of his hand against his forehead

and loped back to his desk, where he picked up a brass paperweight, weighed it absently in one hand and contemplated hurling it at his partner's untidy desk.

He didn't do it—not because he was particularly fond of Mark at the moment, but because he knew that when it came right down to it, the cause of his ill-humor had very little to do with Lee and Lee. He rather enjoyed a challenging account.

When it came to women, though—well, that was a different matter. In the opposite sex he admired stability, loyalty, intelligence and a gentle disposition. Dolores was intelligent, but he didn't see her as either gentle or particularly stable. As for loyalty—maybe in certain areas of her life. Yet he couldn't imagine her trailing around the continent after a man, as his mother had willingly done for so many years. Dolores would follow no man's lead unless it suited her.

He might as well face it. Dolores Rowan wasn't his kind of woman. She was wild, extroverted, she dressed with a total lack of restraint and she attracted far too much attention of the wrong kind.

He was willing to bet she had never even heard of the ubiquitous, "little black dress."

So why was he prowling around his office cursing Mark when what he really wanted to do was pick up the phone and tell that impossible woman he didn't give a damn what she wore—that in fact he wanted her to come over at once and take whatever she was wearing off? Or let him do it for her.

He picked up Mark's fat black file and put it down again. The trouble was, she would probably come—and no doubt have the clothes off *him* before he'd had time to lift a finger.

He groaned involuntarily. Why should that thought

71

bother him so much? Her enthusiasm was flattering in a way. But he had spoken the truth when he told her he refused to be the latest in a long line of conquests.

"You're crazy, Kerrigan," he muttered, prowling back to the window. "What sane man would refuse a gift like that when it's handed to him on a platter?"

He knew the answer to that, although he wasn't eager to acknowledge it. He had been taught to respect women, and it was a lesson he couldn't unlearn.

"Talking to yourself?" The door to the office swung open to admit a short, middle-aged woman who teetered into the room on dangerously high heels. "Better be careful. That's a sure sign of trouble, that is. Who is she?"

Hell. Did Norah, the firm's inquisitive and bossy secretary, *have* to be so damned perceptive?

"No one you know," he said. "Have you finished entering the data on Malahide's?"

Norah tossed her head. " 'Course I have. *I* don't spend my time talking to walls." She stalked back to her office like a dumpling on stilts with her chin at an angle that indicated dudgeon.

Richard grinned at her rigidly offended back. Trouble, she'd called it. Well, Dolores was certainly that. He loosened his tie and, with a compulsion he didn't wholly understand, reached for the phone and dialed the number he had fully intended to forget.

"Richard asked me out again," Dolores told Tamsin that evening. "At first he wanted me to go over to his office right away. But I had clients, so I couldn't."

"Would you have? If you'd been able? And I told you he'd phone, didn't I?"

"Yes, you did. And, no, I wouldn't. I do have my standards. It was odd though—he sounded kind of relieved when I said I couldn't. Anyway, we're going to dinner and a movie. Will you be all right on your own?"

"Of course I will. I'm over Paul, honestly."

"Hmm," Dolores was doubtful. "I'm glad to hear it."

She was glad, but she wasn't sure she believed it. Tamsin might be over Paul, but she certainly wasn't her old self yet. Something was wrong, and Dolores wished her friend would tell her what it was.

"Well, if you're sure," she said.

"Of course I'm sure. You go and have a great time."

Dolores nodded, and went into her bedroom to change.

For once it didn't take her long to decide what to wear. Since Richard had insisted on pulling up her the straps of her dress the last time they'd been together, apparently determined to keep her decent, she would wear the nearest thing she had to a burnoose. That ought to fix him. Plus the sedate pearls Aunt Sadie had left her. And just as much makeup as she chose.

She reached into the back of her closet and pulled out a loose, three-quarter-length black garment with a vee neck and straight, short sleeves that she'd bought to wear to her aunt's funeral. After pulling it over her head, she added the pearls and turned to look in the mirror.

Ugh. Even her red and black quilt would be an improvement over the dress. But the black thing might actually appeal to Richard's sober tastes. The saleswoman in the store had told her it had "classic lines," whatever those were.

When the doorbell rang, she waved good-bye to Tamsin, who was in the kitchen drooping over the paper, and went down to answer it.

"Good grief!" Richard exclaimed. "Who are you planning to bury?"

"You?" Dolores suggested, propping herself against the door frame. "I thought this was the kind of dress you liked. It almost matches your suit." It did, except that his dark suit molded his virile frame to perfection, whereas her dress bore a sorry resemblance to a sack.

"Is that so?" Richard took a step backward, his slate gray gaze traveling over her assessingly. She was about to ask him if he thought he was purchasing a prize heifer, when suddenly he grinned. "I suppose this serves me right for thinking of you in the same breath as a little black dress," he said, adding with what sounded like surprise, "As a matter of fact, the color suits you. Shall we go?"

"You mean you're not going to insist that I go up and change?" Dolores spoke with an edge she intended him to notice.

"I doubt if I could insist you do anything unless it was something you'd already decided to do yourself. Anyway you look very . . . respectable."

Dolores stifled an urge to kick him, painfully, on the shin. If he only knew, in this case, she would have been only too delighted to be asked to change. On the other hand— she bit her lip—the frumpy dress *did* serve him right for being so damn proper.

She took his arm and sailed down the steps as if she were a duchess robed in her most elegant ball gown.

"Who does she think she is?" Mrs. Sawchuk muttered to her son as she lifted a protesting black cat from his perch on the windowsill. "Some kind of princess?"

Barry took advantage of his mother's inattention to remove a five dollar bill from her purse.

Disaster struck almost as soon as Richard and Dolores reached the restaurant.

"Is this where we're eating?" Dolores asked when Richard led her into the marbled lobby of a downtown hotel best known for its famous restaurant in the sky.

"Yes. It's a clear night. I thought you'd enjoy the view."

Dolores's stomach clenched and rolled over. "I'm—um. . . ." she muttered.

"At a loss for words?" Richard teased. "Haven't you been here before?"

"No. No, actually I haven't. . . ."

She had to tell him. It was just a matter of getting the words past the tightness in her throat.

"You haven't?" Richard was saying. "Good. Then I made the right choice. You're in for a spectacle, I promise you."

A spectacle. Oh God, he had no idea. He sounded so pleased with himself too, so certain he was giving her a treat. And why not? This was a man who went para-gliding and white-water rafting for the fun of it. How could he possibly have any understanding of a phobia so ingrained, and so groundless, as her desperate fear of heights.

How could she tell him? He'd think her such a coward. Probably tell her it was all in her mind and just to keep a stiff upper lip and get on with it. Then he'd say she'd love it once she tried it. She knew he would. They all did. She'd been in this situation at least a dozen times before. Only those other times she hadn't particularly cared what her companions thought, so she'd told them she wouldn't love it and to pick another restaurant.

This was different. Richard wasn't besotted with her as those other men had been, and he already disapproved of so much about her. If she told him the truth, he might be politely chivalrous and take her somewhere else, but he'd be disappointed and bored with her and never think of asking her out again.

So what? the craven voice of her deep-seated phobia responded. What does it matter if you never see him again? He's not the only fish in the water.

No, he wasn't. Yet she couldn't give way to her panic in front of Richard. She wanted him to like her, to admire her. . . .

"Are you all right?" he asked as the jaws of the horrible, glass-walled elevator opened to swallow them alive. "You look pale."

"I'm fine," Dolores said quickly. "I didn't wear a lot of makeup," she added pointedly. That much, at least, was true.

They stepped into the elevator along with a thin man with military shoulders, and a small woman, presumably his wife, wearing a beautifully cut green silk suit. If Dolores had been in any mood to care what she looked like, she would have felt like a frump in comparison.

She stared fixedly ahead, her back to the outer glass wall and her eyes on a level with the military man's moustache. He opened his mouth briefly, then closed it like a trout gulping air.

"You'd see more if you turned round," Richard suggested.

The jaws closed behind them, and the elevator began its ascent. "I'm fine," Dolores repeated. Was that her voice, all clipped and sounding angry? She wasn't angry. She was, quite simply, terrified.

The military man puffed out his lip, and Richard moved in front of her and took her hand. It was dripping with sweat, and she tried to snatch it away.

"You're scared, aren't you?" he said, refusing to let go.

"How did you guess?" Terror and embarrassment made her belligerent. Dear God, wasn't this horrible contraption ever going to stop? Her stomach was moving up into her chest, and the sweat pouring down her back was dampening the awful black dress.

"You should have told me." Richard sounded more puzzled than annoyed.

"I know. I couldn't."

"Why not? I wouldn't have. . . ." He paused as the elevator reached its destination and stopped with a small thud that made her gasp. "Never mind, we're here now. You'll be all right once we sit down."

That was all he knew. She wouldn't be all right until her feet were back on solid ground, where they belonged.

"Yes," she agreed in a small voice. "I'm sure I will."

"That's my girl." He was still holding her hand, and she hung on to it as if it were all that stood between her and imminent death.

The military man and his wife squeezed around them and got off first. They glanced at each other and lifted their eyebrows. Dolores didn't care.

"Table in the window, sir?" inquired the maitre d' as they stepped onto a marble-tiled floor that felt like sponge beneath her feet.

"Yes—" Richard began.

Dolores clutched his hand hard enough to cut off circulation.

"No," he amended. "One in the middle will suit us better."

Dolores relaxed her grip but didn't let go. She dared not. Her head was spinning, and she felt as if she were standing on a ship's deck in a hurricane.

When they reached their table with its white linen cloth and gleaming glassware, she sank into her chair and grasped the green leather seat as if it were a life raft.

A waiter came with menus. Richard picked his up. Dolores grabbed the pink napkin from her tall crystal glass and twisted it in her lap. Her clammy hands soaked the crisp linen in seconds.

"Sure you're all right?" Richard asked.

"No," Dolores gasped, unable to pretend courage a second longer. "I'm not. My head—I mean, I feel as if the restaurant's revolving."

"It is."

"*What?*" Dolores dropped the napkin and staggered to her feet, hanging for dear life on to the back of her chair. "I—I'm sorry, I can't—I have to leave." Without waiting to see if Richard was behind her, she made a frantic dive for the exit. The elevator wasn't there, so she stood with her finger glued to the button as if that would somehow summon the car faster.

"There's a freight elevator," Richard's voice said calmly. "The maitre d' suggests we use that."

"No, no. It's all right. I'm fine."

"You are not fine. You're scared stiff, and you've gone a shade of green that doesn't go at all well with black. Now then, here's the freight elevator. No glass walls. You'll feel a lot safer. In you get."

Dolores allowed him to take her elbow and push her inside. The solid-looking floor and walls were reassuring, but the strength that had carried her this far deserted her abruptly, and she collapsed limply against Richard's broad chest.

Steel doors clanged into place behind them, and Richard put both arms around her and held her in the safety of his embrace until they reached the ground.

"Right." Richard lifted his glass and swallowed a

mouthful of the whiskey he considered well earned. "Now tell me what that was all about."

He and Dolores were seated in a dim corner of a downtown pub waiting for their order of fish and chips. His suggestion that they patronize any one of a dozen up-market restaurants in the vicinity had met with Dolores's unspoken resistance. She hadn't actually argued, but her pretty mouth had turned down, and the strain in her blue eyes had been unmistakable. He realized then that what she really needed after her ordeal was somewhere dim and reasonably quiet, where she could recover her composure with a measure of privacy. Hence this small, unpretentious pub with its not unpleasant odor of vinegar and frying.

Dolores was shredding a white paper napkin. "I don't know what it's about," she said. "Not really. I've been scared of heights for as long as I can remember. Richard, I *am* sorry. I should have told you."

"Why didn't you?" He hoped he was hiding his irritation. It wasn't her fault she was frightened of heights, but, dammit, that painful scene had been completely unnecessary. And from what he'd seen of Dolores so far, she wasn't normally the type to be bashful about her needs.

"I wanted to, but I couldn't." The napkin now resembled confetti.

"What do you mean, you couldn't?"

"I felt such a fool. And I didn't want you to think me a coward." She bent her head and crushed what was left of the napkin in one hand. "Now you know I am."

"I know nothing of the sort. It takes guts to do something you're so afraid of."

"But I didn't do it." Dolores raised her head, and he saw that her eyes were unnaturally bright. "I made a complete fool of myself and made you look ridiculous as well."

"You most certainly did not. The only person who can make me look ridiculous is myself. Believe me, I know. I've done it dozens of times. Just ask my partner. Or my secretary."

Dolores sniffed. "You're being nice," she said. "Which is more than I deserve. I'm sorry I spoiled your evening."

"You haven't spoiled my evening, and I like fish and chips. Now. . . ." He swallowed another mouthful of whiskey. "What I want to know is what's happened to the lady who tried to steal my virtue on the dance floor? *She* wasn't sorry about anything."

He heaved a silent sigh of relief when Dolores produced something approximating a smile.

"I guess that lady took a vacation," she said. Tipping her head to one side she made an effort to smile convincingly. "Do you want her back?"

Uh-oh. He'd been asking for trouble, and if he wasn't careful, it looked as though he might yet get it.

But suddenly he didn't care. Dolores, until she'd gone to pieces up there in the restaurant, had been everything he abhorred in a woman. A fascinating little man-eater who gobbled up her victims like peaches, digested them and spat out the pits. But he'd seen a different side of her now, a vulnerable side that until tonight he had only dimly perceived.

"Yes," he said. "Maybe I do want that witch-lady back."

"Oh. Then. . . ." She paused as a baby-faced waitress slammed two hot plates onto the table. "In that case let's forget the movie. Why don't we go to your place instead?"

Delicious, fishy fumes wafted up Richard's nose, and he shook his head as sanity returned. Dolores might be afraid of heights, but she was still the woman he'd spent the last several nights trying to forget.

"I don't think so," he said. No reason to tell her yet that

his apartment was on the fifteenth floor. "I've another idea. My partner's getting married on Saturday, so how about you come with me to the wedding?"

Her chin went up as if he'd punched her. "Why? So you won't have to be alone with me? Or so you can see if I know how to behave in public? Taking quite a chance with your reputation, aren't you?"

Richard laid down his knife and fork. He'd asked for that. It was just as well he'd never doubted her intelligence. "More or less," he admitted. "*Do* you know how to behave?"

Dolores picked up her wine glass, and for a moment he expected her to heave its contents at his face. Instead, she took a thoughtful sip and set it down. "I don't know. I suppose it depends on what you consider good behavior. At the very least, I promise I won't run off with the lucky bridegroom."

"No, you won't," he agreed, concealing his surprise at her cool response to what had amounted to an insult. "For your information, you wouldn't get the chance. Is it a deal, then?"

"Sure." She dealt with a particularly fat chip. "Why not?"

Richard could think of a number of reasons why not, but he didn't express them.

"Good," he said. "That's settled. So tell me, what do you suppose happened to make you so frightened of heights?"

"Nothing I know about. A psychologist once said my acrophobia might be a symptom of some much deeper fear. Lack of emotional support as a kid, or some such nonsense. Tammy thinks so too." She frowned. "Only the thing is, I don't think I'm afraid of much else."

Richard didn't think she was either. He liked that quality about her.

He watched Dolores bite enthusiastically into a crunchy piece of halibut. Good. She was recovering nicely. He smiled and lifted his glass in a respectful salute.

Chapter Five

Nick sat behind his desk studying a seascape by an up-and-coming local artist. He'd bought it just the other day and, on the whole, was pleased with his purchase. Tamsin said it reminded her of Clamshell Bay.

Tamsin again. Nick frowned. What was it about his capable, unobtrusive assistant that had lately become so damned distracting? And why did she keep drifting into his thoughts for no reason? Presumably her neat beige dresses had always covered more than skin and bone. And no doubt the legs he had taken note of for the first time only the other day while helping her into his car had always been borderline spectacular. Obviously there had to be something more. Something he was missing.

He picked up a ruler and ran it slowly through his fingers. Of course, Tamsin was still a dull little mouse in many ways. But when he provoked her into emerging from that stiff, professional shell of hers, she certainly knew how to give as good as she got.

Smiling reminiscently, Nick linked his hands behind his head and contemplated the parchment white ceiling. In his mind, he was looking into gray eyes rimmed with red, a soft, sweet mouth and a nose dusted with gold freckles. . . .

What the hell was the matter with that ex-boyfriend of hers? He'd had no business making her cry. She was fragile, not tough and self-centered like Gloria. Abruptly Nick lowered his arms as a further, more provocative thought struck him.

The infamous Paul was a fool as well as a louse, because only a fool would awaken his Sleeping Beauty and leave some other prince to reap his just reward.

Nick made up his mind.

"Tamsin," he called, leaning toward the intercom. "Tamsin, come in here, please. I have a job for you."

While he waited, he picked up the phone.

Tamsin heard her boss's staccato voice issuing what sounded like orders from God. Great. He was in that sort of mood again, was he?

She rose from her desk with reluctance, taking her time about it, and stopped just inside the doorway to his office.

"Fetch your jacket," Nick said, replacing the receiver in its cradle. "We're going shopping."

"Shopping? Oh, you mean you need help choosing a gift for. . . ." She paused, mentally running down a list of possible recipients. "For Ms. Van Gelder?" she suggested doubtfully. Yesterday he had said Gloria Van Gelder was past history, but he might have changed his mind.

"No." Nick picked up a pen and scrawled a note in his appointment book. "As a matter of fact, I need help choosing suitable evening wear for the young woman who is to accompany me to the Community Foundation's annual fund-raising dinner."

"Oh. I'll do my best."

"I'm sure you will. That's why I've decided to take *you* to the dinner."

"Me! But Mr. Mal—" Briefly, the muscles in Tamsin's throat closed up. Was her boss losing his mind? "Nick, that's very kind of you, but—"

"But you won't be able to accept my invitation? Is that what you were going to say?"

"More or less. Yes."

"Ah, but you see that's where you're wrong." Nick linked his hands on his blotter and leaned toward her as if he were divulging a confidence. "It's not an invitation. I want you to attend on behalf of Malahide's. We're one of the benefit's sponsors, you may remember. And you will, of course, need a new dress for the occasion."

Tamsin stared at him. His unusual eyes held her bemused, helpless, as if she were drowning in their hypnotic green light. "Why me?" she asked finally, with what she was obliged to acknowledge sounded very much like the squeak he had objected to before.

"To represent Malahide's, as I said."

"Yes, but you've always taken one of your. . . ." Tamsin choked back the word bimbos. "You've always taken one of your *friends* before," she amended.

"And is there some reason you can't act the part of a friend?"

"You mean. . . ." Oh, no. Not that kind of friend. Tamsin at last succeeded in tearing her gaze from his. Frantically she scanned the office for inspiration—and found it in the black engagement book beside his phone.

"I'm afraid I can't," she said. "I'll be busy that night. But I'm sure one of your other *friends* will oblige you." She nodded at the book and started to back out of his office.

"Wait," Nick said. "That wasn't a request. I expect you to attend this function as part of your job."

"But it *isn't* my job." Tamsin ran a finger under the round neckline of her dress. "It's after hours, and—"

"Surely as dedicated an assistant as you are wouldn't object to working a few extra hours for the good of the company. You've done overtime willingly enough in the past."

"That's true, I suppose, but—"

"But nothing. Tamsin, look at me."

Reluctantly she lifted her head. He was still leaning across his desk, and the eyes that met hers demanded honesty. "You *don't* have plans for that evening, do you?"

"No," she admitted.

"Then I fail to see why asking you to eat one more-or-less edible, though no doubt unexciting, dinner is such a fearful imposition."

Put that way, it wasn't. But Nick's manner toward her had changed lately, and she was finding herself embarrassingly affected by that change.

In the days before Paul she had resolutely ignored the sexual magnetism that kept women trooping in and out of her boss's life as if he were some kind of human revolving door. But since that disastrous scene on the window seat, she had come to realize that beneath the playboy exterior and autocratic manner lurked something approaching a heart—and that knowledge only made matters worse. If he turned the magnetism on her out of boredom, pragmatism or some other reason, how could she continue to ignore it?

Or was she only imagining Nick's interest because she had liked the feel of his arm around her, liked the sensations inspired by his hard body when he held her close and helped to dry her tears?

"Tamsin?" Nick's deep voice broke into her daydreams. "I asked if it would be such an imposition—"

"No," she said quickly. "No, it isn't that. But—"

"But you'd rather not be seen out with the big bad boss. Is that it?"

"I—no, of course not."

"Good." He sat back, resting his elbows on the arms of his soft leather chair and smiled the smile that set most of his women friends swooning all over the office. When

Tamsin didn't swoon, he said, "Right. Fetch your jacket then, and tell Sally to handle any calls."

"Jacket?" Tamsin said blankly. "Sally?"

"We're going out, remember? To buy you a dress."

"Oh, there's no need for that. I'll borrow something from Dolores." Only after the words were out of her mouth did Tamsin realize she had just agreed to attend his fundraising dinner in a dress that, knowing her roommate, would probably make her look like a hooker masquerading as a seedy duchess of questionable reputation.

Nick appeared to catch something of the drift of her thoughts. "Not if Dolores dresses the way you do, you won't," he said with authority.

"She doesn't," Tamsin replied curtly. Damn him. He ought to be *grateful* she didn't dress like a bimbo. Malahide's was a respectable establishment, not some upscale brothel.

"And will her clothes fit you?" Nick asked.

"She's a bit taller and. . . ." More voluptuous. More curvy and busty. All the things she, Tamsin, was not.

Again Nick caught her hesitation, and a slow smile spread across his face like warm butter. "You see," he said. "It won't do, will it?"

"No," she admitted. "But why can't you find someone else to take to your dinner? Someone who might actually want to go. Sally—"

"Sally is nineteen. I'm pushing thirty-four."

"But if it's purely a business arrangement—"

"Oh, purely," he said, affecting a sudden interest in the delicate glass light globe above his head.

"Then surely her age doesn't matter."

"I'm afraid it does. The idea is to strengthen Malahide's reputation, not ruin it. You, at least, can be counted on not to turn up with studs in your eyebrows or half your hair dyed a putrid shade of orange."

"Sally doesn't dress that way."

"Not at work, no. I wouldn't stand for it. And she's a reliable employee or she wouldn't be here. But I once had the misfortune to run into her in the lobby of the Arts Club Theatre. Her appearance was—well, let's just call it unconventional."

Tamsin sighed. By the standards of "pushing thirty-four," no doubt Sally *was* unconventional.

"All right," she said. "I'll do it. But I'll buy my own dress."

"No, Malahide's will. Consider it advertising."

Tamsin wasn't sure she wanted to be considered advertising. She thought for a moment. If Nick was going to insist on her attendance at this stupid dinner, perhaps it *was* only fair that Malahide's should pay.

"Very well. Thank you." She folded her hands primly in front of her. "I'll pick something out over the next couple of days."

"And where will you go to do your picking?"

"One of the department stores, I expect."

"That's what I thought. Go on, get your jacket." He stood up, all powerful masculine grace, and began to move briskly across the room.

Tamsin froze. He had almost closed the gap between them, and his warm breath was fanning her forehead before she found the strength to scurry into her office, grab the jacket from the back of her chair and hold it in front of her like a shield.

Nick's lips quirked and he shook his head but said nothing.

Tamsin, feeling foolish, took a step backward and started to tug on her jacket.

"Wrong sleeve," Nick said.

She paused and almost immediately felt the sleeve being gently removed. Before she could react, he was expertly sliding both sleeves up her arms and settling the cool beige fabric on her shoulders. When he was through, he didn't at once remove his hands. She could feel them on her upper arms, firm and strong through the lightness of the linen. Then he took her elbow and guided her through the door onto the landing.

Tamsin's legs felt like melting jelly by the time she and Nick had navigated the stairs and stopped to talk to Sally. His hand had remained on her arm the whole time, as if he thought she might try to make a break for it.

When they reached the private parking lot behind the building, trapped heat rose up from the pavement to blast them in the face.

"It's warm." Tamsin gasped as hot air blew the smell of gasoline and rubber up her nose.

"So it is," Nick readily agreed.

Why did she have a funny feeling that he wasn't talking about the weather? She shrugged off her unease, chalking it up to an overheated imagination—something she hadn't been afflicted with until recently.

After his dismissive comment about department stores, she was prepared to endure long lines of traffic as they wound their way to some exclusive little boutique on the North Shore. But Nick surprised her by driving only a few blocks south and stopping outside an unpretentious brick building with nothing in its single window beyond a few multi-hued silk scarves and a delicate bowl of white lilies.

"Here?" Tamsin asked, stepping from the air-conditioned Lincoln back into the suffocating heat of the midday sun.

"This is Lucien's. Yes. He'll know what to do about you."

Do about her? She didn't like the sound of that. Nor did she like the idea of being dressed by a man while another man looked on.

She had, of course, heard of Lucien, the eccentric and famously taciturn designer of very special gowns for very special customers.

"I'm not a Lucien kind of woman," she blurted.

Nick's lips tipped up. "Oh, I think you are. Lucien enjoys a challenge. So do I."

Tamsin swung around and started to scramble back into the car. "I've changed my mind," she said. "Would you please drive me back to work?" She was *not* going to be used as a doll for two grown men to dress up. If that was what Nick had in mind, she wanted no part of it.

Instead of doing as she asked, Nick grabbed the closest part of her, which happened to be the linen belt of her dress. "Oh, no, you don't," he said. "We have an appointment."

"I don't."

"You do. I made one for you."

He was still gripping her belt, and passersby were watching them with amused curiosity. When Nick adjusted his grip and his fingers skimmed lightly across her rear, Tamsin discovered that the heat suffusing her face was beginning to pool deep inside her in a response as instinctive as breathing.

She looked up, horrified, afraid that Nick could tell, but he just smiled amiably and jerked his head at the door of Lucien's.

"Take your hands off me," she gasped.

"Hand. And only if you promise not to run away."

Tamsin guessed that if she didn't promise, he would go on playing havoc with her hormones until she did.

"All right," she said. "I promise." She had always prided herself on keeping her appointments. There was no reason to break the pattern just because Nick Malahide had put her in an embarrassing position.

"Good girl." He let go of her belt and took her arm as gallantly as if they hadn't been scuffling on the sidewalk like a pair of pigeons fighting over crumbs. "Don't worry, it won't be the ordeal you imagine."

As things turned out, it was one of the more fascinating experiences of Tamsin's life.

As the only child of conservative, older parents, she had been expected to dress discreetly and with a minimum of fuss. It wasn't that her parents didn't love her, but they didn't believe in wasting the money her father made as a bookkeeper on unnecessary frills for their child. "Making do builds character," her mother had always said.

Tamsin hadn't seen how being picked on by other children for being different could build character, and in the end she had retreated into her shell and remained there—quiet little Tamsin Brown who always finished her work on time and never caused the teachers any trouble.

Now, here was that same Tamsin Brown heading into the salon of one the most sought-after fashion moguls in town, on the arm of one of the most sought after bachelors.

Over the next fifteen minutes she was measured, draped, appraised and scrutinized until she wasn't sure whether she felt like a princess or a pincushion.

At the end of it all, Nick and Lucien between them had decided on a pale peach silk shot with gold. Tamsin, who up until then had been too dazzled and overwhelmed to take much part in the selection, came to her senses and demanded, "Don't I have any say in what I wear?"

"Don't you like what we've chosen?" Nick asked.

She'd expected impatience, even anger, but detected only disappointment in his voice.

"Yes, I like it very much," she assured him. "The point is, *you* chose it. I didn't."

"No," Nick said, once more in control of his emotions. "The point is, my company is paying, and I'm not a big fan of beige."

Tamsin was so astonished that at first she could only gape at him. At the same time she felt the back of her neck heating up. What was wrong with beige? She'd always thought it perfect for the office, and most other places, too. Practical and not too ostentatious.

"I like beige," she said finally. "But you might give me some credit for knowing what's suitable for a banquet and what isn't."

"I didn't suggest—" Nick broke off to slant her a smile of surprising contrition. "I did, didn't I? You're right." He spoke as if her rightness came as a revelation. "Does that mean you'd like to choose something else?"

Tamsin, ignoring Lucien's indignant twitchings, said she'd think about it.

There was nothing to think about, of course. She loved the peach silk, and, after a reasonable interval, she said so.

The two men exchanged sympathetic glances as Nick and Tamsin left the premises.

"Where are we going?" Tamsin asked, when instead of heading back to the office, Nick pointed his car in the direction of Oak Street.

"I thought you'd like a break. How about tea and a stroll around Van Dusen Gardens?"

"But there's work to be done at the office, and—"

"It'll wait. You work for *me,* remember, and I'm in no hurry."

"Oh, but. . . ." Tamsin tried to come up with a credible "but" and couldn't. When she saw Nick grinning, she said irritably, "Oh, all right. As you say, it isn't up to me."

"No, it's not," he said mildly, and Tamsin squelched an impulse to tell him not to be smug. He *was* the boss, and he wasn't being particularly smug. Just sure of himself, as always.

Her irritation faded once they were seated by one of the garden restaurant's long windows in front of an excellent cup of tea. Outside, the leaves of a kiwi vine brushed against the glass, and multicolored roses bobbed their heads gently in the breeze. The muted babble of conversation and the chink of china provided a restful background to her thoughts.

Nick wasn't altogether impossible. It was generous of him to supply her with a dress from Lucien's, and now, seated across from her, he looked relaxed and unalarming. Not to mention sexy.

That last was unfortunate. She liked relaxed, but sexy was a definite disadvantage in a man she had to deal with every day at work.

"What's the matter?" Nick asked as she bit viciously into a slice of chocolate cake. "You're not, I hope, taking your temper out on your cake because you can't take it out on me?"

Tamsin replied without thinking. "I'm not in a temper. Besides, my appetites don't run along those lines."

Nick choked on a chunk of apple pie. "You're a step or two ahead of me," he murmured. When she frowned, confused, he added abruptly, "That boyfriend of yours had lousy taste."

"In women?" Tamsin asked, lowering her head and pretending to concentrate on her cake.

In the garden outside, a childish shriek turned to gurgling laughter. Nick, who had winced at the ear-splitting noise, studied the dejected droop of Tamsin's shoulders and groaned inwardly. Was she really so unaware of her own charms? If so, it shouldn't surprise him. He had been oblivious to those same charms himself until recently.

"No," he said. "That wasn't what I meant. Why shouldn't a man find you interesting?"

Tamsin shrugged. "Paul didn't. Our relationship was over almost as soon as it began."

"Like I said. He had lousy taste."

Tamsin's eyelids came down like fragile shutters. "Do you mean—"

"I mean you're an attractive woman. His physical preferences must be totally skewed."

"Oh. I wouldn't know about those."

She meant it. He'd stake his life on it. She'd fallen for the creep, but she hadn't fallen into his bed.

"Sorry," he said, noting the spots of self-conscious color on her cheeks. "Perhaps I was out of line."

She nodded with old-fashioned solemnity, and he watched her crumbling her cake as if she needed something to do with her hands. Damn. He'd embarrassed her, when all he'd meant to do was put her at ease with a civilized cup of tea and a genteel stroll around the gardens. She struck him as that sort of woman.

"Look," he said, "if we're going to get through the Foundation's dinner like two sane and sensible people, don't you think we ought to make an effort to get along?"

Tamsin stopped crumbling her cake. "Of course, but I thought we did get along. Most of the time."

"So we do. On a business level."

"I prefer to *keep* things on a business level." She pushed her plate to one side.

Did she have any idea how impossibly and endearingly prim she looked with her nose tilted up and her shoulders soldier straight? Nick found himself hard-pressed not to reach across the table to stroke the seriously flat line from her soft mouth. But he guessed that if he did, she would retreat into her shell like a nervous snail.

"Of course," he agreed hastily. "So do I. But there's no reason we couldn't occasionally acknowledge the world outside the office."

"No, I suppose not." She picked up her cup, stared at its contents, then set it down again so that it rattled in the saucer.

Nick guessed she was thinking she already knew more than enough about his life outside the office and wasn't that anxious to learn more. Normally her suspicions would have amused him, but today, for no particular reason, he found them irritating.

"Let's start with you," he said, making an effort to contain his irritation. "What do you do when you're not keeping me in order?"

Tamsin threw him a quick, harried glance and turned to look at the roses. "Not much," she said. "I read a lot. And sometimes I watch TV."

He knew at once it had been the wrong thing to ask. Surely her life couldn't really be as boring as she made out.

He waited, watching her toy with the handle of her teacup. Would she make an effort to expand on that very dull life she had just described, or would she leave him to think she had no life outside her job?

In the end she swallowed hard, as if something was

blocking her throat, and went on contemplating the roses.

Nick felt like a jerk, though he could hardly be held responsible for his assistant's life after business hours. He experienced an unexpected flare of temper. Dammit, he had no reason to feel like a jerk simply because he couldn't seem to persuade Ms. Tamsin Brown to drop that prim, secretarial armor she persisted in flaunting in his face.

Choking back his momentary ill-humor, he said in what he hoped was a conciliatory tone, "There really is life beyond work."

"You should know."

Oh. So that *was* the way the wind blew. Nick stretched his legs and leaned back, amused and at the same time exasperated. "I take it you don't subscribe to the view that 'All work and no play makes Jack a dull boy.' "

He noted that when his foot accidentally touched her ankle, she immediately tucked both legs beneath her chair.

"*Children* need to play, of course," she said, sounding as if she were a little out of breath.

Nick lifted his napkin to his mouth. That certainly put him in his place. "But not grown men? Or women?" he suggested, purely to tease her.

"I don't know. I. . . ." She stopped, then started again with a noticeable effort. "Were you a very active little boy?"

Ah. That sounded like an attempt to change the subject. Nick smiled. "Yes," he said. "I guess I was. With only transient female influence in our lives, my brother and I hadn't much incentive to stay out of trouble."

Tamsin's answering smile was the most natural expression he had seen on her face since they'd left the office. "Your childhood must have been quite different from mine," she said. "Mine was very . . . restrained. My parents didn't like noise."

"I don't suppose Dad did either unless it was made with a hammer or saw." Nick shifted his chair to avoid the unabashed stare of a scantily clad redhead at the next table.

"Did you lose your mother when you were very young?" Tamsin's voice was low, sympathetic, yet somehow he didn't want to tell her about his mother. Sympathy could too easily become pity, and he'd had enough pity to last a lifetime.

"Poor little boys," they had all said. *"How could she abandon them like that?"*

"Yes," he said briefly. "I did." It was all she needed to know.

"Oh, how awful. Especially for your father."

"I suppose so." He slapped his palm lightly on the table, making the teacups jump.

"Don't you know?"

"I was too young to think about anyone but myself," he replied truthfully. "By the time I was old enough to pay attention, Dad was a gruff old curmudgeon who scared off all the housekeepers and thought the best way to keep our noses clean was to make us work in the shop any time we weren't away at school. I loved it."

"Did you really?" She looked doubtful, still much too ready with her pity.

"Yes," he said brusquely. "Dennis didn't, though. As soon as he was old enough, he took off to sail around the world."

"Really? Is he still sailing?"

"No. He got as far as Australia and stayed there. He's married now. Has two little girls I've never seen."

"So you're all alone?" Her voice vibrated with compassion.

Nick choked back a groan. "When I want to be. I like it that way."

Tamsin stopped looking compassionate and frowned.

"That scowl of yours is likely to wither all the petals off the roses," he warned, becoming impatient with her terminal disapproval. It was almost as annoying as her sympathy. "Come on. If you want to see the gardens we'd better move."

"I thought you weren't in a hurry." She wiped her fingers carefully on her napkin.

"I wasn't. Now I am."

Tamsin shrugged and stood up.

For the next three quarters of an hour they strolled through acres of colorful flowers and winding walks while Tamsin forced herself to chat brightly about roses, water lilies and the relative merits of Japanese versus western style gardening. Nick, who didn't give a damn about gardening, listened in silence and wondered if she would talk as much in bed.

After that he took her back to work.

For the remainder of the week, Nick kept his distance. He was polite, even formal, and as usual relied on Tamsin to cope with all the office minutiae without which Malahide's would not have functioned as seamlessly as it did. If she hadn't caught his speculative gaze resting on her now and then in a way it never had in all the years she had worked for him, she might have believed everything was back to normal, back to the way it had been before she met Paul. Which suited her just fine.

Funny, though, how quickly her feelings for Paul had evaporated. For a week he had lit up her life. Now she could barely remember what he looked like. She must have cried him out of her system that evening in Nick's comforting arms.

She still couldn't pass those curtains without remembering, and what worried her most was that it wasn't Paul she remembered but the feel of her boss's solid shoulder beneath her cheek.

Dolores would undoubtedly tell her she was a fool not to make the most of her opportunities, but Dolores hadn't spent five years watching Nick in action. If she had, she would know that only a fool would look on him as an opportunity.

Tamsin didn't think she was a fool.

Chapter Six

Dolores liked weddings. She didn't suppose she'd ever walk down the aisle at her own, but the smiling faces all around her today made her feel good. Her fellow guests in the small chapel in the park seemed, for a short time at least, ready to believe in love, commitment and happily-ever-after.

Briefly, as she gazed at Richard's back, imposing in a dark gray tuxedo as he stood beside the groom, she even believed in all those things herself. Then she remembered how her parents' commitment to each other and to their careers had so often left their child out in the cold.

Abstractedly she opened her prayer book and began to riffle through the pages.

"Nice-looking fellow, isn't he?" the woman beside her whispered.

Dolores turned to her, surprised. "You mean. . . . ?"

"The best man. Is he your boyfriend?"

"Not really," she whispered back. "We haven't known each other long."

A snub-nosed man in the pew in front of them turned around and glared. "Shh!" he hissed.

Dolores returned to her examination of Richard's back.

The rest of the ceremony passed in something of a daze, and it wasn't until everyone was gathered on the grass in front of the chapel that Dolores finally had a chance to do more than wave at Richard. As best man, he was responsible for bringing the groom, so she had arrived at the church on her own.

"It's a beautiful day. It—the wedding—went well, didn't it?" All at once she was self-conscious. And if he dared to make one of his scathing remarks about the expensive but sober beige dress she had worn at Tamsin's insistence, she would walk off and forget all about him.

"Weddings usually do," Richard replied. "I'm told the problems start later."

"How cynical," Dolores replied lightly, relieved he hadn't commented on her appearance. "I thought you said you believed in marriage and family and all that."

"I do. Very few problems are insurmountable given the will—and the right attitude."

"I suppose not." She glanced at Mark and Carla, two small, round people who couldn't keep their eyes or their hands off each other. "I don't think those two are thinking much about future problems, do you?"

"No," Richard agreed. "They're thinking about bed." He ran a brisk eye over Dolores's slender figure. "You look very nice, by the way."

"Thank you." Dolores spoke stiffly, glad she passed muster in the clothes department, yet unsettled by his comment about bed.

"Come and meet the happy couple," he said.

Smoothing the frown lines from her forehead, Dolores followed him across the grass to shake hands with the beaming bride and groom.

"Your turn next, Dolores," Carla said with a grin after they'd chatted for a while. "It's past time Rick settled down."

Dolores couldn't look at Richard. "We're just friends," she muttered.

"That's what they all say." Mark reached up to pat Richard heartily on the back. "Don't let this one slip through your fingers," he advised.

Richard's muttered reply was noncommittal, but when Dolores attempted to move away, he draped a restraining arm around her waist and laid a cautionary hand on her hip.

"Why did you do that?" she demanded a few minutes later as the wedding party made its way toward the fleet of decorated cars in the parking lot.

"Do what?"

"Make them think we we're a serious item."

"Aren't we?" he asked, leaving her uncertain whether he was semi-sincere or simply being sarcastic.

"You know we're not." She withdrew the arm he held in a light grip and pressed it tightly to her side.

Richard plunged his hands into his pockets. "Have you ever been serious about anyone?"

"No. Well, not since I was very young. What's the point?"

"If you don't see a point, then there isn't one."

He sounded exasperated. She wondered why. So far he was proving a far from satisfactory escort.

They didn't talk much on the way to the reception. Richard seemed absorbed in his thoughts, and Dolores decided nothing was to be gained by mindless chatter. Instead she sat back and watched his long fingers controlling the steering wheel, then imagined them touching her in secret places, skimming over her body, skillfully, softly. . . .

She was jolted from her fantasy when the Corvette slid to a stop in front of an attractive, turn-of-the-century house surrounded by a wooden fence covered in trailing white roses.

Richard helped her onto the sidewalk, and she observed with delight the purple clematis climbing the white stucco walls, and the lush green lawns behind the fence. What a perfect setting for a wedding reception on this cloudless, wonderfully mild June day.

The interior of the house had been remodeled to cater to banquets and receptions, but with its dark paneled walls and coved ceilings it succeeded in retaining something of the charm of a quieter, less frantic era. Dolores relaxed and found herself enjoying the toasts and speeches and the conspicuous happiness of the newly married couple.

Once the obligatory speeches were over, almost everyone except the bride's grandmother, who said it was too cold, drifted into the garden to take advantage of the sunshine.

"Mmm," Dolores murmured, appreciatively sniffing the sweetly-scented air while Richard steered her toward a small arbor wreathed in delicate white pyracantha. "Your partner couldn't have picked a better day."

"He didn't pick it. Carla did. She picks most things."

Dolores laughed. "Are you saying he's henpecked?"

"Yes, but quite happily so. Did I tell you, you look very nice?"

"Thank you. Yes, you did."

In the short, awkward silence that followed, a blackbird perched on a nearby trellis began to sing.

"Stay here." Richard's voice, when he spoke, was unusually curt. "I'll get you some Champagne."

Dolores watched him take long, swinging strides across the grass before he disappeared into the house. A bee buzzed past her nose. She flapped it away. Why did she have to stay here, tucked out of sight in a corner while others celebrated?

The answer, of course, was that she didn't. Tossing back her hair, she wandered over to join a group of men who were discussing a party most of them had attended the night before.

"Hey," one of them said as she approached. "You were there, weren't you? Saw you go off with that little runt with the big teeth. You were wearing a slinky black skirt and a red blouse."

"No," Dolores said. "I wasn't. You must be mixing me up with someone else."

"No, it was you," the man insisted. "Wouldn't forget legs like yours. Or that pair of—"

"Take it easy, Bart," another of the group cautioned. "The lady came with Rick Kerrigan."

"Don't care who she came with." Bart was belligerent, and Dolores realized he was already more than half drunk. "She was there last night, flaunting her—"

"Bart, shut up," said a third man.

"Don't you tell me to shut up." Bart spun around, aimed a fist and lost his balance, stumbling over his own feet to end up face down on the grass beneath a late-blooming azalea. A shower of orange petals tumbled onto his back.

"Leave him there," suggested one of the men. "Let's go get more Champagne."

"Good idea." The group wandered off, some of them none too steady on their feet, leaving Bart stretched out motionless on the ground.

"Wait! You can't leave him!" Dolores cried. "What if he's hurt?"

"He'll have a sore head in the morning, that's all," one of the men tossed at her over his shoulder. "Don't worry about old Bart. He'll be fine."

Dolores gave up on the men. Bart's friends were as useless as he was, and nobody else appeared to have noticed the little drama. If anyone was going to help Bart, it would have to be her. Sighing, she knelt on the lawn beside the sprawled body and touched the back of his neck. It was sticky and he reeked unpleasantly of beer, but she couldn't tell if he was breathing. One plump arm lay stretched across the grass, the other tucked out of sight. Cautiously she picked up his wrist, hoping to feel a pulse as she'd been trained to do. She noticed a green stain on his sleeve. At least it wasn't red.

"Bart," she said, "are you all right?"

"You betcha."

Before she had time to react, Bart had rolled onto his back and clamped his right arm around her waist. His free hand fumbled at the front of her dress.

"Let me go!" she snapped, fury at her own naivete welling up until it threatened to choke her. "At once."

"Now, now, pretty lady. You be nice to Bart, and—"

"I will not be nice." Dolores gritted her teeth. "Let go of me, you creep."

Bart didn't let go. She drew in her breath and put both hands flat against his chest. He narrowed his red-rimmed eyes. It was now or never, she realized, as, pushing with all the force of her indignation, she fought to break his hold.

The drink-addled Bart was no match for her anger. "Ugh!" he grunted, and released her so suddenly that she tumbled onto the grass.

The whole episode lasted only seconds, but as Dolores scrambled to her feet, she saw that at least a dozen people were, belatedly, running to her rescue. Richard, toting two glasses of Champagne and looking lethal, was out in front.

She smoothed down her dress, pushed back her hair and waited.

The small crowd came to a stop, not sure what to do now that the crisis was over. Behind her, Bart made a retching sound. Richard moved toward her, amazingly still holding the Champagne.

"Can't I leave you on your own for two seconds?" he asked in a low voice meant for her ears alone. "What the hell's going on?"

"Nothing," Dolores said. "It's all over. Aren't you going to give me my Champagne?"

She might have known Richard would blame it all on her. Now that she thought about it, he'd probably only asked her to this wedding so he could convince himself once and for all that she wasn't appropriate company for a respectable accountant. She started to turn away, then realized he was holding out a glass.

"Thank you," she said frostily. "Perhaps you'd better see to *that*." She gestured with her head at Bart, who had staggered to his feet and was swaying like an oversized sapling in the wind.

"His friends will look after him—if they think he's worth it." Richard dismissed Bart with a shrug, then put an arm around her shoulders and turned her to face the goggle-eyed gathering of guests. "Excuse me. I'm taking Dolores home."

The small crowd parted as if he were Moses, allowing him to lead her across the lawn toward the house.

"You can't leave," she said. "You're the best man."

He paused to take a sip of Champagne. "So I am. But that's all right. The bride and groom will be on their way before long. I'll leave you with Carla's grandmother for now, and as soon as they're off, we can leave."

"Don't I get a chance to catch the bouquet?" Dolores pushed at his arm, which didn't budge. "Or aren't I a worthy recipient?"

"Put away the acid," Richard replied tiredly. "I don't know if you're worthy, but you're certainly a menace. Just keep still and stay in one place. Please."

Dolores opened her mouth to tell him exactly what she thought of his high-handedness, but changed her mind once she found herself inside and discovered that Carla's grandmother, surrounded by a cloud of blue smoke, was all alone.

"Would you like to come outside and see Carla toss her bouquet?" Dolores called to the old lady through her cloud.

"Nope. No time for that nonsense. Why can't people leave me in peace to have a smoke?"

From the looks of it, she had been left in peace for some time. Dolores refrained from pointing out that there were no-smoking bylaws in effect. Carla's grandmother was the type to insist that the bylaws didn't apply to her. Dolores coughed into her hand, looked around for Richard and discovered he was no longer there.

"Hah," said the old lady. "Had a spat, did you? You'll have your hands full with that young man, my girl."

"I doubt it," Dolores replied glumly. In spite of his continuing disapproval, she wouldn't mind having her hands full of Richard.

"Hah," Carla's grandmother said again, and exhaled three smoke rings in succession. "I know his kind. Had a husband like that once. My second one, and the best of the three of 'em. You hang on to him, girl. You'll find he's worth it."

Dolores was spared the need to answer by Carla's sister, who came hurrying in to urge her grandmother to join the festivities outside. Grumbling, the old lady stubbed out her cigarette and allowed herself to be helped to her feet.

Dolores didn't catch the bouquet.

Half an hour later, after the bride and groom had departed in a shower of pink confetti, Dolores again found herself seated next to Richard as he pulled the Corvette

107

onto the road. One look at his face convinced her that, after all, she'd just as soon keep her hands to herself.

"Where are we going?" she asked when she realized he wasn't taking her straight home. She had expected to be dumped outside her door like a parcel of no commercial value.

"Stanley Park. We have to talk somewhere, and I don't feel like sitting in some poky little cafe where everyone can hear us."

By now Dolores knew better than to suggest that no one would hear them in his apartment.

"There are usually a couple of people in Stanley Park," she pointed out instead.

"So there are." He half turned his head. "Want me to take you home?"

"No. Not really. But what's to talk about?"

If he was going to dump her, why not get on with it? What was the point in prolonging the agony? Except, of course, she wasn't going to go through any agony. Maybe a slight disappointment, nothing worse.

"Damned if I know," Richard admitted with a funny, sideways smile. "Something will come to me."

"I see," said Dolores, who didn't see at all.

She spent the rest of the drive to the park watching the inhabitants of Vancouver as they strolled along the sidewalks, making the most of the unusual evening warmth.

They might as well. She ran the back of her hand across her eyes. Rain would follow soon enough. It always did.

Richard took off his jacket and spread it on the grass beneath the shadow of a venerable fir tree. Then he gestured at Dolores to sit down, and waited for the inevitable protest.

To his astonishment, she made no objection. He raised

his eyebrows. Most women of his acquaintance, including Elizabeth, would have twittered on about the mess the grass would make of his jacket. Dolores merely sat on it as if she were a princess who expected nothing less.

Richard smiled and lowered himself beside her, observing that her linen skirt had ridden up to the point where it barely covered her thighs. She seemed unaware of it and certainly unconcerned.

"Okay," she said. "Better get on with it then."

Richard blinked. "On with what?"

"Telling me it's all over between us. That's why you brought me here, isn't it?"

Was it? He honestly didn't know. All he'd been sure of was that he had to get her away from other people—away from the Barts of the world.

"Aren't you over dramatizing a bit?" he asked, taking his time before answering. "There hasn't been enough between us for anything to be over yet."

She pressed the tips of her fingers to her temples. "Perhaps you're right."

Richard watched her, puzzled. What was it about this lovely, pleasure-seeking seductress that had the power to turn his normally logical thought processes both inside out and upside down, leaving him confused and uncertain of his own motives? Perhaps he had planned to break off with her. So why had he felt positively murderous when he'd seen her grappling on the ground with the repulsive Bart? And why, after that, hadn't he just taken her home, thanked her for her company and driven off into the sunset? It was a particularly vibrant burnt orange this evening.

"What made you think I planned to end it?" he asked, though that wasn't what he'd meant to say.

She smiled, an odd, sad, bitter little smile. "I'm an expert, remember? I know the signs. Except that up till now, I've always been the one who did the ending."

What was he supposed to say to that? Richard stretched out his legs, placed his hands behind his head and watched a small boy chase a ball bigger than he was across the grass. The rough bark of the tree rubbed against his knuckles.

"Maybe being dumped yourself would be a salutary lesson," he said. "People have feelings, you know."

"Of course, I know. Why do you think I'm a massage therapist? I *like* helping people feel good. Or at least better." She heaved a small sigh. "Even though some of them get the wrong idea."

"About what?"

"About what I do, of course. Men, in particular, often think I'm in a different kind of business altogether. Or at least they pretend they do. Have *you* ever been to a party and found yourself being hustled off for a grope in the coat closet the moment you tell some woman what you do for a living?"

Richard turned his head away to hide a smile. He had a feeling this was the wrong time for levity.

"No," he admitted. "I'm afraid the average woman doesn't find accountancy an aphrodisiac." He eyed her endless legs, smooth in silk against the grass, watched the evening breeze lift her hair and decided he couldn't entirely blame those men for trying it on.

"I bet those low-life's didn't get far," he remarked. "I can't imagine you allowing anyone to hustle you off amongst the coats against your will."

"You're right. They didn't." Dolores tugged at the hem of her skirt to no effect.

He twisted himself sideways to examine the rest of her. She had a cute little mole at the base of her throat that he'd never noticed before. . . .

"Well?" she said, rousing him from his scrutiny. "Have you made up your mind?"

"No," he admitted, deciding honesty was the only possible policy.

"Oh." Dolores's tone was flat, bored even. "I suppose that means I didn't come up to scratch at the wedding."

Richard breathed in the scent of freshly cut grass—a natural, uncomplicated smell. He wished his feelings were equally uncomplicated.

"You were fine," he said. "Although I could have done without Bart."

"So could I," Dolores said with feeling.

Richard plucked a blade of grass and ran it down her arm. "I know you could. And if you'd stayed where I told you to, you *would* have done without him."

She shrugged, and he saw her wince as the bark of the tree scratched the bare skin of her neck. "I'm nearly twenty-six, Richard. I make my own decisions, and I don't need anyone else to tell me what to do."

Richard could come up with no satisfactory answer to that. This afternoon she had proved beyond all doubt that at times she most definitely did need someone to tell her what to do. Bart and his group were poker friends of Mark's, and anyone but Dolores would have known they were trouble to avoid when they'd been drinking. On the other hand, Dolores herself was trouble, so what did he expect? Not that he could hold her responsible for the power cut at Bentley's. And it wasn't her fault she was frightened of heights. But, dammit, it ought to be possible to be in her company for more than an hour or two without some minor catastrophe erupting.

You're a fool, Kerrigan, he told himself for at least the

tenth time that week. You knew from the moment she grabbed on to you in the mall that Dolores Rowan wasn't the woman for you. You should have ended it right there, before it began.

So why was he hesitating? Why didn't he just admit the truth and let her find some other idiot to bewitch?

Richard was still trying to come up with a rational answer to his own question when he realized his silence had lasted too long and that Dolores had risen to her feet.

"Wait," he said, rolling onto his side as a small gray squirrel scampered past his hand and ran up the trunk of the tree. "We haven't finished our conversation."

When she didn't reply, he reached over and caught hold of her ankle.

She looked down at him, blue fire sparking from her eyes. "Conversation?" she said. "We weren't having a conversation. And now, if you wouldn't mind letting me go. . . ."

"Sorry." Richard shook his head, surprised to find he had no intention of releasing the silk-covered flesh he held between his fingers, no intention of letting her go. Not yet.

The blue fire faded to smoke as he looked up at her, and a moment later she dropped back onto his crumpled jacket and, either deliberately or by accident, brushed a delicate hand across his thigh.

His body's reaction was instant and overwhelming. She seemed to guess, because instead of pulling back she began to trail her fingers slowly up his leg. She stopped only when he made a grab for her wrist.

"Stop it," he said in a voice he barely recognized as his own. "This is a public park, not some sleazy motel."

"I know that, and I wasn't—"

Whatever else she might have said was cut short by an

unexpected shower of pine needles loosened from the tree by the squirrel.

Richard swore and sat up. "Squirrels," he muttered, glaring into the blazing orange sunset. "Damn pests."

Dolores, looking annoyingly cool, sat up, too, and brushed the needles off her dress. "I think we're about to be interrupted," she said.

"What? Oh."

He collapsed back against the tree as an enormous inflatable ball came floating toward them on the breeze. Behind it came the little boy he'd noticed earlier. Reaching out, Richard caught the ball and balanced it on his knees.

The child, who looked to be about three, came to a halt with his thumb in his mouth.

"Hi. What's your name?" Dolores asked.

The thumb came out briefly. "Zachry," he said.

"Zachary? That's a nice name. Where are your parents?" When that elicited no response, she explained patiently, "I mean your mommy or daddy."

"Somewhere." Zachary waved vaguely in the direction of the seawall.

"Wonderful," muttered Richard. "Now what?"

"I guess we've inherited a kid." Dolores, unruffled, jumped up and held out a hand to the child. "Come on, let's go find them."

"Ball," Zachary said, refusing to budge. "Mine."

"I'll carry it for you," Richard said resignedly as he, too, rose to his feet. "Okay?"

The child thought about that for a few seconds, then made up his mind. "Okay. Mine."

"Yes, definitely yours," Richard agreed with a smile.

The three of them started across the grass, Richard's upper body partly obscured by the huge ball.

They had taken only a few steps when a piercing voice shrieked, "Zachary! Don't you go with those people. You stay right where you are!" And a young woman wearing thick pink glasses rushed over and scooped up the little boy as if she expected them to snatch him from her arms.

"I believe this belongs to you." Richard, at his most icily polite, held out the ball to the outraged mother.

The woman gave him a suspicious look, grabbed the ball and succeeded in clamping it under one arm.

As certain parts of Richard's body were still causing him considerable discomfort, he was in no mood to be glowered at by a distraught and misguided mother who seemed to be blaming him for the fact that she'd mislaid her child.

He opened his mouth to say so, but Dolores placed a hand on his arm and gave the woman the kind of smile he was willing to bet would knock over a whole roomful of men. "We were coming to look for you," she said. "The wind caught Zachary's ball, and he was chasing it."

The smile had little effect on Zachary's mother, but she did manage a grudging thank you before bearing her son rapidly away.

If Richard had been wearing a hat, he would have raised it in a sarcastic salute to the departing woman's back. As it was, he took Dolores's elbow, turned her around and steered her toward the parking lot and his car.

Dolores, accurately reading his mood as they pulled onto the road out of the park, said, "You can't altogether blame her. So many horrible things have happened to children lately, it's not surprising she got the wrong idea."

"I know." Now that they were on their way, the heat had gone out of him. "All the same, she should have been watching the damned kid."

"Easier said than done sometimes. My little cousin, Kitty, used to disappear at least once a week in spite of everything my aunt did to keep her in. Harry—he was my favorite cousin—and I were always being sent to bring her back."

"Hmm." Richard was concentrating on the traffic along West Georgia and wasn't prepared when Dolores asked suddenly, "Don't you like kids?"

"What?" He narrowly avoided an oblivious cyclist who, without warning, swerved into his path. "I suppose so. I haven't thought about it much. But, yes, I guess I like kids."

"So do I," Dolores said.

Richard slammed on the brakes and nearly hit the Mercedes in front of him. Was she saying what he thought she was?

No. She couldn't be. Of course not. It was just an innocent, tossed off remark.

Except that the one thing he was sure of about Dolores was that she wasn't, by any stretch of the imagination, innocent.

"Goodness," said Tamsin, wandering out of the bathroom with a towel wrapped around her head. "You're back early, Doro."

"I know." Dolores threw her borrowed brown purse onto a chair. "Richard's gone home. Without me."

"Is that a first?"

"It is, as a matter of fact."

She looked so stricken that Tamsin said quickly, "Sorry, I didn't mean to be sarcastic. You mind, don't you?"

Dolores nodded. "I seem to." She sounded more bewildered than unhappy.

"Did you quarrel?"

115

"Not really. Oh, Tammy, I'm so—I mean, he's not the same as the other men I've been out with. I don't think he likes me the way I am."

Tamsin had only glimpsed Richard briefly, but she'd seen enough to know that his reaction to her friend was exactly the same as that of other men.

"He likes you," she said. "Don't worry, Doro, he'll be back."

It felt odd to be reassuring Dolores, the confident one, the one who never gave her heart to any man—and who was never without a Saturday night date.

"Maybe he will." Dolores sighed. "I thought he was going to kiss me—really kiss me—but he changed his mind and left me standing on the doorstep with my mouth hanging open." She reached around to unfasten the back of her dress. "I felt like a fool."

"But you probably looked beautiful just the same." Tamsin tried not to sound wistful. "If I'd been the one standing with my mouth open, I'd have looked like a fish catching flies."

For the first time since she'd come home, Dolores's gloomy expression lifted, and she laughed. "Don't be so down on yourself," she advised. "You'll be the toast of the evening at that dreary banquet you're going to next weekend. Just you wait and see."

"I wouldn't count on it," Tamsin said.

"I would." Dolores wandered into her bedroom, sliding the beige dress off her shoulders as she went.

Tamsin watched her go and shook her head. The more she thought about it, the less she wanted to wait and see. Not that she had a choice. Not now. And she'd be happy to settle for dreary provided she got through the banquet without letting Nick down by spilling food on the peach-colored dress or running out of things to say about the weather.

She crossed to a small mirror hanging in the kitchen, pulled the towel off her head and spent the next five minutes practicing her best inane party smile.

Dolores, emerging from her bedroom, burst out laughing. "You look like the Cheshire cat on Ecstasy," she gibed.

Tamsin stopped smiling long enough to pick up her damp towel and throw it at her friend.

They spent the rest of the evening munching popcorn, watching sitcoms on TV and assuring each other that sensible modern women could get along just fine without men.

Chapter Seven

Tamsin half hoped Nick would forget to collect the dress from Lucien's after her final fitting, but of course he didn't.

That night, as she prepared to head home carrying the big box containing the most expensive item of clothing she had ever owned, she saw that Nick was still seated at his desk, scoring red lines through his head carpenter's latest purchase order.

"I'll pick you up at seven tomorrow," he said without looking up. "Try not to be late."

As if she ever was! Tamsin turned her head sharply but didn't respond. She just kept walking.

Nick laid down his pen. He didn't even try to suppress a grin as he watched his assistant march out the door with her nose in the air and her neat bottom tight with indignation.

She was such a quiet, subdued little thing most of the time, and this past week there had been few signs of that bright glow she had exhibited during her brief romance with—what had she said the creep's name was? Paul? Yet even though she was obviously unused to moving in the social circles of the rich and self-important, he was fairly confident she would hold her own with the worst of them. Not that worrying about it would make a difference at this stage. Tamsin would either sink or swim tomorrow.

The door to the street closed with a bang that carried all the way up the stairs. Hearing it, Nick knew he ought to feel guilty. But he couldn't. He wondered if Tamsin had any idea how much fun she was to tease.

After a while, when no further sounds came from the showroom, he picked up his pen and went back to scoring lines through the purchase order.

The doorbell rang. Automatically Tamsin's eyes flicked to the practical chrome clock her mother had given her as a going-away present. Seven o'clock on the dot. Her nerves, already on edge, jolted her out of her chair.

"Doro," she gasped, "would you mind answering it? I have to—um—check my face."

"Uh-huh," Dolores said. "It's still there. Not much you could do if it wasn't."

"I know, but—"

"Okay, okay." Dolores grinned and headed for the door. "I'll get it. I want to check out loverboy anyway."

Feeling like a fool, Tamsin followed her roommate to the top of the stairs and hovered there. What, after all, did she have to be nervous about? She was going to a boring dinner with her boss. That was all. There was no reason for her to behave like a scared rabbit.

She watched Dolores, in skin-tight silver satin, throw open the door with a flourish. "*You're* Tammy's boss?" she heard her say.

"Yes," replied Nick's familiar voice. "I'm Tamsin's boss. Shouldn't I be?"

"Not from the way she spoke about you. I figured you were at least forty and short."

Oh God, Doro! Must you? Tamsin buried her face in her hands.

"Short? Why short?" she heard Nick ask.

"She said you could never lay your hands on anything

except women and that you kept her climbing the walls looking for missing files."

Like a damn bluebottle! Tamsin groaned silently. *Doro, for heaven's sake!*

"As you can see," Nick said, "I'm not short. And I promise I won't lay my hands on Tamsin. Is she ready?"

Tamsin lowered her arms, took a deep breath and started down the stairs. She had to face him now, before Dolores did any further damage. "Yes, I'm ready," she called.

When Nick saw her, he went unusually still. She caught just a glimpse of his face before she looked away.

Was something the matter with her dress? She glanced down just to make sure, resting a hand on the peeling, pond-green wallpaper.

All was well. Everything was the way it was meant to be. Pale peach that flattered her complexion, or so Dolores said. Soft folds of fabric that shimmered and clung as she walked. Bare arms and shoulders set off by the thin gold chain that had long ago belonged to her grandmother. She had to admit that from the waist down the dress looked as though it had been sewn while she was in it, yet it flared out from her knees so that she was able to walk gracefully and with ease.

Tamsin lifted her head proudly. She might be quaking inside, but she was damned if she would let Nick Malahide know it. Tonight she was a duchess, and she was going to walk down these creaking stairs as if they belonged in a ducal palace. She might not be beautiful, but that was no reason not to move as if she were. She smiled at Nick as she reached the bottom step.

He put a hand into his jacket pocket and stepped forward. "You look stunning," he said, favoring her with the kind of smile he usually reserved for his Glorias.

"So do you," she whispered, and was disconcerted to see his eyebrows go up.

All the same, what she'd said was true. She was used to seeing Nick in office suits and, occasionally, in casual slacks and shirts. But in his superbly tailored tuxedo, he was a walking sex symbol in black.

Tamsin took the last few steps toward him and once more raised her eyes politely to his face. At least now he was smiling the familiar office smile. That she could handle.

Taking a deep breath, she moved forward to place her hand on the arm he was holding out. But the moment she touched him, he stiffened, as if her fingers had transmitted some kind of electric surge.

She tensed, waiting for what would come next. But Nick said only, "Ready?" as if no lightning had forked between them. They might have been getting ready to go over the company accounts.

"Yes," she said with a nonchalance meant to match his. "I'm ready. Good night, Doro."

"Have a dynamite evening." Dolores, who had retreated up a step, was observing the two of them with a smug little smile that would have made Tamsin want to hit her if she'd suffered from a tendency to violence.

"Oh, we will," Nick replied drily. "Provided Tamsin can stomach rubber chicken."

"Ugh." Dolores shuddered. "Dead bird. Enjoy your veggies, Tammy."

Tamsin, her color high, ignored her roommate as she and Nick made their way down the shabby steps to the front gate.

"Oh!" she exclaimed when they reached street level without incurring further parting salvos from her friend.

"That's not ours, surely?" No wonder Mrs. Sawchuk's eyes were popping out of her head from her vantage point behind the curtains.

"What? The limo?" Nick sounded amused. "Why shouldn't it be?"

Why indeed? She had often ordered limousines for his use.

"I guess I'm not used to the high life," she explained, smiling ruefully.

Nick laughed and helped her in while the driver held the door.

Tamsin soon found there was more she wasn't used to about riding in style—such as sitting in the subtle intimacy of the limo's soft interior, inhaling the potent scent of man mixed with leather. She shifted along the seat, as far from Nick as she could get.

"Would you like a drink?" he asked, leaning toward the bar.

Tamsin jumped as his hand brushed her knee.

"N-no thank you."

He turned to look at her then, his face half hidden in the shadows cast by tall buildings along the route. "Sherry?" he suggested. "You look cold."

"I'm not cold."

Nick reached for her hand and, finger by finger, began to pull off one of the long gloves Lucien had insisted she wear with his dress.

"Yes, you are," he said, curling his palm around her fingertips. "What's the matter, Tamsin? You're not scared of this rather dull dinner, I hope. There's no need to be."

She flinched and tried to draw her hand away. "No. Why should I be scared?"

"Of me, then?"

122

She laughed, a brittle, unconvincing sort of laugh. "Of course not. I've known you too long."

"Or not long enough," he suggested, echoing her own erratic thoughts.

She pressed herself back into the corner.

Nick shook his head. "Tamsin, I haven't tried to seduce a woman in thc back seat of a car since I was sixteen. And even then I didn't succeed."

"You didn't?" She blinked and relaxed just a little.

"Don't sound so surprised. No, I didn't."

"I am surprised," Tamsin admitted.

"How flattering," he murmured in a voice that sent shivers across her skin. She was acutely conscious that he was still holding her hand.

"I didn't exactly mean—" She broke off. What had she meant?

"If it helps at all," Nick said, "I have kissed in the back of a car more recently. I'm not too old for that."

He sounded brisk now, almost as if kissing were part of the job. Tamsin wasn't sure whether to laugh or slap him. The other alternative didn't bear thinking about.

"Yes, you are," she said. "Much too old. Would you mind letting go of my hand?"

The limo turned a corner, and his face came fully into the light. Was that faint curl at the corner of his mouth meant to be teasing or malicious? And why was he holding her hand anyway? She felt as if she were drowning in his eyes and in his scent and in the warmth of his fingers clasping hers.

Nick laughed and began to ease the glove back onto her fingers.

Five minutes later the limo passed through tall wrought-iron gates and drew up in front of a low cedar-frame building overlooking the waters of Burrard Inlet. In the background, a profusion of colored lanterns threw dim lighting over softly scented gardens. In front, Vancouver's rich and philanthropic were being disgorged from a profusion of Lincolns, Cadillacs and limousines.

Tamsin, still feeling dazed and disoriented, walked beside Nick toward the building she recognized as the well-known Cypress Club. But when a piercing female voice shrieked, "Nick, darling, you came!" and her boss disappeared in a cloud of midnight blue silk, she returned to reality with a jolt.

The last time she'd experienced such instant disillusionment had been on the day Paul told her that what had not yet been between them was over.

It was too much. Nick wasn't Paul, but the feeling of betrayal was startlingly similar. Nick had asked her to play the part of his partner for the evening, and now it seemed that honor should have gone to this woman who called him darling.

Blindly, without pausing to consider what she was doing, Tamsin extricated herself from a trailing wisp of blue silk and began to run back toward the gates.

Seconds later a firm hand descended on her shoulder. "And where do you think you're going?" Nick's voice inquired conversationally.

She tried to shrug him off, but he only turned her to face him and held on to her upper arms so she couldn't move.

"Home," she said. "I'm going home."

"Are you? And how do you plan to get there?"

"The same way I came, of course." Why wouldn't he just let her go?

"In the limo? I don't think so. Especially as it's already left."

Tamsin followed the direction of his eyes. In the spot where the limo had parked, a black Rolls was releasing a purple-rinsed dowager in pink accompanied by a hairless man who looked as though he'd just been taken out of mothballs.

Tamsin turned back to Nick. "I can take the bus," she said, clutching at the only straw that presented itself.

"Dressed like that?" He inserted a finger beneath the thin strap of her dress. "Why would you want to?"

"Why not? You don't need me here."

"What makes you think that?"

She frowned. In the light from the lanterns, Nick's eyes gleamed dark and inscrutable, yet she could have sworn she heard laughter behind the seemingly bland inquiry.

"Your *friend,*" she said. "The one who squeals like a rabbit and calls you darling. She makes me think so."

"Squeals?" Yes, he was definitely laughing. "I assure you Marriette is no rabbit. A kitten perhaps, but certainly not a rabbit. Now stop behaving like an idiot, and I'll take you inside and introduce you."

"I'm not an idiot. I saw her kiss you."

"Lots of women kiss me. It doesn't mean anything. And if you'd been looking, instead of running away, you would have noticed I didn't kiss her back. Marriette didn't come here tonight to be with me. She's married to a good friend of mine, one of the other sponsors."

"Oh." Tamsin put a hand over her face to hide her embarrassment, hoping that in this light he couldn't see much anyway. "I thought—look, I wasn't running away—"

"Yes, you were."

"All right, I suppose I was. But I didn't think you'd mind."

"Don't be ridiculous. Of course I'd mind." He leaned

forward until his nose was almost touching hers. "As a matter of fact, I'd mind very much."

His deep, midnight voice curled around her like rich, smooth cream, and for no good reason Tamsin felt tears pricking at her eyes. She blinked them away. Once before she had cried in front of Nick. It wasn't going to happen again.

"Thank you," she said formally. "In that case I won't let you down."

"Good." Nick tucked her hand securely in his elbow and marched her toward the brightly lit doors. "And now, if you could just manage not to look as if you're approaching a particularly daunting scaffold, the two of us ought to get through this evening quite well."

Tamsin squared her shoulders. She didn't look *that* scared, did she? Lifting her chin, she offered him a bright, brittle smile. He smiled back and gave her hand a squeeze.

All at once she felt comforted, warmer—even attractive. Tonight she was Ms. Tamsin Brown of Malahide's, chosen by Nick Malahide to represent the firm. And represent it she would.

Inside the long, panelled reception room with its rough stone fireplace and pots of summer foliage, the gathering of dark-suited men and expensively dressed women drifted about chattering, appraising each other and waiting to be seen.

Nick, with an encouraging nod, led her over to Marriette of the midnight blue silk, and the short, moonfaced man who stood beaming beside her.

"Tamsin," he said, "I'd like to introduce you to Bill and Marriette McCrosky. Bill and I have worked together on quite a few of the Foundation's fund-raising campaigns."

And Marriette had worked on several of her own private

campaigns, Tamsin thought, watching the way the other woman eyed Nick, who gave every appearance of being totally oblivious.

Tamsin smiled brilliantly and was surprised to see a look of startled admiration in Bill's eyes.

"Where did you find this lovely lady?" he demanded of Nick before turning to Tamsin and asking, "Haven't seen you at any of the usual functions, have I?"

"No, you haven't." Tamsin decided she could easily get to like Bill.

"In the office," Nick said. "I found her in my office."

"Don't tell us!" Marriette tittered. "You *haven't* brought your secretary to the banquet."

"His assistant," Tamsin said, bristling. "But I promise not to drink from my finger bowl or put ice cubes in my wine."

Beside her she heard what sounded like a snort, then Nick leaned down to growl into her ear, "Keep it up, and you won't get any wine."

Marriette, who hadn't been able to hear him, frowned. "I'm sure you won't," she said condescendingly to Tamsin. "Do let me know if I can be of any help."

Tamsin dug her fingers into Nick's elbow.

"Isn't that Guy Gatesby over there?" he said at once. "Tamsin, I'd like to introduce you to the Foundation's president."

He drew her away from Bill and Marriette with a smoothness she guessed was born of long practice in avoiding awkward scenes.

"I figured I'd best get you out of there before Marriette went for your eyes," he said. "I'd no idea she was that much more cat than kitten."

"Hadn't you?" Tamsin wondered if he recognized that

jealousy was at the root of Ms. Blue-Silk's venom. Maybe not. She'd learned from Dolores that men could be extraordinarily obtuse.

Until tonight she had never come close to inspiring jealousy in another woman. It was a heady feeling—especially when she saw the same look of admiration in Guy Gatesby's eyes that she had seen in Bill's.

Further introductions followed, and the pattern was repeated. Appreciative glances from the men, suspicious ones from many of the women. Tamsin felt as if she'd grown six inches and sprouted a tiara, especially when Nick patted her hand and told her she was the toast of the evening.

Dolores had been right. She could hardly believe it.

The meal, in spite of its exclusive surroundings, was as uninspiring as Nick had predicted.

As a waiter removed the remains of a sickly pink raspberry mousse, the most edible part of the dinner, Nick leaned over and whispered, "Good for you. You even managed to look as though you enjoyed that."

"I did," Tamsin said, surprised. "It was quite a nice mousse."

"Good grief, don't tell me you have a sweet tooth."

"What's wrong with that?"

"Nothing. You don't show it, that's all."

"No," she agreed. "It's genetic. Bones instead of curves."

"Oh, I don't know." He ran a pensive eye over her figure. "Some parts of you are very nicely covered."

Tamsin, feeling absurdly flattered, bit her tongue, at a loss for an appropriate response.

As it turned out, she didn't need one, because at that moment the president stood up to make his obligatory speech about the importance of contributing to the community, and what a good job the Foundation had done over the past year. Further congratulatory speeches followed, along with the presentation of a number of awards. Then Nick stood up to introduce the main speaker of the evening, a serious young man whose specialty seemed to be the production of lengthy application forms calculated to ensure that the Foundation's funds never left the bank.

As soon as the speaker sat down to relieved applause, Nick took Tamsin's hand and led her back to the reception room, where a small band was now tuning up.

"You didn't tell me there would be dancing," she accused him.

"Didn't I?"

He knew he hadn't. And she knew why. "You were afraid I wouldn't come if I knew, weren't you?"

"Not afraid, no. I just wasn't taking any chances."

Tamsin thought of refusing to dance with him, but she'd already made a fool of herself once this evening. It would be better to respond to his duplicity with cool civility.

The trouble with cool of any sort was that she already felt much too warm, and when Nick put his arm around her waist and led her onto the dance floor, her body reacted as if he'd lit it with a match.

The musicians found their rhythm, and Nick swung her out and away from him, spinning her gracefully on her toes. Tamsin, who had always thought herself clumsy on her feet, felt light as a summer breeze, as if she'd been whirled about by handsome men all her life.

After a while the music slowed, became softer, more sensuous, and Nick drew her back into his arms and held her close. The provocative pressure of his thighs combined with the subtle scent that she had always vaguely been aware was a part of him, created an unusual melting sensation deep in her abdomen.

When Nick slid his hand down her back and pressed her against the flatness of his stomach, she gasped.

She hadn't felt anything remotely like this when she'd danced with Paul.

When she looked up, she saw that Nick's eyelids were half-closed, and his lips only inches from her own.

"Nick—?" Someone bumped into her back, and she broke off, no longer sure what she'd meant to say.

"Yes?" His breath was a feather tantalizing her cheek. The hand on her back slipped lower. "What is it?"

"Please. . . ."

Her plea was never uttered. The music came to a thrumming halt, and at the same moment Bill tapped Nick on the shoulder and announced that it was time to change partners.

Before Tamsin could recover her senses, she was hauled away in Bill's arms, while Marriette hurried into Nick's, her blue silk bottom swaying in what looked like invitation.

Tamsin tried to see if the invitation was likely to be accepted, but as far as she could tell before Bill waltzed her behind an oversized rubber plant, Nick's hand remained discreetly on his partner's waist.

For the remainder of the evening, Tamsin was whirled from partner to partner while Nick did his duty by a procession of eager young women, middle-aged matrons, and a few over-painted dowagers who had a tendency to pat him on the cheek.

It wasn't until the very last dance that she found herself back in his arms.

"Well? Did you enjoy yourself?" he asked, pushing a stray wisp of hair behind her ear.

The beat of the music was slow, soft, erotic, making her

forget that she and Nick were not the only couple in the room. "Yes," she said, surprised to realize it was true. "I did. Did you?"

"Not much," he admitted, maintaining a careful distance between their bodies. "I never do at these affairs. But it's the kind of evening I've learned to survive."

Funny, she had never thought of Nick as a survivor. To her, he had always been a man who did as he pleased and, in most cases, got what he wanted. But perhaps she was wrong about that. Considering he'd been raised by a father who sounded as though he'd had a greater affinity with furniture than with his motherless sons, Nick had grown into a surprisingly well-adjusted man. Oh, he was arrogant and impatient, certainly, but on the whole he had accepted life's obligations with good grace—which was why the two of them were here now, gliding around the dance floor to a beat that was once again inspiring feelings she didn't think her parents would approve.

Or would they? She had often wondered how she'd happened to be born.

"You make 'surviving' look so easy," she said as Nick maneuvered her around a stout couple doggedly trying to waltz to the contemporary rhythm. "As if you like being the beau of the ball."

His frown was so fleeting she might have imagined it. "It is easy, but that doesn't mean I particularly enjoy it. Given a choice, I'd prefer to be in Malahide's workshop drilling holes."

"Sorry," Tamsin said lightly. "I can't turn into a drill or a chisel at midnight."

Nick shook his head. "I haven't the least desire to exchange you for a chisel."

Tamsin was still trying to come up with a smart answer

131

when the music stopped. After that the president climbed onto the small stage to thank the assembled guests for coming and to wish them all a good night.

"We've been dismissed," Nick said cheerfully. "Where's your coat?"

"I didn't bring one."

"Didn't you?"

She remembered then that when they had left her apartment he'd been so busy appraising the rest of her that neither of them had stopped to think about a wrap.

"Never mind," he said, putting an arm around her shoulders to steer her outside. "I'll make sure you're warm."

On this balmy night Tamsin suspected she'd have a full-blown fever if he went on making comments like that.

The moment they were through the door, she pulled herself out of the protective circle of his arm. To her surprise, she immediately felt a chill.

Bill and Marriette passed them, waving as they hurried toward the gates. All down the driveway good-byes were shouted and car doors slammed as, duty done, the Foundation's guests turned their thoughts in the direction of home.

The limo, engine purring, was waiting for them.

"In you get," Nick said.

Tamsin wriggled into a corner.

Nick laughed softly. "You couldn't sit farther away, could you?"

Tamsin was on her guard at once. "I'm your assistant, not Ms. Van Gelder."

"Good. I don't want you to be Gloria." Nick stretched an arm along the back of the seat. "I prefer you as yourself."

"I am myself," Tamsin said.

"Ah, but which is the real you? My competent, unobtrusive assistant or the pretty Cinderella I met tonight?"

Tamsin hunched into her seat and made no answer. Had he actually called her pretty?

"I'd find it easier to make up my mind if you'd stop trying to melt into that corner," Nick said.

Tamsin sat up so straight that her back felt like a fence post. "Don't bother," she said, "I'm your assistant, nothing more."

For five years she had watched women parade in and out of Nick's life. She wasn't about to join the ranks of his discards simply because something about the evening had awakened the Romeo in him. If nothing else, Paul had taught her how it felt to be tossed aside, and she wasn't anxious to repeat the experience.

"Thank you for a lovely evening," she said, when Nick made no response to her pronouncement.

"Is that what your mother taught you to say?" He spoke with more than a hint of exasperation.

"No. I thought of it all by myself."

"I see." He turned away as if he'd lost interest, and for the remainder of the drive acted as if she wasn't there. Only when the limo drew up in front of her home did he stop impersonating a stone.

"I suppose you're not going to ask me in," he said as he escorted her up the steps to the battered door.

"How can I? Your driver's waiting for you."

"As he's paid to do. Any other excuses?"

"Dolores . . ." she muttered.

"If I'm any judge of character, your Dolores wouldn't hesitate to entertain her friends whether I was there or not."

"True, but—" Tamsin turned away.

"But you don't want to ask me in. Okay. Message received." He touched her bare shoulder, and she jumped. "Turn around, Tamsin. Please."

Reluctantly she did as he asked.

Nick gazed down at her in the light from the street lamp, then raised a hand and cupped it around her cheek. Somewhere an owl hooted softly in the night.

"You look like a field mouse about to be eaten by a hawk," he said. "Would it be so terrible if I kissed you good night?"

Tamsin gasped. Nick was her boss. If she allowed him to kiss her now, everything would change.

It was changing already. She couldn't let it go any further.

"It—it wouldn't be terrible," she stammered. "At least I don't think so. But—"

Nick put his free arm around her waist.

Tamsin took a deep breath. "But I don't want to kiss you," she lied.

He released her at once, but as she groped in her purse for her key, she heard him murmur without apparent rancor, "Coward."

Tamsin ignored the gibe, let herself in and murmured a quick, "Good night" as she closed the door. Seconds later she heard Nick running down the porch steps, then the limo door closing and the purr of its engine as it took off down the street.

She kicked off her shoes and hurried up the stairs. A field mouse, Nick had called her. Maybe he was right. But if so, he was the hawk she had escaped. She pushed open the door to the apartment.

Dolores was lying on the sofa with Richard. When the door hinge creaked, she raised a languid arm from his back and waved. "Hi, Tammy. Have a good evening?"

Tamsin watched, fascinated, as the long-legged Viking lying half on top of her friend slowly extricated himself from her grasp and rolled elegantly onto the floor.

She took a hasty step backward. The Viking was not Richard Kerrigan.

"Hey," Dolores protested. "No need to get up. It's only Tammy."

"Makes no difference. We weren't getting anywhere anyway." The man's voice, rough and resentful, didn't fit with the rest of him.

"It's all right. Really," Tamsin muttered. "I'm off to bed."

"Should have brought your hunk of a boss along," Dolores said. "He'd keep you warm."

"I'm already quite warm enough, thank you."

"I'm out of here." The Viking grabbed the edge of the sofa and pushed himself to his feet.

"No need," Tamsin and Dolores chorused in unison.

"Right. Tell me another one." He scowled at Dolores, then swung around and stalked toward the door.

Tamsin stepped hastily aside. She waited until she heard the downstairs door slam before turning back to her friend.

"Sorry," she said, although in truth she was more exasperated than sorry. In Susie's day she had never had to worry about coming home to late-night entertainment of the X-rated kind.

"Doesn't matter. I didn't like him much. I'm glad you came back when you did." Dolores pulled up the strap of her silver dress and tried to comb her hair with her fingers. "How did you make out with the big bad boss?"

"I didn't 'make out.' We went to a respectable charity dinner dance and then he brought me home."

"That's it? Did you at least dance with him? And why on

135

earth didn't you ask him in? I'll take him if you don't want him."

"No you won't. I don't want him, but you wouldn't either. He'd only dump you. He dumps everyone."

"Including you?"

"Of course not including me." Tamsin produced an unconvincing laugh. "Ours is purely a business relationship."

"Oh, yeah? I saw the way he looked at you. That kind of 'business' I could handle. And don't be surprised if you find his desk cleared off and ready for action when you go into work on Monday morning." Dolores grinned and stretched her arms above her head. "Does he have one of those nice big desks with a leather top?"

"Doro! Don't be ridiculous." Tamsin glared at her friend, but Dolores only shrugged and threw herself back onto the sofa.

"Okay, how about a table in the boardroom? You do have a boardroom, don't you?"

Tamsin battled to keep her face straight—and failed. "Yes," she admitted. "It has a very *hard* table."

"Perfect." Dolores closed her eyes.

Tamsin chuckled in spite of herself, but a moment later she frowned. "Doro . . . ?"

"Hmm?"

"What were you doing with that fellow?"

"Jake? What did it look like I was doing?"

"You know what it looked like. But you weren't, were you. Not really."

Dolores's mouth turned down. "No. I told him nothing like that was going to happen. He was trying to change my mind."

"Yes, but why were you even. . . . ? I mean you just said you didn't like him. I thought—"

"You thought I'd hang about waiting for Richard." Her roommate's voice was flat. "What's the point? He's not going to call. And no way am I going to call him. Besides, what would the Sawchuks have to talk about if I stopped dating?"

"Me going off in a limo, maybe. But, seriously, it hasn't been that long—"

"Long enough." Dolores sat up. "There's plenty more where Richard Kerrigan came from."

Her indifference was so patently false that Tamsin's exasperation turned to sympathy. "Oh, Doro, don't. Don't rush off looking for love in all the wrong places. Give Richard time to—"

"I'm not looking for love. Believe it or not, I'm looking for a good time. Besides, I just had a call from Mom and Dad. They're coming to see me sometime soon. That's all the love I can handle right now."

"Doro, that's great. But—"

"Nothing's hurt except maybe my pride," Dolores interrupted, wriggling a little as she attempted to straighten her dress.

Tamsin gave up. There was no talking to her friend in this mood. The trouble was, Dolores had spent a lifetime learning how to bury her hurt. Now, when she needed comfort and support, she had no idea how to ask for it.

"Okay, I'm going to bed," Tamsin said.

"But not to sleep, I bet," Dolores called after her.

Tamsin paused long enough to smile. "Probably not," she agreed. "Good night, Doro."

Dolores's prediction proved accurate.

As Tamsin slid between the sheets and tried to tell herself that all she wanted was sleep, images of the evening kept flickering through her mind like disconnected film clips.

Nick enfolded in clouds of blue silk. Nick whispering "Good for you," in her ear as they ate that doubtful dinner, holding her in his arms as they danced so that she was aware of every seductive movement of his body. Then, at the end, Nick suggesting he might kiss her.

It had surely been an evening to remember. An evening she would hold in her heart when her hair turned gray and she was a tired old lady living with a cat. . . .

No! She sat up suddenly. Damned if she'd allow that to happen. When the time was right, she would make a life for herself. A full life. Tonight had helped prove she could do it.

Tamsin pushed back the sheet, allowing the mild breeze blowing through the open window to fan her heated skin.

Dawn was brightening the sky with its soft pink light by the time she finally fell asleep.

On Monday morning, when Tamsin walked into Nick's office, he was wearing jeans and a sweatshirt instead of his usual suit, and he was perched on the edge of a desk that had been swept totally clean. Even his computer was on the floor and pushed against the wall.

When he raised a finger and beckoned to her, Tamsin opened her mouth, closed it, tried to speak and failed.

Nick, observing her reaction, spoke instead.

"Tamsin?" He watched in disbelief as his sensible assistant tripped over her practical beige pumps and stumbled out of his office as if she'd been swigging the firm's brandy.

Now what was the matter with the woman? Was she ill? Or merely suffering from some kind of female problem? He didn't know much about those, but he hoped she wasn't going to start having them around the office.

He heard the sound of her body thumping into her

chair—followed by silence. He waited. Did she need help, or would she rather be left alone? Women were so unpredictable. Gloria, with nothing worse than a cold, had expected flowers and fuss and anxious faces hovering over her sickbed. It had infuriated her when he failed to oblige. In contrast, her predecessor had told him to go away if she so much as sneezed. That he had found easier to take.

But this was Tamsin. He couldn't ignore funny, beige Tamsin who had turned his loins to porridge in her sexy peach dress.

The silence continued. No clicking computer keys, no banging drawers, no soft voice answering the phone.

Right. He couldn't sit here doing nothing any longer. Maybe she'd fainted.

Mentally rehearsing his knowledge of industrial first-aid, Nick stood up and strode into her office.

She was seated at her desk staring at the fax machine as if it were a bomb.

He followed the direction of her gaze. The fax was squat, lifeless and definitely not ticking.

"Tamsin," he said. "Are you all right?"

She nodded without looking at him.

"Then why are you sitting there like a zombie?"

Her only answer was to reach for a pile of mail.

"You've lost your voice?" Nick wasn't sure whether to be angry or alarmed.

"No. No, I'm fine." Tamsin shook her head as if she needed to clear it. "I just felt dizzy for a minute." She picked up her letter opener and attempted to split open an envelope that was already open.

Nick waited, leaning against the door frame. What was going on? He moved to the center of her office and planted both fists on her desk. "Come on, let's have the truth."

Tamsin pinched her lips together and refused to look at him.

Frowning, he studied the pale, silky cap of her hair. It smelled fresh, like peaches—or was it apple blossom? Without actually forming the intention, he raised a hand and stroked a few strands back from her brow.

She flinched, as if he'd touched a much more private part of her, and cried, "Don't! Don't do that."

Nick decided he'd had enough. "Look," he said, "I'm not about to ravish you on my desk. Too public. Uncomfortable as well."

At first he thought it had been the wrong thing to say, because in seconds Tamsin's skin turned from white to a startling shade of gray. Then she surprised him by putting a hand to her mouth to stifle what sounded remarkably like a giggle.

"I could have you charged with harassment for saying that," she said.

"Charge ahead." Nick gazed at the tip of pink tongue protruding between her lips. "Are you okay now?"

"I'm fine," she said softly.

"Good. Oh, by the way, I'm having a crew from the workshop deliver another desk later on this morning, while I have Dad's old one refinished. Let me know when they get here."

He watched with interest as her skin turned back to pink and then to crimson. Finally he sauntered into his office, shutting the door behind him with a snap. As he sank into his chair he favored his new painting with a broad grin.

Did Tamsin have any idea how cute she looked when her feathers were ruffled? Definitely cute enough to kiss. He contemplated the prospect for several pleasant moments, then leaned back and gave his undivided attention to the ceiling.

Impossible toad of a man! Tamsin pounded her computer keys as if she had Nick's scalp beneath her fingers. He had nearly made her laugh with his outrageous comment about the office being too public for seduction. The idea of a man as successful and businesslike as Nick ravishing an employee on a desktop—sandwiched in between phone calls, appointments and interruptions from staff—was ludicrous. Totally absurd. If only Dolores hadn't suggested the possibility. No, that wasn't fair. It wasn't Dolores's fault. It was her own. She should have known better than to pay even temporary attention to her dizzy roommate's nonsense. How could she have made such a fool of herself in front of Nick? All because, just for a second when she'd walked into his office, she had imagined Dolores's prediction was about to come true.

Tamsin's head jerked up as a voice from the landing yelled, "Watch that corner, Al. The boss'll have our backsides for target practice if we smash up his new desk before we get it delivered."

Another voice mumbled something lurid and unprintable, then she heard a thud.

Tamsin crossed the room to knock on Nick's door.

"Yes? Come in," he replied, in a voice that clipped like scissors.

She poked her head inside. He was standing with his hands behind his back, staring down at the street. "Your desk is here," she said.

"Good. Have it brought in."

Tamsin withdrew, passed on Nick's instructions to the men with the desk and went downstairs to talk to Sally. With all that crashing and thumping going on, there wasn't much point in trying to work.

By the time she returned to the office, the new desk had been satisfactorily installed and Nick was seated behind it looking bosslike.

"Where have you been?" he demanded.

"In the showroom. I had something to discuss with Sally."

"Did you indeed?"

Tamsin waited to see if he had anything more to say. When he hadn't, she turned away.

"Tamsin?" His imperious voice stopped her in her tracks.

"Yes?"

"I'd like you to have dinner with me tonight."

Help! What was it he'd said earlier? About the office being too public and too uncomfortable? And yet, this invitation seemed more peremptory than personal.

She spoke without turning around. "Thank you, but I already have plans." Nick might rule Malahide's, but that didn't mean he had a right to rule her.

"Have you? Look at me, Tamsin."

Why was he always telling her to look at him? Not that he was hard on the eyes. She hesitated, then turned around, allowing her gaze to settle on his mouth.

How strange that lips as seductive as Nick's could look so hard.

"Now," he said, "tell me again that you have plans."

"I have. I plan to wash my hair and catch up on my reading."

He nodded. "Ah. I thought so. Another dynamite evening on West Sixteenth."

Tamsin, hurt by his sarcasm, was determined not to show it. "Please don't misunderstand me, but I'd rather not."

"Why? Because washing your hair and reading is more stimulating?"

"No, because I prefer to keep my business and my social life separate."

"Ah. So if I'm to have the pleasure of your company I'll have to fire you. Is that it?"

Was he serious? She didn't think so—but with Nick you never knew.

"If you fire me, you certainly *won't* have the pleasure of my company," she pointed out. "And what's more, you'll have to train a new assistant."

A corner of Nick's mouth tilted wryly. "Good point. So if I'm to retain your services, I'm not allowed to ask you out. Is that it?"

"Yes. Dolores says—"

"That roommate of yours needs her backside kicked," Nick remarked.

"I'll tell her you said so." Tamsin gazed with feigned innocence at his gold pen and pencil set, the only items he had so far placed on his new desk. "She'll probably invite you over for an evening."

Nick brushed a hand across his mouth. "I think not," he replied.

Tamsin waited for what would come next, but after a few seconds he waved her away, and she retreated to her office with a feeling that she had somehow cut off her nose to spite her face. Dinner with Nick would have been . . . interesting, at the very least.

No. Shaking her head, she picked up a pencil and tapped it sharply on her desk. Interesting or not, she couldn't allow herself to get too close to Nick. Not as long as she wanted to keep her job. Which she did. It was convenient, she was good at it, and after her rather Spartan childhood it was nice to work around furniture and accessories so beautifully designed they were almost art.

When, or if, it became necessary to her peace of mind to leave Malahide's, she would do so. Until then her best option was to maintain a discreet and professional distance from a boss who attracted women as easily as a snapdragon attracts bees.

Tamsin went back to assaulting the keys on her computer.

Chapter Eight

Dolores slammed the front door behind her and stomped up the stairs with rain dripping from her eyebrows. It wasn't supposed to rain like this in July. Especially not on a day when she'd had one client who smelled like a brewery, another who was stoned and a third who had missed her appointment altogether.

Hoisting an overloaded shopping bag onto her shoulder, she pushed open the door to the apartment and paused to glare at the runnels of water streaming down the two narrow windows.

"Tammy?" she called when only silence, punctuated by the relentless dripping of rain on the roof, greeted her entrance. "Are you home?"

No answer. Her roommate must still be at work. Or maybe she'd finally succumbed to the lures of that gorgeous boss she pretended not to notice.

Dolores dumped her shopping bag onto the kitchen counter and marched into her room to unbutton the uniform-like dress she wore to work. After that she collapsed wearily onto her bed—and saw that directly over her head a damp stain was oozing its way across the ceiling.

Perfect! Just perfect. Pretty soon it would be raining onto her bed.

Disentangling her legs from the red and black quilt, she swung her legs to the floor and padded into the front room to call the landlord.

He was out, of course. It figured. It was that sort of day.

She left a message on his machine and stood frowning at the arrow-shaped mark beside the phone while she tried to decide what to do next.

She could, she supposed, phone that man she'd met out dancing two nights ago and get him to take her somewhere. It would beat staying home waiting for the rain to start pouring through the ceiling. The only trouble with that idea was that she couldn't remember the man's name, and hadn't liked him much in the first place. She didn't seem to like any man particularly these days. Not since Richard, who hadn't phoned her since Mark and Carla's wedding in June. She'd given up hoping he would.

Dolores slid her dress down her arms and went on staring indecisively at the wall. He *hadn't* been indifferent to her; she knew he hadn't. So why had he refused to give her a chance? The fiasco at the wedding hadn't been her fault.

Maybe it was just that she wasn't like his true-blue Elizabeth, who had probably stayed by herself in corners when he told her to.

Dolores draped the dress over her shoulder and rested a hand on the peeling cream paintwork. She was being unfair, of course. How could Richard help mourning the woman he'd loved for two years and then lost? Any more than she could help comparing every man she met to Richard? Damn his icy gray eyes.

A forceful gust of wind blasted another sheet of rain against the windows. She swivelled around, glowering, then directed her bleak gaze at the phone.

All she had to do was pick it up.

Slowly, scarcely admitting to herself what she was doing, she reached for the receiver.

"Yes? Hello?" Richard's unforgettable baritone purred

down the wire after the second ring. He sounded distracted.

Dolores hesitated. She hadn't thought about what she would say.

"Hello?" he repeated, impatient now.

She opened her mouth to speak, but before she could say anything, another voice, a woman's this time, said, "Ricky, where do you keep your coffee?"

The words were quite distinct, spoken with the confidence of someone who knew Richard well and was standing right beside him . . . perhaps even with her arms around his neck.

Ricky. Dolores replaced the receiver, crossed to the nearest window and dropped her forehead against the cold, damp glass.

"Hello?" Richard said for the third time.

The sound of the line disconnecting hummed maddeningly in his ear. Frowning, he turned to his sister, Janet, who was rifling through his varnished kitchen cupboards in search of coffee.

"I keep it in the fridge," he said.

"Oh." She switched her attention to the refrigerator. "What was that? Wrong number?"

"No." He wasn't sure how he knew the identity of his silent caller, but he did. He also had a fair idea why she'd hung up.

Dolores Rowan. How many times over the past weeks had he thought of calling her? Even to the point, once, of dialing her number. No one had answered, and, surprisingly, neither had a machine.

He wanted to see her again. There was no getting away from that unpalatable truth. It had very nearly killed him not to kiss her the day he brought her home from Mark's wedding, when she had stood on the porch of that dilapidated house she lived in with her full lips parted in expectation. He had been about to fulfill that expectation too. Then a face with a cigarette attached to its lower lip had appeared at the downstairs window. Somewhere down the street a woman laughed, and he was reminded that Dolores, too, would laugh and move on to someone else once she had him as enslaved as all the others.

Men had looked at Elizabeth that way too, but Elizabeth had never dressed to drive them mad. Nor had she tried to grope him on a darkened dance floor—

"Ricky?" His sister's voice cut into his thoughts. "Do you plan to sit there brooding all evening? Because if you do, I think I'll take myself off to the beach to watch the rain. The sea gulls might make better company anyway."

"What?" Richard, who was lounging in his favorite high-backed brown leather chair, twisted around and caught a glimpse of Janet's plump behind in white slacks on the other side of the door to his small kitchen.

"I said, do you plan to sit there brooding all evening?" she repeated.

When he chose not to answer, she popped her curly ginger head around the door and asked worriedly, "It wasn't bad news, was it? Your call, I mean?"

Bad news? Yes, Dolores was undoubtedly bad news. But he wanted to see her. More than he would have thought possible. And, for the moment at least, he was certain she wanted to see him.

"Not bad news, no," he said. "Just bad timing."

Janet wiped her hands on her slacks, leaving mottled streaks on the white fabric. "I don't have to stay, you know. I've got lots of friends in town who'll be glad to have me."

Damn. He'd offended her. "I didn't mean *that*," he said,

mustering a reassuring smile. "I meant I wished that particular caller hadn't phoned on a night when my sister has come all the way from Calgary to visit me." He tipped his head against the back of the chair and crossed his legs.

Janet shook her head at him, but he knew she was over her pique when she couldn't hold back a grin. "I didn't come to visit you," she scoffed. "I came to sell our customers on our new line of scientific textbooks. *You're* just a handy source of bed and breakfast."

Richard removed a brown tweed cushion from the sofa and aimed it with deadly accuracy across the room.

"Ouch." Janet caught it against her chest. "I see you haven't lost your touch. Now tell me who phoned."

"Dolores. At least I'm almost sure it was." He closed his eyes, as if the subject wasn't sufficiently inspiring to hold his interest.

Janet wasn't fooled. "Uh-huh. So who's Dolores? And why did you hang up on her?"

"I didn't. She hung up on me."

"Why?"

"I've no idea." He raised a finger and removed a speck of dust from the corner of his eye.

"All right, who is she then?"

Janet had always been a bulldog, Richard reflected. "She's a woman I went out with a couple of times. Very sexy and about as reliable as a firefly."

"Sexy's good. You want reliable as well?" Janet disappeared into the kitchen and started banging about with mugs and spoons.

"I'm an accountant. The tax department takes a dim view of it when our clients' figures don't add up the way they're meant to. So, yes, I'm into reliable."

"Yes, but women aren't taxes. Is she nice?"

Nice? He'd never thought of Dolores as nice. But she was carelessly kind in her own way—except, he guessed, when it came to men. She didn't seem to understand that the game of love wasn't all one-sided, that men hated being jilted just as much as she had hated being abandoned by her parents.

"No," he said, "I wouldn't call her nice. In a lot of ways she's never quite grown up."

"But you care about her."

"I didn't say that."

"No, but I can tell. Maybe you could help her grow up."

Richard shuddered. "That's a task for a better man than I am."

"Garbage." Janet emerged from the kitchen carrying two white mugs of steaming black coffee, which she set down on his rectangular coffee table. "The trouble with you is that you're still hung up on Elizabeth. No, wait a minute." She held up a hand as he tried to interrupt. "You think all women ought to be like her, and when they're not, you find some excuse to get rid of them."

"You make me sound like Bluebeard," he snapped, then abruptly recollected that he'd said something similar to Dolores. "And you don't know what you're talking about. You haven't met Dolores, and I doubt you'd like her. Also, she's afraid of heights, which would mean—"

"That you'd have to move? Good. This place is much too Spartan anyway."

"I happen to like it."

"You would." Janet dropped into a second brown leather chair that matched the brown leather sofa and regarded her brother with a critical air. "Wouldn't I like her?" she demanded when Richard's gaze strayed toward an accounting periodical on the coffee table.

"Dolores? I doubt it. You'd say she was a bimbo."

"Ah, I see." Janet nodded wisely. "You're probably right, in that case. But still, I don't see why you shouldn't have some fun. You've been altogether too celibate since Elizabeth. It's unhealthy."

"Easy for you to say." Richard uncrossed his legs and leaned forward to pick up his mug. "You've got a perfectly good husband—who doesn't even complain when you travel all the way to Vancouver for the sole purpose of aggravating your brother."

Janet ignored the last part of his speech. "You could have a perfectly good wife if you wanted one. Or at least a steady girlfriend. You're thirty-six, Ricky. You need to settle down."

"Heaven preserve me from women who know what's best for me," Richard groaned. "And especially from sisters. Now can we please change the subject? Tell me about James's new job."

"All right, you asked for it." Janet, who had always known when to give up, spent the next half hour regaling him with the details of her husband's recent promotion to head of sales and marketing for a national bookstore.

Richard allowed his attention to drift.

No, Dolores wasn't nice. She wouldn't suit him in the long run. Yet, as he sprawled in his chair only half listening to his sister, he was sorely tempted to reach for the phone.

Janet was right. His bed was altogether too empty. Dolores might be a man-eater, but that was no reason she couldn't fill a temporary void. . . .

Richard closed his eyes, only opening them again when he awoke to find Janet shaking him by the shoulders and threatening never to visit him again.

In the morning, after he'd kissed her an apologetic good-bye, he knew he wouldn't make the call to Dolores.

The price of filling that particular void could prove too high.

"Doro? What's the matter?" Tamsin closed the door behind her and took a couple of steps into the apartment, her transparent raincoat dripping water onto the threadbare green carpet. "Doro, why are you staring at the phone? Are you trying to put a hex on it, or something?"

"What?" Dolores, wearing only a slip and a bra, turned slowly to face her. Her eyes, usually so bright and filled with laughter, were unfocused. "Oh," she said. "No. No I'm fine. Just a wrong number."

"Richard?" asked Tamsin, undeceived. Her friend had been putting a brave face on for weeks, but to anyone who knew her well it was apparent that her sparkling good humor was no more than a veneer brushed on to hide her hurt.

Dolores made a face, then nodded. "Oh, all right. Yes, as a matter of fact. I phoned him awhile ago. I know I shouldn't have, but I did. There was a woman with him. She called him *Ricky*."

"Doesn't suit him," Tamsin agreed. "Do you suppose she could have been his sister?"

Dolores's eyes snapped instantly back into focus. "I hadn't thought of that. Do you think she could be?"

"Why not? Probably an older sister who still looks on him as her little brother."

All at once Dolores's soft features lit with hope. "You could be right. Oh, Tammy, what would I do without you?"

"What you've always done. Find another man," Tamsin replied drily, and she went into the bathroom to hang up her raincoat.

When she came back, Dolores had put on jeans and a shocking pink T-shirt and was lounging on the sofa painting her nails purple.

"That's better," Tamsin said.

Dolores looked up. "Glad you think so. By the way, we're having a flood."

Tamsin blinked. "What are you talking about?"

Dolores wiggled her painted fingers. "Go see for yourself. The roof's leaking. Don't worry though, I called the landlord."

Tamsin hurried into her friend's bedroom. Sure enough, a damp patch was spreading like mold across the red and black quilt covering the bed.

"Honestly, Doro," she exclaimed, marching back into the living room to find her roommate engaged in a critical examination of her nails. "Why didn't you put a bucket under the leak? Or move the bed? Your quilt is soaked."

"Is it? Doesn't matter, I haven't been sleeping much anyway."

Tamsin gave up and went to find a bucket herself. Her friend's mental state must be worse than she'd thought.

"It's Monday, isn't it?" Dolores said when Tamsin returned with her arms full of wet quilt.

"Of course it is. Why?"

"I was just wondering what kind of flowers Nick brought you today."

Oh. Trust Dolores to remind her of the one person she'd been trying not to think about.

"Wild flowers," she said tersely, and went to hang the quilt over the shower rod in the bathroom.

"What's the matter?" Dolores called after her. "Don't you like wild flowers?"

Tamsin waited as long as she could before emerging

from the bathroom, but it did no good. Her roommate wasn't about to let the subject drop.

"*Don't* you like wild flowers?" she repeated, missing a nail and dabbing a streak of purple across her thumb.

"Yes, of course I do." Tamsin opened her mouth, started to speak, then thought better of it and plumped herself into the rocker. Its chintz cover was beginning to rip across the seat.

How could she explain to her friend, who would undoubtedly tell her to make the most of her opportunities, that she wasn't open to bribery by her boss? Even if he *was* every woman's fantasy in a suit.

For several weeks now Tamsin had been aware of Nick watching her.

He hadn't initiated any further personal conversations, and communication between them had remained on the strictly-business basis she had assured him she preferred. But still she knew he was watching, with an amused, predatory speculation that made her want to forget all about keeping her distance and demand to know what he was plotting.

Every Monday morning he arrived with flowers and told her to put them in water. The first time it had been roses, yellow ones. The second, red carnations artfully mingled with greenery and baby's breath. The third time she'd had to scurry around looking for a vase long enough to contain a boxful of creamy gladioli.

Today, as she was bent over the photocopier unblocking a paper jam, Nick had turned up with a stunning profusion of wild flowers and told her he was giving her a raise.

"Thank you," she had said, straightening cautiously, accepting the flowers and making an unsuccessful attempt to quash a flare of suspicion. "I appreciate that."

"Do you now?" Nick rapped his knuckles on the edge of her desk. "On one condition, though."

Of course. She'd known there was a catch. "Yes?" Her eyebrows lifted in inquiry.

"Use part of it to buy yourself some new clothes."

Tamsin took a step backward and collided with the photocopier. "I don't need new clothes," she said, grabbing the machine for support.

"Ones that aren't beige," he explained.

"I like beige." Hadn't they had this conversation before?

"I know you do. I don't, and I have to look at you all day."

"Gee, thanks." Tamsin switched on her computer. She was hurt, but damned if she meant to let him see it. "You don't *have* to look at me."

"Hard to avoid. Besides, I like looking at you. That doesn't mean the view can't be improved." He grinned, presumably to take the sting from his words.

"How gallant of you," Tamsin jeered lightly.

"No offense meant," he assured her.

Tamsin was inclined to believe him. Nick had always come directly to the point without much thought for the effect he had on others.

"Didn't your mother teach you—" She stumbled to a stop. For a moment there she had forgotten that Nick hadn't had a mother's guidance.

"Don't worry about it," he said. After a brief silence he added as if he still believed he had the right, "Green or blue ought to suit you. Don't even think of black."

Tamsin wasn't thinking of black. She was thinking of informing him, in words of one syllable, precisely where he could stuff his green and blue. But he chose that moment to deliver one of his killer smiles, and when it reached his eyes

155

she heard herself saying instead, "I'll think about it."

"Good." Nick raised a hand as if he meant to pat her on the cheek, but when she frowned, he let it drop against his thigh.

"I'll talk to accounting about that raise," he said, and was gone before she had time to blink.

"So," Dolores said, after Tamsin had given her an abbreviated version of the events of the day. "Are you going to buy something sexy and gorgeous? Nick's right, you know. You'd look good in green. A silk skirt with a slit up the back, maybe—and a jacket that shows off your—"

"Breasts?" Tamsin interrupted ruefully. "I haven't any to speak of. And even if I had, I wouldn't be parading them around the office. Nick wouldn't approve, and neither would I." She sneezed as the caustic smell of nail polish tickled the end of her nose.

"I wouldn't be so sure about Nick." Dolores put down the purple polish and surveyed her shiny nails with approval.

Tamsin shook her head and went to change out of her beige suit.

Nick, stuck in rush-hour traffic on the Lions Gate Bridge, wasn't in the best of moods.

He knew he'd hurt Tamsin's feelings. He hadn't intended to. The flowers had been his way of showing her he valued her as more than an office drone. Had the raise, well-deserved as it was, been the next step in a campaign which, as yet, he hadn't made up his mind to carry to its logical conclusion? Certainly ordering Tamsin to change her wardrobe had never been part of any plan.

He had spoken on the spur of the moment, irritated by

the suspicion she hadn't been able to hide when she thanked him for the raise—and by the fact that her neat backside bent over the photocopier had induced a spasm of desire that he was well aware was unlikely to be satisfied any time soon.

Tamsin had every reason to be suspicious of his motives. Nick glared at the driver of a van in the next lane who had one arm draped around a girl. It occurred to him, as he rolled up the window to shut out the smell of exhaust fumes, that if Tamsin did, in fact, purchase a new wardrobe, he must remember not to compliment her too extravagantly.

He was beginning to understand how her mind worked—at least he thought he was—and because he understood, he knew he might have to postpone the half-formed plan that had been lurking at the back of his mind ever since the day he had held her on his knees and discovered she wasn't all skinny efficiency beneath her eternal beige.

Waiting wouldn't be easy. He wasn't a patient man, and Tamsin Brown, all unconsciously, was getting under his skin.

The next day Tamsin bought a soft turquoise dress with short sleeves that Dolores said made her look glamorous.

When Nick saw it, he nodded. "That's the idea," he said. "Much better."

Tamsin refused to admit she was disappointed.

The following week, she bought a smart Nile green suit, and again Nick nodded approvingly before snapping the door to his office firmly shut.

She didn't buy any more new clothes.

Nick noticed, but he didn't comment.

★ ★ ★ ★ ★

As the weeks passed and the turning of the leaves hinted at the coming of autumn, Nick continued to bring flowers to the office every Monday and to treat his assistant with perfect courtesy and respect.

Tamsin noticed that Gloria Van Gelder no longer came into Malahide's, but a redhead called Loralee Spring sometimes did.

She told herself that everything was exactly the way she wanted it as she went about her work and kept the office running as smoothly as her boss's expensive car.

Dolores told her she was a fool.

"I'm telling you, Tammy, all you have to do is lift your little finger, and you'll have him," she said one evening as the two of them were getting in each other's way in the small kitchen.

"No, I won't."

"You could though. Remember the night you went to that snooty dinner? There was I, in my best knock-'em-dead silver, and all he could do was look at *you*. He was yours for the taking, Tammy."

"All right, what if he was? I wouldn't have kept him. Nobody can." Tamsin took an absentminded bite of the carrot she was peeling.

"I wouldn't be too sure of that. Anyway, you might not want to keep him. I've decided not to keep Jackson." Dolores bent down and peered into the fridge. "What happened to my tofu?"

"It grew greeny gray legs and walked away. Who's Jackson?"

"He's a client of Yoko's. Not mine, so it's all right to go out with him. But I don't think I will anymore. If the tofu's gone off, I'd better have lentils and beans."

"Yes, I suppose so." Tamsin wasn't much interested in her friend's rigidly healthy diet. "What's wrong with Jackson?"

"Nothing."

Tamsin didn't press the matter because she already knew the answer. Jackson wasn't Richard. Dolores had at last met a man who refused to be her doormat, and it was driving her unfortunate friend crazy. Thank heaven she was no longer moping around the apartment shooting desperate glances at the phone and refusing all invitations to go out. That phase had been mercifully short-lived.

All the same, Tamsin worried about her roommate, and she knew Dolores worried about her. For no reason, of course. *She* was perfectly content.

Yet only a few days later, when she went in to work and found Nick sitting on the edge of her desk swinging a leg and looking at his watch, contentment plummeted to her knees and took her stomach with it.

"Another two minutes and you'd have been late," he informed her.

Uh-oh. He was in one of those moods, was he? And ready to take it out on her.

"I'm never late," she said.

"Hmm." Nick frowned. "So what have you done with the designs for the Hagan Building's vestibule and boardroom?"

"You had me take them down to the workshop. Yesterday." Tamsin went to hang up her jacket.

Nick stopped swinging his leg. "Did I? Yes, so I did."

He didn't move, so she hung her jacket behind the door and asked politely, "Is there something else I can help you with?"

"You sound like a salesperson trying to sell me an overcoat to go with the underwear I just bought."

Tamsin laughed and said she'd bear that in mind if she ever decided to go into sales.

Nick, having failed to get a rise out of her, said, "As a matter of fact, there is something you can help me with. I'm going over to Victoria next week for a few days. A couple of bureaucrats need some help using up their budgets, so they're getting Malahide's to refurnish their offices."

Tamsin nodded. "I see. And you want me to keep things running here."

"No." Nick flicked a piece of lint off his sleeve. "I want you to come with me."

Tamsin's heart fluttered as if a moth had become trapped in her chest. A few days? On the Island with Nick? She eyed his wide shoulders and confident posture with an admiration that was partly unease. Did he mean it? Yes, of course he did. Nick didn't say things he didn't mean. But she couldn't go. Because if she said yes, he might take it as agreement of another sort, and she was not, ever, going to join his collection of interchangeable women.

"I'm sorry," she said. "I can't. Take Ms. Spring with you."

Nick shook his head. "Nope. I want my assistant for this trip, not a pretty airhead. Someone who can keep track of details and handle a laptop computer. That means you, Ms. Brown."

"But—"

Exasperation flared in his eyes. "Don't argue with me, Tamsin. Please. I need your help. You look very nice in that suit, by the way."

Was that miserly bit of flattery supposed to make her go limp with gratitude and fall obligingly in with his plans? Nick Malahide was altogether too used to getting his own way.

160

"You've never needed me on a business trip before," she pointed out.

"This particular situation hasn't arisen before."

Was he telling the truth? It wasn't likely that this was some devious ruse to get her into bed, given his current interest in Loralee Spring. Or was Loralee already a back number? An airhead, he'd called her. The moth in Tamsin's chest gave a little skip.

"Precisely what would my job be?" she asked, edging around him and pulling out her chair. She might as well find out where she stood.

"Oh, arranging appointments, transportation and dinner reservations, noting measurements and special requests, handling phone calls and generally seeing to my care and comfort."

"I'll think about it," Tamsin said, stalling.

Nick shook his head. "Can't we cut out the preliminary skirmish? I'd like you to make our hotel reservations as soon as possible."

He was strumming his fingers on his thigh, a sure sign of diminishing patience. Obviously it hadn't even occurred to him that he might possibly lose this clash of wills.

"What, exactly, do you mean by seeing to your comfort?" Tamsin asked.

"I've just told you that. Making phone calls, et cetera—"

"Yes, I know. Just as long as it's clear that I'm not tucking you into bed or standing in for your teddy bear."

Nick's face was a study in astonishment followed, eventually, by an expression she couldn't quite pin down.

"I never had a teddy bear," he said. "And to the best of my knowledge, no one has ever tucked me up in bed. So I expect I'll manage."

"Oh!" Instinctively Tamsin stretched out a hand. Her

own parents hadn't been demonstrative or overly generous with presents, but they *had* provided a teddy bear and shown her affection when she needed it. Perhaps Nick's father hadn't known how.

"Don't look so stricken. I had a baseball bat and a football and toy soldiers." He stood up and moved toward the door. "Let me know when you've made the reservations."

"Wait a minute," Tamsin called after him. "I didn't say. . . ."

But Nick, whistling under his breath, was already halfway down the stairs.

"Tammy. Tammy wake up."

"Mmm?" Tamsin blinked and opened her eyes. Why was Dolores shaking her like a jelly? "Whatsa matter?" she mumbled. "Are we having an earthquake?"

"Tammy! Don't be silly. Wake up. Your boss is here. And he's fit to be tied." She giggled. "Not, unfortunately, to my bed. There was a power cut and our alarms didn't go off."

"Damn. Today of all days." Muttering, Tamsin threw her legs over the edge of the bed and pulled at the hem of her brushed cotton nightshirt.

If only she had stuck to her guns and refused to accompany Nick to Victoria, she wouldn't be in this position. Instead, she'd given in, partly because she wanted to, and partly because it seemed an act of cowardice not to. She was, after all, a sensible modern woman who was entirely capable of defending her virtue if it came to that. Which, of course, it wouldn't.

Tamsin gave her friend a baleful look, pulled on a rumpled cotton wrap and stumbled barefoot to the door to tell Nick he'd have to wait while she got ready.

He was standing against the far wall with his arms folded across his chest and one ankle hooked over the other. "Is that what you plan to travel in?" he asked before she had a chance to say anything.

Some devil inspired by the power pose and the incendiary look in his eye brought Tamsin instantly awake. "Do you have some objection?" she asked sweetly.

Hazel-green eyes raked over her in a way that should have been insulting but wasn't—because it was flatteringly obvious Nick liked what he saw. "No," he said after a long, tension-filled pause. "Why should I? It's not me that every man on the ferry will be ogling. Where's your suitcase?"

Tamsin turned her back on him so he wouldn't see the color in her cheeks. "In my room. I have a couple more things to put into it."

"Well get your a—" Nick cleared his throat. "Get moving, please. We don't have a lot of time."

Dolores, glamorous in a pink satin negligee, drifted over to seize Tamsin by the arm. "Hang on," she said to Nick over her shoulder. "She won't be a minute. Tammy, come on. Don't just stand there."

"Hey! What do you think you're *doing?*" Tamsin demanded when Dolores pulled her into her bedroom and shut the door in Nick's impatient face.

"Getting you ready," Dolores replied, unperturbed. "Your heavenly hunk out there is in a hurry." She opened a drawer, pulled out a pair of neatly folded jeans and tossed them onto the bed. "Put these on."

"But—"

"Tamsin!" roared a voice from the other side of the door. "If you're not out of there in ten seconds, I'm coming in."

By the time Tamsin had on the jeans and a dark green

sweater that Dolores said looked reasonably attractive, at least thirty seconds had passed and Nick's solid frame was filling the doorway.

Dolores took one look at him and swooped under the bed to pull out Tamsin's half-packed suitcase.

"Cosmetics," she said. "Perfume. Those'll be in the bathroom. Tammy, get on with it. Go and fetch them."

"I can't," said Tamsin, who was now fully awake and suffering from a hysterical urge to laugh. "There's an—an obstacle in the way."

Dolores swung around, hands planted on her hips. "Now don't start—oh, I see." She nodded at Nick, who was still blocking the doorway. "Better move, boss-man."

Nick, who had been watching the proceedings with an unusually bemused eye, stepped aside and said, "Right. One minute and we're out of here. Okay?"

Ten minutes later Dolores dragged Tamsin's green suit and turquoise dress out of a closet and told Nick to take them downstairs and hang them in his car. "I'll get Tamsin ready for you," she promised.

"Check." Nick touched his fingers to his forehead in a smart salute. His smile of amused gratitude made Dolores pick up the morning paper to fan her face.

Once he was headed downstairs bearing Tamsin's clothes, she said, "If you pass on that one, Tammy, you'll deserve to be put out of your misery."

"You're a fine one to talk," Tamsin said. "You've just passed on two perfectly nice men. Jackson and—I forget the other one's name."

"Armand."

"Right. Anyway, Nick's all gorgeous packaging. Just like Paul."

"Maybe. But I'd settle for the packaging myself." Dolores rolled up a silk scarf and tucked it into a corner of the suitcase. "There, that should do it."

By the time Nick reappeared, Tamsin was waiting for him, suitcase in hand, and wearing her friend's yellow windbreaker over her jeans.

"Nice job." Nick nodded approvingly at Dolores. "Thank you."

He didn't say anything to Tamsin as he took her by the arm and hustled her down the stairs and into the Lincoln. He didn't need to.

The admiring look in his eyes said it all.

Tamsin cast a quick backward glance at the house. Dolores was standing at an upper window waving madly, and all at once Tamsin felt a shiver of unease. Odd, that. She wasn't unduly nervous about this trip. Yet something about that solitary figure in the window disturbed her, made her feel she ought to stay.

She waved back frantically until she could no longer see Dolores or the house.

Chapter Nine

Dolores didn't work Mondays, so she was home when the doorbell rang.

At first she ignored its persistent summons, but eventually it was borne in on her that whoever was out there didn't mean to give up until she answered. Grumbling, she stumbled out of the shower and stubbed her toe on the edge of the bathtub.

"Damn salespeople," she muttered, wrapping a bath towel around herself and dripping her way down the stairs to put a stop to the irritating noise.

The last thing she noticed before her world came crashing in on her was that the Sawchuks' cat had been sick on the front porch.

"Tell her I'll call her back," Richard said to Norah when she buzzed to tell him he had a call on line one from a woman who sounded frantic and incoherent.

The last thing he needed this morning—or any other morning, for that matter—was some unhappy client with a cash flow problem telling him she was about to go bankrupt.

"Right." Norah's clipped voice was reproachful.

Richard didn't care. He wasn't in the mood for incoherent, and he knew from experience that his caller's problems would be solved more efficiently once she'd had time to calm down.

Besides, why spoil the good humor left over from a particularly satisfactory weekend? The winds had been perfect for gliding, and as he'd drifted below the occasional soft clouds over Howe Sound, he had experienced a sense of freedom and well-being the likes of which he hadn't known in months.

There, high above his world, he had come to the conclusion that as far as Dolores was concerned there could be no going back. Dolores was over, a bittersweet might-have-been if he, or she, had been different people. Now it was time to take his sister's advice, stop comparing every woman he met to Elizabeth and start looking for new opportunities.

That advertising executive two floors down, for instance—the one with the cropped blond hair and the promising smile. She'd been sizing him up in the elevator for weeks.

The intercom buzzed again.

"Yes, Norah?"

"You can't call her back, because she can't remember her number," Norah informed him with infuriating complacence. "She's kind of hard to understand, but I think she said her name is Dolores."

Dolores? It couldn't be. Not after all these weeks. This must be some other woman who happened to have the same name.

"You want me to talk to someone who can't remember her own phone number?" he asked, trying to maintain his patience because Norah was good at her job and he didn't want to offend her.

She didn't answer. Her silence was in the nature of an accusation.

Richard gave in. "All right," he said. "All right, I'll talk to her." Might as well get it over with.

"Won't let you alone, will they?" Mark gibed from his desk across the room.

Richard mouthed an expletive at his partner, who knew damn well his phone calls at work were strictly business, and reached for the receiver.

"Yes?" he said guardedly. "Richard Kerrigan here."

"Richard?" The unmistakable voice on the other end was barely audible.

He took a handkerchief from his pocket and wiped it across his forehead. "Dolores? Is something wrong?"

"I—yes. I'm sorry. I shouldn't have called. But I didn't know who else . . ." The rest was drowned out by a maddening crackle of static.

"Dolores? What's happened?" Concern as well as irritation made his voice sharper than he'd intended.

"I—I'm sorry."

"Stop saying you're sorry and tell me what's the matter."

Her response was a sound that might have been a moan, followed by the crack of a receiver clattering back into its cradle.

Richard rubbed his ear, then dialed Dolores's number. When there was no answer after twelve rings, he swore.

Mark, red head cocked to one side, grinned and raised his eyebrows. "Woman trouble? How is the gorgeous Dolores?"

"I don't know," Richard said. "I haven't seen her."

"But you're about to."

"How the hell did you know?" Richard pushed himself to his feet and prowled across to the window. Was the man psychic? Was that why he was such a good poker player? The mountains, still clear of their winter frosting of snow, rose craggy and gray against the morning sky. He stood for a moment, admiring their remoteness, remembering how they had looked from above. Then he turned and prowled back to his desk.

"Because Norah's voice carries. So does yours, and I haven't seen you so bent out of shape about a woman in eons, that's how," Mark replied smugly. "You're leaving *now?*" he added, when Richard picked up his briefcase and swung toward the door.

"Yes, and heading into deep glue, I expect. Dolores seems to be in some kind of trouble."

"What kind of trouble? If it involves the police, you shouldn't—"

"I don't know what it involves. I'll call you." Without stopping to listen to his partner tell him what he shouldn't do, Richard stalked into the elevator and waited for the door to close behind him.

It seemed to take forever to reach the ground.

He kept hearing the note of desperation in Dolores's voice and that odd little moan as she'd hung up. He wouldn't be able to live with himself if he ignored such a poignant plea for help.

Nobody answered when he rang the doorbell on West Sixteenth. Had she gone out? Somehow he didn't think so. She'd sounded too distraught to make the effort. He went around the side of the house and rang the Sawchuks' bell.

After a long pause followed by the sound of teenage swearing, Barry Sawchuk pulled open the door.

"Dunno," he grunted when Richard asked him if Ms. Rowan was all right. "Mom's out, but she didn't say nothin' about them two upstairs. Stuck up pair, they are. One of 'em went off in a limo."

"Today?"

"Nah. Weeks ago."

Richard noticed that the unprepossessing youth was

169

holding something concealed behind his back. He hoped it wasn't a gun.

"Does your mother have a key to the upstairs?" he asked, without much expectation.

"Huh. Fat chance. Wish she did." Barry turned sideways, and Richard saw that the concealed object was a bottle of beer, no doubt purloined from his mother's stock.

Recognizing that he would get no help from Barry, Richard returned to the front of the house. No sign of life in the upstairs windows. He thought for a moment. Didn't most of these older houses have fire escapes?

Peeling off his jacket and tie, he slung them onto one of the battered wicker chairs that cluttered the porch and made his way around to the back.

At first glance the oblong of scrubby lawn surrounded by broken-down cedar fencing didn't look encouraging. But when he advanced to the far side of the house, he discovered a moss-covered wooden ladder descending from a small platform several feet above his head. Maybe it would hold.

Richard drew in his breath and jumped, grasping the bottom rung with both hands. It shuddered but held firm. Cautiously, bracing his feet against the once-white wall, he shifted his grip to the next rung. It, too, held.

Slowly he eased his way up to the platform, then hooked an arm, followed by a leg, over the low wooden railing. As he did so, something black and furry shot past his face and landed on his shoulder before letting out a yowling screech and skidding down his back onto the ladder.

Damn cat. Courtesy of the Sawchuks, no doubt. He'd heard about that family from Dolores. Thrown off-balance, Richard clung precariously to the railing. It didn't give way, and moments later he was standing on the platform peering into a room that contained a bed with a blue chenille bedspread piled with what looked like half the contents of someone's dresser. A quick glance told him the slips and panties were of the white and sensible variety.

This must be Tamsin's room then. Had there been a burglary? Was that why Dolores had sounded so distraught?

There was no door leading from what was obviously an old-fashioned fire escape, but the low window was slightly open at the bottom. He pushed it up and swung himself inside.

"Dolores?" he called. "It's Richard. Are you all right?"

No answer.

Wasting no further time, he strode through the bedroom into the living room, pausing in the doorway to take stock.

At first everything seemed the same. The faded chintz rocking chair, the sofa with its sagging, mud-colored cushions, and the photographs of Vancouver Island on the walls. Tamsin's, presumably. The faint scent of sandalwood hung in the air.

Sandalwood. Dolores's scent. Richard lowered his eyes, and only then did he notice the white, near-naked figure huddled on the floor beneath the phone.

Dear God! The burglar had attacked her. And he had callously told Norah to tell her he'd call back.

In two strides Richard was across the room and kneeling beside Dolores. She lay on her side in the fetal position, a damp pink towel twisted around her body. Her soft white flesh was deathly cold, but she was still breathing easily and gently, as if she were asleep. Thank heaven it was a reasonably warm day.

"Dolores?" He touched a hand to her frozen cheek. "Dolores, wake up."

She stirred, and again the scent of sandalwood teased his nose.

171

"Dolores?" He put an arm under her shoulders and lifted her against his chest, cradling her to him as if she were a baby. Her long blond hair was damp and smelled of scented shampoo.

Her eyelids fluttered, and a moment later she lifted her head. "Richard? What are you doing here?" She smiled drowsily as her body curled into his, creating a familiar throbbing ache between his thighs.

Within seconds her smile faded, and she dropped her forehead against his chest. Richard kept holding her as she made a sound that chilled his bones. It was part howl, part heart-wrenching cry for help, as if she were in more pain than she could bear.

"Sweetheart? What is it?" Richard held her close, rocking her gently as he stroked her cheek, his bodily urges forgotten in the need to give comfort. She was still unnaturally cold, and he rose to his feet and carried her into the bedroom—the one with the red and black quilt that wasn't strewn with sensible underwear and stockings.

Setting her on the edge of the bed, he forced his gaze from her breasts while he removed the damp towel and wrapped her in the quilt.

She stared at him, white, silent and anguished.

"Hey now, what's happened here?" he asked softly.

She didn't respond, but her big blue eyes fastened achingly on his.

Richard felt a painful swelling in his chest. "I'm trying to help you," he said.

Dolores shook her head. "You can't. No one can. I shouldn't have called you."

In this state, she looked like a breakable china doll, but he felt he had to give her a gentle shake to make her talk. He had to find out who had done this to her.

"I can't help you if you won't tell me what happened," he said.

Her lower lip started to quiver, and Richard, feeling like a rat for insisting, said, "Come on, sweetheart. Talk. Then we'll see what we can do to fix things."

He waited.

"The police came," Dolores said at last, her voice pitched so low he had to strain to hear.

"Yes? And?"

"It—they said my parents. . . ." Her voice trailed off, and she hung her head.

Richard put a fist under her chin and made her look at him. "Has something happened to them?" he asked.

"Yes. They're dead."

"Dear God." Richard stared into her agonized blue eyes, appalled at the bald finality of her words. Then, acting purely on instinct, he enfolded her in his arms and lifted her, quilt and all, onto his knees.

It was several seconds before either of them spoke.

Dolores sat unnaturally still, her arms clasped around his waist and her face buried in his neck. She made no sound, but as his collar grew progressively wetter he knew she was at last finding an outlet for her grief. She had passed out on the floor because her mind couldn't cope with the tragedy that had befallen her. Tears, at least, were a healthier release.

When at last she raised her head, he said, "Do you want to tell me about it?"

She sniffed. "It—makes no difference. Thank you for coming. I'm sorry—"

"Dolores." Richard's tone was now deliberately harsh, "if you tell me you're sorry one more time, I swear I'll walk out and leave Tamsin to look after you. I'm *glad* you phoned me. Do you understand?"

It was true, he realized with some surprise. He *was* glad. Not that she'd lost her parents but that she'd called on him in her time of need.

"Yes." Once again Dolores buried her face in his neck. "But Tamsin isn't coming home. She's gone to the Island with her boss. She won't be back till the weekend."

"I see." Richard frowned. Now what? Dolores was in no condition to be left on her own. "Do you have any relatives in Vancouver?" he asked.

"No. My aunt here died, and the rest of them are scattered all over."

"Can't anyone come?"

"No. I haven't heard from them for ages. Not even Harry."

Richard stroked her hair. It felt like damp, sweet-smelling silk beneath his fingers. "That's all right. I'll stay with you."

She sat up then. "You will? Oh, Richard, I . . ."

"It's all *right,*" he said, patting the closest part of her, which turned out to be her bottom, then quickly raising his hand to her lower back. "Of course I'll stay. Have you had any breakfast?"

"No. The police came before . . . but it doesn't matter. I'm not hungry."

"You need to keep up your strength. Look, you get yourself dressed and I'll go and cook us up some bacon and eggs."

"I don't eat bacon."

"Eggs? Do you eat those?"

"Sometimes."

"Fine, poached eggs on toast it is. Do you think you can manage to get dressed?"

"I suppose so." Her reply was so listless that Richard wondered if he ought to do something to shake her out of her apathy. But in the end he hadn't the heart. "Okay, then," he said, and went to find the eggs.

Ten minutes later Dolores joined him in the kitchen wearing tight blue jeans and a startling orange and green shirt. That was something, he supposed. She was still Dolores.

Hunched over the white kitchen table, she ate her eggs dutifully but without any evidence of enjoyment, or even awareness of what she was doing. When she'd finished, Richard, who was sitting opposite her nursing a cup of coffee, said, "Good girl. *Now* do you feel strong enough to tell me?"

She picked up her fork and made tracks in what remained of the egg yolk on her plate. "They came to the door," she said, in a dull monotone more chilling than any outburst of hysterics. "The police. I didn't believe them at first. They wanted to get a neighbor to stay with me, but I couldn't face the Sawchuks, so I said I'd be all right until Tammy came home from work. I forgot she wouldn't. Then I phoned you, but you. . . ."

"I know." Richard reached across the table to take her hand. "I snapped at you. My turn to be sorry."

"You didn't know." Dolores's long hair fell across her plate. She seemed unaware of it, so he brushed it back behind her ears.

Richard swallowed a mouthful of bitter tasting coffee while he waited for her to tell him the whole story. He wouldn't press it. She was having a tough enough time as it was. A car accident, he supposed. It usually was.

In that he turned out to be wrong.

Half an hour later, after she'd allowed him to draw her

down beside him on the sofa and into the safety of his arms, she told him the whole tragic story as she knew it—not all at once, but in short, uneven sentences that he eventually pieced together into a whole.

Eddie and Edie Rowan had been driving from Spokane to a gig in Seattle. From there they had planned to travel north for a brief reunion with their daughter, but somewhere in the Cascades they had stopped for a picnic lunch. Afterward other picnickers had heard Edie insist on going for a hike to walk it off.

"She was worried about her weight," Dolores said with a choked little laugh.

Richard pressed her head against his shoulder and stroked her cheek.

In a little while Dolores blew her nose and went on to explain that while there were well-marked trails through the mountains, a man walking some distance behind her parents had seen Edie wander off the trail to look over the lip of a ravine. As he watched, she had slipped and fallen, landing near a stream that wound it's way over the rocks several hundred feet below.

"The man said she was watching a butterfly instead of her feet," Dolores whispered.

Richard fixed his gaze on a framed print of waves rushing up a wide, sandy beach. "Then she saw something beautiful at the end," he said, hoping it would help.

"Yes. That's good, isn't it?"

Dolores fell silent, but he felt some of the tautness go out of her. When she spoke again, it was to say, "My dad tried to get down there to save her, but he slipped, too. The man behind them went for help, but by the time the rescue team got there they were both . . . dead. Dad had an arm around Mom, the policeman said."

Brakes squealed on the street outside as someone took a corner too fast.

Dolores blinked and lifted her head. "Tomorrow," she said, "I have to go down to Seattle—to . . . to identify them."

"I'll go with you." The words were out before he knew he meant to speak them.

She didn't answer, but when he took her face in his hands he saw that her big eyes were brimming with tears. He touched his lips to her forehead.

"They've left me again," she whispered. "I was going to see them at last, but they've left. And this time they won't be coming back. Not ever."

There was nothing Richard could reply to that, and he didn't try. He simply held her.

For Dolores, the remainder of the day passed in a kind of vacuum. She phoned her partners to tell them she wouldn't be in, arranged to take the rest of the week off and ate whatever Richard put in front of her.

Feeling, when it came, turned out to be two-thirds grief for the parents she had never really known and one-third a crushing anger that now she never would.

How *could* they leave her this way? Alone, with no one of her own left in the world? The collection of scattered aunts and uncles and cousins had never taken the time to keep in touch. Even Harry had drifted away once he married. There was Tammy, of course, but she was in Victoria. And Richard, who was only being kind, doing what he thought was his duty. When this was over, when all the practical things had been done and the memory of her mother and father locked away in some private recess of her heart, Richard would leave her to get on with her life. Without him.

Dolores dashed the back of a hand across her eyes. When she looked up, he was standing over her, holding out a glass of brandy. She accepted it without argument, and the golden brown liquid slid smoothly down her throat.

After a while she felt stronger, better able to cope, and when she glanced at the clock on the wall she discovered to her astonishment that it was evening. That must have been supper Richard had made her eat an hour ago after he'd made a brief trip to the store. Somehow she had survived this horrible day.

"Tired?" Richard asked when she placed her elbows on the kitchen table and dropped her head onto her hands. "It's time you went to bed."

"I won't sleep."

"Maybe not, but I think you'd better try." He helped her to her feet, turned her gently around and placed a hand on her back. "Go on. Bed."

Dolores was horrified to feel a traitorous flaring of desire.

Richard lowered his arm. "Go on," he repeated.

She hesitated, wondering if he, too, had felt that shock of forbidden electricity. When he gave no sign that he had, she shuffled into her bedroom and shut the door. She would have to sleep sometime, and she hadn't the energy to argue.

An hour later sleep still hadn't come. Vaguely she wondered where Richard was sleeping. On the sofa probably. She twisted onto her side, feeling the top sheet wind around her legs.

Her parents were gone. Eddie and Edie Rowan would sing no more. The thought, unreal and unbelievable, kept spinning around and around in her head like one of the bittersweet songs they had sung. Now they would never have the chance to tell her again that they had loved her, that they had left her with relations so often not because they didn't want her but because singing was the only thing they knew. A child couldn't fit into their transient way of life, they had explained patiently whenever she protested. The explanations had never been enough. Yet they *had* been coming to see her when. . . .

Dolores pulled her pillow over her head to muffle the sounds coming from her throat.

Richard was almost asleep when the disturbing noises began. They pierced the outer layers of slumber until he found himself fully awake and lying with his feet over the end of the sagging sofa. He blinked at the moonlight glimmering through the unlined curtains, touching the shabby room with silver.

"What the . . . ?" He sat up, running his hands through his hair.

Was that Dolores? Crying? Or, more accurately, sobbing her heart out? She seemed to be trying to muffle the sounds so he wouldn't hear.

He made his way to her bedroom. When he opened the door, moonlight beaming through the open window revealed that she was lying on her stomach wearing something white and shiny with narrow straps. A pillow hid her head.

He crossed to the bed, pulled the pillow aside and sat down beside her.

"Hey," he said, stroking the tangled sweep of her hair. "Sweetheart, don't cry."

"I c-can't seem to stop." She drew in a great gulp of air, held it, then started to cry again.

"I know." Richard stroked some more.

Eventually Dolores squirmed onto her back and choked

out, "I think I'll be all right now. Thank you."

"No need to thank me. Sure you're okay?"

"Yes. I didn't mean to wake you."

"You didn't," he said. "I wasn't asleep."

"I should have given you a blanket."

"I'm fine. I found one in a closet."

"Good." She reached up to touch his bare chest. "You're not cold?"

He took her hand and laid it on the quilt. "No, I'm not cold. Do you want me to get you something? Tea? Hot milk?"

"Hot milk?" Dolores shuddered. "What kind of a heathenish drink is that?"

He smiled briefly. That sounded more like the Dolores he knew. "When we couldn't sleep, my mother used to make us drink hot milk," he explained.

"Ugh!" Dolores gazed up at him in the pale light, her eyes shadowed pools in her white face. After a while she said, "At least I never had to endure that."

Damn. Richard cursed himself. He shouldn't have mentioned his mother—although it seemed as though Dolores was working through her initial shock. Soon she would have to face what came after.

"There's nothing you want then?" he asked. "Sure you'll be okay?" He didn't want to leave her but knew he must.

She put a hand on his knee. "Yes, I'll be okay. Only . . . please don't go."

Richard covered her hand with his own. "I'm not going. I'll be in the next room."

"No, I mean, stay with me here. Please."

"I can't. But you only have to call, and I'll come. I promise."

"I know you will. But, oh, Richard, I keep seeing their faces, wondering if they knew . . . They were coming to see me, you see." She turned her face into the pillow, and after that her voice came out muffled. "If you stay with me, maybe it won't be so bad."

"Here? Where do you expect me to sleep?" he asked.

"There's room in the bed."

"That's not a good idea."

As if she'd read his thoughts, Dolores said, "I didn't mean we should—"

"No, of course not."

"Richard, please. I only want you to hold me. Just until I fall asleep." She blinked, and her blond eyelashes glinted silver in the moonlight.

She was going to cry again.

Richard hesitated but eventually he said, "All right. Just until you fall asleep."

She nodded and scooted to the other side of the bed. As he climbed in beside her, Richard thanked his stars he'd kept his pants on, hiding his unwanted arousal.

Dolores gave a little sigh and settled herself against him. He held his breath and counted to ten. Moments later, as his senses were engulfed by the scent of sandalwood, he heard the soft, gentle breathing of sleep.

Richard awoke to the feel of long limbs wrapped around his legs, soft breasts encased in satin pressed against his chest, and a woman's scent tantalizing his nose. He must still be dreaming.

"Mmm," he murmured, inhaling the scent of sandalwood as his hand slid down the satin to uncover a smoothly curving thigh.

The thigh moved, and a leg was thrown over his. There was something wrong with this dream. Why did he still have his pants on?

Slim, capable hands unfastened his zipper even as the thought crossed his mind. Then the hands were on his hips, the pants were sliding toward his knees and he heard a faint thud as they landed on the floor.

His turn. He reached for the straps of a white satin nightgown, slipped them down to expose full, rosy breasts. The woman beside him raised her arms and helped him toss the nightgown to the end of the bed. He smiled. Once before he had noticed that endearing little mole at the base of her throat . . .

So perfect . . . so beautiful. Richard raised himself on one elbow to gaze down at the soft, slender body lying beside his. If he touched it, would the dream turn to smoke?

He had to touch.

With a little moan, she linked her arms around his neck and drew his mouth down to her breasts.

Nectar of the gods. Richard groaned. If the dream ended now. . . .

It couldn't end. Not yet. With a wild sense of urgency, he covered the quivering body beneath him with his own.

He heard a gasp, then a woman's voice calling, "Richard!" Then another voice that might have been his own cried, "Dolores!" and the passion he had repressed for so long exploded in an agony of release.

The shadows of the night vanished into the glory of a blazing September dawn.

A sparrow was greeting the day from the plum tree outside the window when Dolores came fully awake and realized what she'd done.

She hadn't meant to, hadn't thought—but she had woken with a great emptiness in her heart, and when she turned to the man beside her, seeking comfort, all at once the only comfort was in his arms. If either one of them had been totally aware of what they were doing, the prohibitions of a lifetime would surely have kicked in.

What they had done was probably wrong, but it hadn't seemed so at the time. It had seemed beautiful.

"Richard?" she murmured, turning onto her side to find him lying with his hands behind his head and his gray gaze riveted on the damp stain above the bed. "Richard, I didn't . . . that is, I wouldn't have. . . ."

"I know." His voice was gentle, comforting. "You mustn't be sorry. Not if it helped." He reached beneath the sheet and found her hand.

Dolores nodded. "I never knew. . . ." She paused. "Was it really wrong? It didn't feel it."

"No." Richard squeezed her hand. "It didn't, so perhaps it wasn't. Perhaps it was right at the time."

But you still don't like me much, Dolores thought, hearing what sounded like doubt in his voice. Any moment now you're going to say it mustn't happen again. She pulled her hand away abruptly, disentangled herself from the sheet and swung her legs over the side of the bed.

Aloud, she said, "Do you want breakfast? There's a lot I have to do today."

"I'll make it." Richard, too, pushed back the sheet and swung out of bed so that they were sitting with their backs to each other. "As you say, you have a lot to do." She didn't answer, and as he stood up and pulled on his crumpled pants, he asked, "How are you feeling?"

"I'll make it through the day."

"Yes," he said quietly. "I believe you will."

Dolores did make it through the day, with Richard's help. He drove her to Seattle, assisted her through all the ghastly formalities that go with dying, and eventually drove her home to her apartment and blessed sleep.

Richard stayed for the rest of the week.

Eddie and Edie Rowan had requested in their wills that there be no funeral service held for them, no formal farewell for fans, family or friends. Richard said it might have been easier for Dolores if there had been.

Insisting that she was still suffering from shock, he refused to leave her on her own. Yet, although he was kind and helped with all the sad and unexpected things that needed to be done, he wouldn't hold her again or come closer to her than the opposite side of the table while they ate.

That was all right with her, Dolores decided. She didn't want him close. Not when he was so obviously reluctant.

Once, when she said she loved hockey, he took her to a pre-season game, but she couldn't concentrate the way she usually did. Twice he took her out to eat in dark, quiet little restaurants where she could rub her eyes and weep into her food if she liked, but always he avoided the intimacy they had shared that first morning.

Dolores didn't try to change his mind. For now it was enough that he was with her.

She made no attempt to think about the future beyond the end of the week, when Tammy would be home.

How hard it was to believe that only a few days had passed since her friend had left town with Nick Malahide in a flurry of objections and confusion.

The world had become such a different and, in a way, more frightening place since that morning.

Chapter Ten

"What do you mean, we didn't reserve a suite?" Nick's aggressive baritone turned heads as the harried clerk behind the desk of the luxurious hotel across from Victoria's Inner Harbor poked anxiously at the keys on his computer.

"I'm sorry, sir. The booking is definitely for two single rooms on opposite sides of the corridor."

"Then the booking's wrong. As you can see, we're a double."

"Nick. . . ." Tamsin tugged at his arm.

Nick brushed her away. "Right," he said to the clerk. "Now let's get this settled. Cancel the single rooms, and book us into a suite. With a view of the harbor, please."

"Yes, sir, but I'm not sure—"

"Nick!" Tamsin raised her voice and contemplated stomping on his autocratic foot. "Will you listen to me? I didn't book a suite."

"You didn't?" Nick stopped glaring at the clerk and glared at her. "Why the hell not? I told you we'd need a suite with two bedrooms."

"I didn't think it necessary." Tamsin avoided Nick's eyes and smiled apologetically at the clerk.

"I see," Nick said through teeth that would have done credit to a tiger. "But I'm afraid it *is* necessary—unless you're comfortable with the idea of taking notes, answering the phone and sorting out orders while the two of us perch on my bed."

Oh. He had a point there. "I didn't think of that," she

185

admitted, maintaining her composure with difficulty. "I suppose an extra room might be useful."

The ironic gleam in her boss's eye convinced her he knew exactly what had been in her mind when she'd booked those single rooms.

Nick turned his attention back to the clerk. "My apologies for the confusion. Meanwhile, if you can find us a suite, I'll be grateful." He glanced meaningfully at Tamsin and exchanged an expressive you-know-what-women-are-like look with the clerk, who nodded understandingly, punched a few keys, and announced that a suite had unexpectedly come vacant.

"Surprise, surprise," muttered Tamsin as a bellman escorted them to the elevator.

Minutes later she was gazing around a spacious, beautifully appointed suite with floor-to-ceiling windows and a breathtaking view of the harbor.

"Suit you?" Nick asked.

Tamsin swallowed, watching him as he tossed his jacket over a chair and loosened his tie. What would suit her at this moment was a cold shower.

"Yes, it's fine," she said, turning away. "I'll go and unpack, if you don't mind."

Nick nodded and picked up her battered brown suitcase. It looked terribly shabby beside his smart black luggage.

"This one all right?" he asked, heading for the bedroom on the right.

"Yes, quite all right." She waited until he came out again and tried not to think about the fact that all that separated her bedroom from his was a rose-colored carpet, some good hotel furniture, and a fridge.

When she returned to the sitting room, Nick had his shirt unbuttoned to the waist and was sprawled in a fat brown armchair with his eyes closed.

She moistened her lower lip. "Nick?"

Hadn't he said they were supposed to start work this afternoon? Not that the sight of him all relaxed, male and sleepily sexy made it easy to think about work.

He didn't answer, and she moved closer. "Nick? Are you asleep?"

Still no answer. She took another step forward. He was breathing deeply, rhythmically, with the hint of a smile on his lips.

"Nick!"

"Mmm?"

At last a sign of life. "You can't go to sleep. We have work to do."

When that produced no response, she grabbed his shoulder and shook him. Immediately his arm shot out and wrapped around her waist. The next thing she knew, she was sitting on his knees and his hand was resting lightly on her thigh. It felt nice. . . .

Tamsin gave herself a mental shake. Right. Nick was awake and up to no good. She ought to have known.

"Stop it," she said, pushing his arm away and leaping to her feet. "Stop it this minute, Nick Malahide."

"Hm?" Nick opened an eye. "Seems I have stopped. No need to sound the alarm."

"You weren't asleep at all. You did that on purpose," she accused.

"No, I didn't. I thought you were part of a dream. The best part." He grinned, that familiar, oh, so guileless grin that made her want to kick him.

Tamsin took an extended breath, not sure whether she believed him or not. Did he *have* to look so maddeningly desirable? For a moment there, when he'd held her on his knees, she had felt as if she were burning up inside.

Folding her arms across her chest, she said, "Nick, it's time we got something straight."

"I was afraid of that. Personally I'm in favor of meandering."

No, he wasn't. It was a good line, but Nick had never meandered in his life. He always went directly for what he wanted and helped himself. Dolores had been like that until recently.

Cautiously, keeping her eye on him, Tamsin pulled out the chair in front of a dark mahogany desk and sat down facing him with her ankles crossed. "This was precisely the reason I didn't want to come here," she told him.

He said nothing, yet she knew she had his whole attention. "I'm not going to have sex with you," she said. Bluntness was the only way to handle Nick, yet she knew that if she looked him in the eye she would blush.

His shoulders lifted just enough to show puzzlement rather than indifference. "I don't remember asking you."

"You didn't. Not precisely."

"Then I don't see the problem." He looked at his watch. "And now that we have that settled, we'd better have some lunch. I have an appointment with a deputy minister at two."

"There isn't a problem," Tamsin said. "I just wanted to be sure we had things clear."

"Perfectly clear." His voice was flat, and she had a sense that she was missing some important message, that something was happening here she didn't understand. Nick's eyes, when they rested on her, were opaque as green marble. Yet he'd been gentle when, briefly, he had held her on his knees—as if he cared about her. . . .

"I'll just go and change," she said, jumping up and

stumbling toward her bedroom. "I won't be long."

"Good."

As she tripped on the edge of the carpet in her haste to escape, Nick murmured, "No need to break your neck on my account."

"No danger of that." Tamsin closed the door firmly behind her.

From the next room she heard the sound of muffled laughter, and would have stuck out her tongue if Nick had been able to see her.

"What would you like to do now?" Nick asked, removing his tie and tucking it into his pocket. He and Tamsin had just completed a very satisfactory government contract with a deputy minister who was anxious to inflate his budget to the maximum so it wouldn't be cut.

Tamsin blinked in the sunlight shining on the lush green lawns of the Provincial Parliament Buildings, reminding him of a near-sighted owl.

"Do? Nothing," she said. "You have another appointment."

"No, I haven't. I canceled it. We have the rest of the week for appointments. I thought you might like to see something of the city."

When Tamsin frowned and didn't respond at once, he began to regret his well-intentioned impulse to put her pleasure before his business.

"I have been here before," she said finally in what he had come to think of as her touch-me-not voice. "But we could go for a walk in Beacon Hill Park if you like."

Amazing woman. His mild irritation vanished without trace. She hadn't mentioned shopping or anything else that was likely to cost him money. It was probably more than he deserved.

Half an hour later, after taking a leisurely stroll through the bright greens and golds of the park, they found themselves standing on a grassy cliff top overlooking the Straits of Juan de Fuca.

A strong gust of wind almost lifted Tamsin off her feet. When she staggered and fell against Nick's shoulder, his arm slipped quite naturally around her waist.

She didn't tell him to take it away.

Far below them on the beach, a small brown and white dog was dashing up and down, barking excitedly at two sea gulls on a rock.

"I had a dog like that once," Nick remarked. "A Jack Russell terrier who thought he was a guard dog. He'd have defended Dennis and me from Lucifer himself, I think, though usually he concentrated on terrorizing the neighborhood cats."

"Oh," Tamsin said softly. "I am glad. You *did* have something to love. I thought perhaps you hadn't."

Nick scowled down at the mousy brown head resting on his shoulder. Good grief, had he made his childhood sound as grim as that?

"I had a father and a brother," he reminded her. "We didn't have Toby for long."

"Oh, dear. What happened to him?" Tamsin's gray eyes were luminous with sympathy, and Nick had to restrain himself from bending down to kiss her parted lips.

"He was hit by a car. After that my father refused to let us have another dog. He said we'd be away at school and he'd be the one left with all the work."

"Oh, Nick. That's terrible."

For one horrible moment he thought she was going to

cry, and wanted to kick himself for bringing up the subject of his long-dead pet.

"Nonsense," he replied brusquely. "Dad was right."

She gave him a reproachful look that made him feel as if he'd stolen a toy from a child. Then, to his relief, she changed the subject.

"Did you like boarding school?" she asked.

He waited for the roar of a passing seaplane to fade to a distant hum before replying, "Not particularly. People kept giving me orders, and I discovered early on that I much prefer giving orders to taking them."

"I can't imagine you as a boy." Tamsin ran a sensible brown walking shoe over a small pebble lying in the grass. "Not that you've changed much. About giving orders, I mean."

"No. Unfortunately some of my staff haven't learned to take them." He focused his gaze reflectively on a small gray cloud shaped like a snail.

"I suppose you mean me." She attempted to push away his arm.

He responded by dropping it lower so that it curved around her hip. "In most respects I find your services entirely satisfactory," he replied, knowing his deadpan expression would leave her in no doubt as to precisely where her "services" failed to measure up to his expectations. He waited with interest for her reaction.

There wasn't one, and Nick began to wonder if his teasing had upset her. "Did *you* like school?" he asked, feeling his way.

"I endured it," she said. "My parents expected me to do well, so I did."

"That doesn't sound so bad."

"It wasn't, I suppose, but I was always the odd one out.

191

Mom didn't approve of following the latest fad, so everything I owned was either too grown up or out-of-date."

"Ah," Nick murmured, unable to resist. "Hence your current predilection for blending in so nicely with the woodwork." He smiled to show he meant no serious offense.

After a short, startled pause, she said, "You know, you may be right. I never looked at it that way before."

Nick, having made his point, decided not to rub it in.

"Look!" Tamsin cried as he was about to suggest they move on. "That little dog is swimming out to sea. Do you think he'll be all right? The water's so cold."

"Of course he'll be—" Nick broke off as the dog disappeared beneath a larger than usual wave.

Tamsin's hand flew to her mouth. "He's not coming up," she whispered.

"Of course he will."

She stared, petrified, at the spot where the dog had disappeared. The wind was growing stronger, and the waves seemed bigger and more ominous than before. He'd never make it. . . .

"Oh!" she cried as a particularly tall wave crashed onto the beach.

Her cry was caught up by the wind, and when she turned to look at Nick, she saw that he, too, was shouting.

"Toby! Hold on."

Before Tamsin could take in what was in his mind, he had thrown off his jacket and was hurtling down the slope, tripping over rocks and clumps of grass, tearing across the blowing sand until he came to the very edge of the waves. There he tore off his shoes and plunged into the sea.

Tamsin stood stunned, watching him, knowing the turbulent waters were famous for their bone-numbing cold. A movement at the edge of her vision drew her eyes to the right.

At the far end of the beach a small dog was dancing out of the water, giving itself a good shake and prancing up the sand toward a teenage boy holding a ball.

Nick must have seen the dog too, because he waved and, moments later, was striding out of the water, picking up his shoes and plowing his way back up the beach.

Tamsin took a few steps down the cliff to meet him, not sure what kind of mood he would be in.

She needn't have worried. He was laughing when he came up to her.

"Don't say it," he said. "I've just made a first-class fool of myself."

"No, you haven't." She swallowed an annoying tightness in her throat. "You tried to save a little dog's life. That's not foolish."

"The dog didn't need saving," he pointed out.

"I don't care." Tamsin lifted her chin. "I think it was heroic."

Nick smiled wryly and looked down at his saturated clothes. "In that case," he said, holding out his arms, "how about my hero's welcome?"

Tamsin shook her head. "You never miss a trick, do you?"

"Not if I can help it. Come on." He beckoned with the fingers of both hands, and Tamsin laughed and allowed herself to be swept into his arms.

The moment she felt his freezing, damp thighs pressed against her skirt, she knew she'd made a serious mistake. This was Nick, her boss, the man whose lips had launched a thousand brief affairs. Yet her hunger for him was growing with every day that passed.

He had looked so tortured in those brief moments when the past came back to haunt him in the shape of a little dog he'd called Toby that she longed to give back to him some of the warmth and affection he refused to admit he'd missed. But she mustn't do it. Not if she meant to protect herself from heartbreak.

"I'll call a taxi," she muttered, breaking free of his embrace before it was too late. "You'd better get out of those wet clothes."

As she held his hand and hurried with him to the top of the cliff, she was almost certain she heard him murmur, "Anything to oblige, darlin'. Anything to oblige."

Damn him.

Odd, Nick thought when they emerged from the hotel an hour later. In spite of his foolish attempt to rescue that idiotic dog, he couldn't remember enjoying an afternoon so much in years. Most of the walks he'd taken as a child had been in school crocodiles being marched to church. Later on, the women he'd known had been more interested in shopping and nightclubs than exercise and air. Tamsin wasn't like that. As the afternoon progressed, he had watched her unwind, become less prickly and suspicious, more inclined to smile.

She was almost beautiful when she smiled.

They ate dinner in a quiet restaurant down by the water where, unless he was mistaken, Tamsin continued to take pleasure in his company. He certainly took pleasure in hers.

Their unusual amity showed no signs of fading until Nick remarked, without intentional innuendo, that since they had a busy day ahead of them tomorrow, they had better think about making tracks for bed.

"Bed?" Tamsin repeated in a voice that made the woman at the next table giggle and choke on her food.

"Mm," Nick said. "You know. Soft, flat surface with sheets. Usual purpose sleep, but can be used for more stimulating activities."

"I *know* what a bed is," Tamsin said.

He waited for her to tell him not to get his hopes up, but she surprised him by coolly swallowing the rest of her coffee and rising to her feet. He was reminded, briefly, of the poised, confident young woman he had escorted to the Community Foundation's annual banquet.

Taking his cue from her, Nick rose, too, tucked her hand in the crook of his arm and escorted her out of the restaurant as if no unexpected tension had sprung between them to shatter the harmony of the evening.

Ten minutes later he opened the door to their suite.

Without looking at him, Tamsin darted across to the window and stood with her neck bent and her forehead just touching the glass.

"It's a long way down," Nick observed. "I'm not that terrifying, am I?"

Tamsin shook her head and turned stiffly around. "No. No, of course not. Um, good night then. Thank you for dinner."

Nick, who was used to willing women and didn't appreciate being looked on as a possible sexual predator, was still contemplating his reply when she edged past him and vanished into her room.

He shrugged, thought for a moment and then strode to her door to rap sharply on the wood with his knuckles.

"What?" Tamsin asked, opening it just a crack.

"You forgot to tuck me in."

She shut the door in his face.

★ ★ ★ ★ ★

That night Tamsin fell asleep with the memory of Nick's laughter ringing in her ears and his sexy voice murmuring through the door, "Sleep well, darlin'. Don't let the bogeyman get you."

For the remainder of the week their routine didn't vary. They ate breakfast in the suite without much conversation, saw customers in the morning, visited gardens and museums in the afternoon, and in the evening ate a leisurely meal before retiring to bed. Separately.

By Friday, contrarily, Tamsin was beginning to resent the gentlemanly restraint Nick had shown toward her since that first afternoon. He made no attempt to move her into his bed, and he treated her with a propriety worthy of the stuffiest Victorian.

On the last day, after dinner, the pattern changed. Over poached salmon followed by a deliciously creamy dessert, they discussed the day's business as usual. But as Nick smiled at her over the rim of his wineglass, Tamsin was astonished to hear herself saying, "You didn't really need me here, did you? All I've done is attend a few meetings and take notes, make a couple of phone calls and order extra coffee—all things you could have done for yourself at far less expense."

"I could. I didn't choose to."

"I know, but. . . ." She stopped. What was there to say? Nothing had happened. And Nick's smile, which had been warm and non-threatening, was now a cynical curl that made her feel awkward and insecure.

She eyed him warily and subsided into silence.

When they returned to the suite, she said, "Good night," at once.

Instead of answering, Nick strode to the window and stood with his fists pressed against the sill.

"Good night," Tamsin repeated.

Without turning, he held out his hand. "Come and look at the stars."

Instinctively Tamsin stepped backward, feeling the slim skirt of her turquoise dress pull tight against her knees. Suddenly the big room seemed airless and much too hot.

"I won't bite," he said. His voice was hypnotic, dark, irresistible. So was he in his almost black suit as he swung to face her, his full lips smiling an invitation.

Tamsin took a step forward. And then another.

When she was close enough, Nick curled his fingers around her wrist and drew her to him. "See?" he said, waving an arm at the night sky.

"Yes," Tamsin whispered. "I see stars."

Nick laughed and ran his palm lightly up her spine. "I told you I'm not dangerous."

Oh, but he was. Wickedly, gloriously dangerous, and he had lured her to him with a subtle magnetism she was powerless to resist.

"But. . . ." she whispered, opening her mouth to protest because she knew she must.

Nick closed it with the first serious kiss she had ever known.

His lips were warm, gentle, exquisitely seductive. Tamsin forgot then what she had wanted to protest, and allowed the surprising responses snaking through her body to lead her on.

She returned his kiss with eager passion. Nick's tongue, when it tangled with hers, tasted of wine and warm man— and she couldn't get enough of either.

Then he was carrying her across the soft rose carpet to

his room, lowering her onto a bed with a crimson striped cover. She watched, enthralled, as he removed his jacket and tie with swift, economical motions.

It wasn't until he started unbuckling his belt that she came to her senses and cried, "No!"

Nick paused with a hand on the belt.

Tamsin, gazing up at him, felt like a rabbit mesmerized by the approaching talons of a bird of prey. Something of the sort must have shown on her face, because his purposeful, piratical stance altered subtly, and his arms dropped in slow motion to his sides.

"No?" he repeated.

"Please." She moved her head on the striped bedspread. "We can't."

Nick pushed a lock of damp hair off his forehead, and his body shuddered as if he were in pain. "We can," he said. "But only if you want to. I thought you did."

"No. No, I don't." She moved her head back and forth on the pillow, frantic to convince herself she meant it.

"What are you afraid of, little field mouse? Surely you know I won't hurt you." Nick's crooked smile taunted her with its blatant sensuality, yet she heard disappointment and a kind of hunger in his voice that made her want to hold out her arms to him in welcome.

No, Nick wouldn't hurt her. Not physically. He was no pink-cheeked boy attempting to fumble his way through his first experience of sex. But he was right when he said she was afraid—not of him, but of what he was doing to the remnants of her willpower. That smile of his had captured too many unwary hearts.

Nick moved suddenly and sat down beside her on the bed.

She flinched.

"Don't be scared." With two swift tugs he pulled off her black, high-heeled shoes, then leaned over to press a fist into the covers beside her head.

"I do know you won't hurt me," she blurted before he could make further practiced moves.

"Then why . . . ?" He blew a wisp of hair gently off her forehead.

She searched wildly for an answer that would make sense. "Because . . . because you're still my boss."

"What?" His frown was quick, genuinely puzzled. "Of course I am, but that doesn't mean I expect you to take off your clothes as part of the job."

Tamsin relaxed marginally. "What do you expect then?"

He touched a finger to the tip of her nose, and if she hadn't known better, Tamsin would have sworn there was bewilderment in his smile. "I hope you'll take them off because you want to. For me, as a man. Not for Mr. Malahide, your boss."

Tamsin closed her eyes. "But I *don't* want to," she moaned. Even to her own ears her protest sounded unconvincing.

Nick slid his left hand slowly down her thigh. Her turquoise dress had already ridden up to the point where it was less than useless in defense of her modesty, and the sheer nylon of her stockings did nothing to detract from the tantalizing play of his blunt fingers on her skin.

"Open your eyes and look at me." Nick spoke in the kind of voice he used in the office when he was giving her instructions for the day.

Hesitantly, she did as he said.

"Now tell me again you don't want to."

Tamsin looked up at him helplessly. It would be so easy to give in, to wrap her arms around those powerful shoulders and tell him what he wanted to hear. Part of her longed to do just that.

The other part knew she didn't dare.

"I can't tell you that," she admitted, her gaze on the lips so close to hers. "But I *can* tell you I'm not going to take off my clothes."

"Then let me take them off for you."

Help! She pushed away the tempting images inspired by Nick's words, and for the first time since he had picked her up and carried her to his bed, she felt the stirrings of indignation. It wasn't fair of him to sit there, all confident and sexy and smiling, just because this was a battle he'd fought and won so many times before.

"No," she whispered. "It's not going to happen, Nick."

"As you wish." He lifted his arm abruptly and stood up.

Was he angry? He had no right to be. Or was he just frustrated, as she was? "Look," Tamsin said with a kind of desperation. "I'm your assistant. I do my job to the best of my ability. But that job does *not* involve warming your bed. You said so yourself."

"I know." He took a deep breath, held it and made a crooked attempt at a smile. "Seems I made a mistake there."

Tamsin slid her feet into her shoes, then stood and pulled down her skirt.

Nick was lounging against the wall with his thumbs hooked into his belt. Watching him, Tamsin felt a pang of compunction. She had responded to his kiss with passionate enthusiasm, even admitted that, under different circumstances, she might not be reluctant to share his bed. Perhaps she did owe him some sort of explanation.

"I can't sleep with you," she said, backing away from him and moving to the other side of the bed. "Everyone at work would guess. And when it was over, I'd be out of work." She didn't add that when that day came she would stand to lose a whole lot more than the job she loved.

Nick's nostrils flared in that way they sometimes did when he was on the verge of losing his temper. "Tamsin, what kind of a louse do you think I am? I realize that when—no *if*—it ended, it might be hard for you to remain at Malahide's. But of course I'd find you another job. A damn good one, too. You wouldn't be worse off, I promise you."

Tamsin made an attempt to smooth the wrinkles from her skirt. He didn't understand that she would be much, much worse off if she gave him what he wanted—what they both wanted—and then had to wait to be discarded like all the rest. She could tell him, of course, but her pride wouldn't let her admit that what she had come to feel for him was very different from the lustful affection that was all he felt for her.

"I don't want another job," she said. "I want the job I have. You'll have to find someone else to look after your other needs."

"My *other needs?*" Nick unhooked his thumbs and plunged his hands deep into his pockets. "Dammit, I don't want someone else—"

Tamsin averted her head. "That's too bad. Because I'm not interested in being another one of your fly-by-night affairs. I've watched the parade, Nick, but I've never wanted to be a part of it. You'd better go back to Loralee Spring."

Damn. Why did it hurt so much to say the woman's name?

"That's over. In fact it was never really on."

"Really? She didn't last long."

Nick threw her a look that made her glad they had the

201

bed between them, but all he said was, "What do I have to do to change your mind?"

"There's nothing you can do. I just don't seem to want a temporary affair."

Footsteps passed by in the hall, and a man called to his companion to hurry up. In the silence that followed, Tamsin lowered her head and discovered a stain on the carpet.

"I see." Nick walked across to the window and hitched a hip onto the sill.

Tamsin, unable to bear the frustrated bafflement in his eyes, said good night and pushed herself to her feet.

"Good night," Nick said when she reached the door. He spoke as politely as if they had just finished a boring conversation about the weather.

When she left the room he didn't try to stop her.

Nick, his forehead creased in a scowl, prowled along the seawall with his hands shoved deep into the pockets of his pants.

It was cold out here with the breeze coming in off the water, but he didn't care. He welcomed the cold. It helped to cool the fire rampaging through his blood.

Dammit, he hadn't meant to scare Tamsin, had meant to wait until she showed him she was willing. And she *did* want him. Her response to his kiss had proved that.

As Nick passed a middle-aged couple walking arm in arm, a startling thought hit him between the eyes.

Was Tamsin holding out for marriage?

No, she couldn't be. The idea was absurd. He hadn't reached the ripe old age of thirty-four without hearing even an echo of wedding bells, only to start hearing them now over an efficient but insignificant field mouse of a woman who had lately turned unyielding as a mule.

He hunched his shoulders against the wind. It seemed that, inconvenient as it was, somewhere along the line he had come to develop a taste for field mice.

He paused to glare at the outline of the Parliament Buildings sketched in a thousand fairy lights against the sky. Tamsin had said they were magic, but he couldn't see any magic in this night. Only a small, obstinate woman with a soft, sweet body that drove him wild . . .

Nothing in his life had prepared him for this.

"See ya later, alligator. My place or yours?"

A raddled blond in a short, shiny skirt stopped in front of him and peered into his face. Cheap perfume assaulted his nostrils as he stepped around her.

"In your dreams," he said, and walked on at a faster clip than before.

What a contrast to Tamsin that pathetic creature was. Nick stopped abruptly and narrowly avoided a lamppost. Tamsin. Lately everything came back to Tamsin.

He couldn't remember ever wanting a woman as he wanted her. What in hell did it matter that she worked for him? He'd wouldn't toss her out on her ear the moment she'd given him what he wanted. He'd look after her. This wasn't the nineteenth century.

Swearing softly, Nick swung around the lamppost and continued his walk. He went on walking until his blood had cooled sufficiently to allow him to return to the hotel. Yet it wasn't until the early hours of the morning that he finally fell asleep.

When he did, he dreamed of a small, stone church and Tamsin in a short, shiny skirt walking down the aisle toward a man wearing an alligator head.

In the morning he awoke feeling as if he'd spent the

night in a swamp wrestling a whole family of alligators.

His mood wasn't improved when the phone rang in the middle of breakfast.

It was Dolores, sounding unusually subdued, and asking to speak to Tamsin.

Chapter Eleven

Nick's Lincoln glided to a stop at the curb in front of the house on West Sixteenth.

"I'll see you in," he said to Tamsin. It was a statement, not a suggestion, and she didn't bother to argue. She was saving all her energies for Dolores, who had phoned that morning to break the news of her parents' death.

"I would have phoned before, but there was nothing you could do, and I didn't want to spoil your trip," she had explained.

"But you should have called. Then you wouldn't have had to bear it all alone," Tamsin, horrified, had protested. "I could have taken the next ferry—"

"I'm not alone," Dolores interrupted in a funny, tight voice. "Richard's here."

"Oh. That's . . . good."

Tamsin had been shaking as she hung up the phone, and the receiver had slipped from her hand and crashed onto the hotel's antique desk.

Nick picked it up and restored it to its cradle, all calm efficiency once he knew what had happened.

The Lincoln's engine was still running as Tamsin leaped onto the sidewalk and ran up the steps to the porch. She rifled through her purse for her key and had just discovered it in an inside pocket when the door swung open and Richard walked out.

"How is she?" Tamsin asked at once.

"She's doing quite well—better than I expected. I'm sure

she'll do even better now you're back."

Tamsin glanced at him doubtfully. That sounded altogether too crisp and dismissive, as if he meant to put the whole unpleasant business behind him.

"Are you leaving then?" she asked.

"For the present. I have a business I've been neglecting of late."

"Yes, of course. Will you be back later?"

"I told Dolores I'd phone."

She nodded, puzzled by his curtness, and stood to one side as Nick's heavy footsteps sounded behind her, followed by an indignant meowling as the Sawchuk cat came flying off a dusty wicker chair.

"Kerrigan! What are you doing here?" Tamsin heard Nick exclaim.

Surprised, she looked around in time to see Nick put down her suitcase. The two men exchanged businesslike handshakes.

"Dolores is a friend of mine," Richard explained.

"And Tamsin is an employee of mine," Nick responded, glancing at her with a pointed little smile.

Tamsin paused in the doorway. "You two know each other?"

"Richard is the Kerrigan in Kerrigan and Fletcher," Nick replied. "Malahide's new accountants."

"Oh." Tamsin turned to Richard. "You're *that* Kerrigan. I didn't know."

What she did know was that the auditors had found several errors in the previous accountants' books, and Nick had fired them within the hour and hired Kerrigan and Fletcher to replace them. He had never taken kindly to incompetence, and the whole thing had happened so fast that she'd never actually met Kerrigan *or* Fletcher—or so she'd thought.

A door slammed upstairs, and Tamsin jumped. "There's no need to come in," she said to Nick. "You can leave my suitcase here if you like."

"I don't like. It's heavy."

Tamsin shrugged and left the door ajar as she hurried up the stairs.

Behind her she heard the murmur of male voices and the words, *bank* and *payroll* and *audit*. Couldn't men ever get together, even casually, without discussing sports or business?

Dolores was in the kitchen stirring something green into a stainless steel bowl.

"I'm back," Tamsin said quietly.

Dolores dropped her spoon with a clatter. The next moment Tamsin's arms were around her friend and she was hugging her as if friendship alone could ease her pain.

Neither of them spoke. They didn't need to.

When Nick came up with the suitcase a few minutes later, he found the two women seated at the kitchen table drinking tea.

"My sincere condolences on your loss," he said formally to Dolores.

"Thank you," Dolores replied.

Tamsin glanced at her, caught a surprising gleam of amusement in her eyes and found herself wanting to defend Nick. He was doing his best. He just had no idea how to express the genuine sympathy she knew existed behind the shuttered green eyes. He too had lost parents. He likely knew better than most what Dolores was suffering.

"I'll leave you two to talk," he said. "Will you see me out, Tamsin?"

Tamsin frowned doubtfully and thought of refusing, but she didn't want to provoke a scene in front of Dolores, who had enough to bear already. In the end, she followed Nick down the stairs.

When he reached the bottom, he swung around. Tamsin waited for him to leave, puzzled by the unusual emptiness in his eyes.

"Good-bye," she said, running her tongue along her upper lip. "Thank you for—" She stopped. Why was she thanking him for a business trip?

Nick smiled—not the hard, confident smile she was used to, but a rueful, lopsided smile that made him look younger, less formidable. For a few seconds she saw him as he must have looked as a boy, before his father's bitterness had turned him into the man he was today.

When he raised his right hand to curl it around the back of her neck, Tamsin had to dig her nails into her palms to stop herself from reaching out to smooth away the lines etched into his face.

Yet she didn't need to touch him to know she wanted him, to know exactly how his lips would taste if . . .

If Dolores wasn't waiting for her upstairs.

She took a step backward, and Nick shook his head slightly and allowed his hand to drop back to his side.

"I'll see you on Monday," he said as if nothing more intimate than a handshake had passed between them.

Maybe she'd only imagined that it had.

"You *didn't?*" Dolores gasped. "Tammy, you have to be out of your mind."

"Why? Because I turned down the chance to lose a good night's sleep?" Tamsin reached for the teapot, discovered it was empty and stood up.

"No, because you turned down the chance to get your hunk of a boss into bed." Dolores stood, too, wandered into the living room and collapsed onto the sofa.

Tamsin followed her as far as the kitchen door. Her friend had drawn her knees up under her chin and was studying her with the pitying look of one who had always been able to pick and choose her chances. Dolores didn't understand that, for Tamsin, getting her hunk of a boss into bed and then losing him would leave her a thousand times more bereft than she'd been before.

It didn't matter, of course—wasn't even the point. Dolores was concentrating on her problems with Nick because she didn't want to think about her own, far more tragic, loss.

Maybe that was okay. Richard had said Dolores was coming through it surprisingly well. While they talked over tea, Tamsin sensed a quiet acceptance in the way her friend talked about her parents, as if the best of the memories were bringing their own kind of peace to the pain of remembrance.

As Dolores said, she had spent most of her life without parents. Aside from the shock of their unexpected deaths, letting go of her childhood dreams of one day being part of a real family remained the hardest part.

Tamsin, seeing her friend surreptitiously brush a finger across her eyes, guessed those dreams had not been dreams at all, but a lifelong hunger for love.

"Well?" Dolores pushed a lock of hair off her face and rested her chin on her knees. "Aren't you going to tell me why you turned Nick down?"

"There's more to life than bed, and he's my boss," Tamsin said, opening the fridge and pretending an interest in its dubious contents. "I'm not like you, Doro. When it was over, I wouldn't be able to forget him and move on to someone else." She wrinkled her nose. "What have you left in here to die? Boiled socks again?"

Dolores shook her head. "Probably the macaroni I made last night. Richard took me out to dinner when he smelled it."

"It couldn't be," Tamsin objected. "Day-old macaroni doesn't smell like that."

"Mine does." Dolores sighed. "And stop trying to change the subject."

"I'm not. There's nothing more to say. You asked me why I didn't share Nick's bed, and I told you."

"There has to be more to it than that. He's crazy about you, Tammy. If his eyes could undress you, you'd be walking around that office in your birthday suit."

Tamsin gave a short laugh and slammed the door to the fridge. Dolores might still be in shock, but she was definitely going to survive.

"I doubt it," she said. "Not good for Malahide's reputation as a respectable and exclusive establishment."

"Believe me, Nick would forget about Malahide's reputation if you give him the ghost of a chance." Dolores extracted a nail file from the pocket of her tight black pants and began to work on her left thumb.

"Hm." Tamsin was noncommittal.

Without giving her roommate a chance to press her further, she picked up the suitcase Nick had carried upstairs, said she wouldn't be a minute and staggered off to her bedroom.

Dolores meant well, of course. Tamsin dropped the suitcase, substituted a clean white blouse for the one she'd worn on the ferry and went to the mirror to comb her hair. The trouble was, her friend's continued championing of Nick's cause was fast becoming something of an irritant—especially as Nick had barely spoken to her today. On the

210

ferry back he had disappeared behind the *Financial Post*, emerging only when it was time to disembark.

Except for that brief moment when he had asked her to see him to the door, last night might never have happened.

Was it possible that once again she was to become useful, invisible Tamsin Brown who ran Nick's office with clockwork efficiency and was only missed when something went wrong?

She had told him that was precisely what she wanted, so she had no real right to complain. Yet she had spent the journey home staring at the back of his paper and dreaming of ripping it down, kicking him in the shins and forcing him to talk to her.

The only thing that had stopped her from carrying out her fantasy was the knowledge that in the five years she had worked for him, she had never once seen anyone succeed in forcing Nick Malahide to do anything he didn't choose to do.

Tamsin kicked her suitcase and watched it crash onto its side.

"Hey!" Dolores shouted. "Keep that up, and you'll have the whole place collapsing around our ears."

Which would solve both our problems, Tamsin thought morosely. And yet she smiled. It was impossible not to smile at Dolores.

Funny, she had come home prepared to lend support and comfort to her friend. She had done that, and now Dolores, with her humor and courage, was lending that strength back to her.

Perhaps that was the nature of friendship.

The next day was Sunday, and Richard spent it alone in his office catching up on the work he'd neglected all week.

211

Finally, at around four o'clock, he switched off his computer, swung his feet onto his desk and leaned back to gaze reflectively at the ceiling. Immediately a vision of Dolores's face as it had been when he'd said good-bye to her materialized on the dull white surface.

He had promised to call her, and she had nodded and thanked him for his help, a confused, hopeless look darkening the blue of the eyes that wouldn't quite meet his. He hadn't known how to break through the barrier he had deliberately erected between them.

He knew why he had built it, of course. Allowing himself to make love to Dolores almost by accident, because she needed him, and because his body had craved release, was one thing. Allowing it to happen again would mean making a commitment he wasn't sure she was capable of returning. Nothing in Dolores's experience had taught her to believe in love between one man and one woman. Her parents' love for each other had, in essence, been a selfish thing, and their daughter had suffered for it. Had their deaths only reinforced her conviction that relationships weren't meant to last?

There was only one way to find out.

As he reached for the phone, dialed and waited for someone to answer, a purple cloud drifted across the sun.

Dolores opened the door to Richard without a word and immediately led him upstairs. She could feel him watching the pearl gray satin stretched across her rear.

After his phone call she had contemplated putting on jeans and a plain white blouse of the type he seemed to favor—she could always borrow one from Tammy—but in the end she'd made up her mind to suit herself. Why not? Richard didn't own her.

The satin skirt and low-cut red chiffon blouse were the result.

"Where's Tamsin?" Richard asked, looking around as they came to the top of the stairs.

"After you phoned, she arranged to go to a movie with Sally from her office. I told her there was no need, but she insisted."

"I see."

Dolores's smile was brittle as she sat on the sofa and patted the seat beside her. He didn't seem particularly pleased by the news that the two of them were alone.

Richard remained standing.

Dolores leaned her head against the back of the sofa. Lord, Richard was gorgeous from this angle. He was gorgeous from any angle, of course, but with his long, jean-clad legs set elegantly apart, his hands on his hips, and his dark blue shirt exposing the sinews of his neck as he loomed above her, he was, if possible, more devastating than ever.

She had spent the past week mourning, crying herself to sleep every night. Perhaps now it was time to move on—to allow the healing to begin.

She held out her hands. "Come and sit with me. Please."

Richard didn't take her outstretched hands. Instead, he lowered himself onto the opposite end of the sofa, removed a cushion from behind his back and crossed his legs.

Okay, so he was going to take persuading. Before Richard she had never met a man who needed persuading. In a way, it added zest to the game.

She slipped off her high-heeled black sandals, extended a leg and ran a nylon-sheathed toe down his calf. When he didn't react, she did it again.

Richard reached down and grabbed her ankle. "That's enough," he said, and Dolores knew from the tension in his grip that he was no more immune to her than any other man—which was good, because it had been a long time since she'd wanted any other man. She wasn't at all sure she ever would.

"Get your coat," he said, standing abruptly. "I'll take you out to dinner."

"No need. I'll make it. Later."

Richard smiled for the first time since he'd walked into the apartment. "You forget, I spent nearly a week not eating your cooking. What makes you think I'm going to start now?"

Dolores tried to scowl but ended up grinning. "You sound like Tammy. She won't eat my cooking either unless it's salad. Haven't you two ever heard of healthy food?"

"Yes, and it doesn't come in packages labeled *organic*. Dolores, go and get your coat. We're going out."

Oh, no, they weren't. Not if she had her way. And she was very determined to have her way.

"Let's have a drink first," she said. "Whiskey?"

Richard brushed a hand across his mouth. "All right, but I didn't think whiskey came under the heading of *Healthy*."

"It doesn't. I'm having mineral water," she announced blithely, and went into the kitchen to pour the drinks.

"Here's to a better week than the last one," he said, raising his glass to her when she handed him his whiskey.

"Yes." Dolores resumed her place on the sofa. She didn't want to talk about the past week—didn't want to think about it. If this evening went as she hoped it would, it could be the start of a whole new life.

"Will you be going back to work soon?" Richard asked.

"Oh, yes. On Tuesday." She stared down into her glass of mineral water. "My parents left me a bit, but I'll still have to work."

"Don't you want to?"

She recrossed her legs and shifted a little along the sofa. "For a while, yes. But I'll quit once I have a family. At least until the kids start school."

Richard choked and spilled a few drops of his drink onto his jeans. "A family? You expect to have kids?"

As the meaning of his words sank in, a hard ball of anger began to form in the pit of Dolores's stomach. Did he think she was incapable of raising children? Or of staying true to one man?

She pushed away the thought at the back of her mind that it wasn't an unreasonable supposition. Just because she had always rejected permanence in the past didn't mean she had rejected it for all time. He had no right to assume she couldn't change.

"Of course I do," she said. "Why not?" Then, seeing the doubt in his slate-gray eyes, she couldn't resist adding, "For all we know, I could be starting a baby already."

She watched with considerable satisfaction as every scrap of color drained from Richard's face.

"You're not . . . ?" he began.

"On the pill? No. These days it's safer to insist my partners take precautions. Except once," she amended when she saw the horrified dawning of realization in his eyes. "I wasn't thinking clearly that morning."

Richard swiped a hand across his face. "Obviously neither was I."

"No."

She wondered if the silence that followed was the origin of the phrase, *pregnant pause.*

"You can't possibly know yet," Richard said at last.

"No."

"If you are . . . pregnant . . . will you have it?"

215

Dolores hadn't actually thought about it before. The likelihood of pregnancy had seemed so small. Now she did, however, and the answer was a dizzying revelation. "Yes," she said. "Yes, I will."

Richard gulped down the last of his whiskey. "It probably won't happen. If it does . . ."

"If it does, I'll let you know." She had no intention of sounding desperate. Because she wasn't.

His color had returned, Dolores noted, and after the first shock he seemed to be taking the possibility of fatherhood with surprising composure.

When, after another short silence, he said, "Right, let's go get something to eat then," the knot in her stomach twisted until she was ready to scream. Was that all he had to say? She didn't honestly believe she was pregnant, but that was no reason for Richard to act as if food was more important than their child. She bit her lip. He wasn't usually that sort of man. In fact his strong sense of responsibility was one of the traits she most admired in him.

So did his lack of passion, his detachment, mean that, unless there was a child, he planned to leave her for good?

She studied him covertly while pretending absorption with her drink, and detected no tenderness in his gaze, no sign that he held her in more than a casual affection. She put down her glass and slid her hand along the back of the sofa until her knuckles brushed his neck. No man had ever been given the opportunity to break off with her before—and Richard Kerrigan needn't think he was getting the chance to be the first.

"I have a better idea than food," she said, controlling an urge to scratch his face and provoke him into some kind of reaction.

He caught her wrist. "I'm sure you have. But let's not go looking for trouble."

Dolores considered her options. She could continue the sultry vamp routine, which obviously wasn't working, or she could give up all hope of a grand finale and end it now. If she was wrong, if that wasn't what he wanted, she would know. Wouldn't she?

She waited until he released her wrist before saying, "You're right, of course. I don't want trouble either. Good-bye, Richard. Thank you for all your help this past week." She held out her hand, keeping her disappointment in check by the sheer force of her will, and favored him with what she hoped was a careless smile.

Richard frowned at her hand. "Good-bye? You're telling me good-bye?"

"Yes. Better to end things before we both get bored, don't you think?" She had no idea how she kept her smile in place, but she did.

A spark flared in Richard's eyes. "Bored?" he said. "I've never found you boring, Dolores. Confusing, yes. Exasperating and maddening, yes. But not boring."

Dolores covered a yawn. "That's good."

"And what's more," he said, picking up her hand and placing it, palm down, against his thigh, "I don't believe you've ever found me boring."

She kept quite still and said nothing.

All at once Richard moved, trapping her knees between his, then sliding them slowly, erotically up the length of her thighs. Dolores gasped, her hand clutching his jeans. When he could move no closer, the ball of hurt and anger burning in her stomach dissolved into delicious ripples of desire.

"Damn you," she whispered.

"Bored?" he asked.

217

Dolores reached for his belt, and when he would have stopped her, she slipped her palm down to cup his groin.

He flinched and lowered his eyelids, but he didn't push her away.

With the blood singing triumphantly in her veins, Dolores began to move her fingers in slow, sensuous exploration, teasing and stroking until she forced a groan from Richard's throat.

Without warning he leaned forward, seized her shoulders and pressed his lips to the vee of her cleavage. Seconds later he was sliding the sleeves of her blouse down her shoulders.

"You're so beautiful." His voice was unusually thick as he expertly unhooked her bra.

Dolores laughed, and this time Richard offered no resistance when she put her hands on his belt.

Then he was pulling her to her feet, sliding a hand smoothly across the gray satin covering her bottom, drawing her toward him to cover first one peaked nipple, then the other with his mouth. Her hips began to move beneath his touch, and when he pulled her hard against the length of his body, she reveled in the fierceness of his desire.

In that moment she forgot that he might have meant to leave her, forgot everything except that he was here now, and hers for the taking. She began to tug at his shirt as his fingers closed on the zipper of her skirt. Seconds later gray satin skimmed down her legs and came to rest around her ankles. She was wearing nothing but stockings now, and Richard—Richard was as magnificently naked as the day he was born. She moaned as he sank to his knees to peel off her stockings, sliding them down slowly, too slowly, pressing his lips between her thighs. Finally her hosiery joined the heap of discarded clothing on the floor.

Richard rose to his feet. His pupils widened briefly, then he held out his hand.

Hypnotized by the sight of his naked glory, she didn't at once take it, and immediately he moved forward, swept her up into his arms and said, "Where?"

"Anywhere," Dolores cried. "But *now*. Please."

Richard laughed, bore her over to the rocking chair to set her astride his knees. She gasped as his long fingers curved around her waist, easing her forward.

"Please," she moaned. "Oh, please . . ."

The chair creaked and tilted beneath them until at last they slid together onto the carpet. Then he was inside her, and she was all around him, her straining breasts pressed against his chest. Behind them, the rocking chair creaked then slowed gently to a stop. Moments later, in one final ecstatic explosion, their bodies shuddered to the ultimate release.

As the fading waves of pleasure mingled with the sound of their breathing, Dolores looked down at the fine blond hairs on Richard's chest and murmured, "I'll never be able to sit in that chair again without remembering."

Richard ran a finger down her spine. "Not bored?" he asked.

Dolores gasped as reality came crashing into the make-believe game they were playing. No, she wasn't bored. And he'd just proven it. But she had already said good-bye to him. Nothing had changed simply because they had once again made glorious, passionate love. He might stay with her if she asked, out of a sense of duty. But she wouldn't ask. Richard had too many doubts for the two of them to work.

"I wasn't bored," she said dully.

"But it's still good-bye?"

She turned her head away so he wouldn't see the pain reflected in her eyes. "Yes," she said. "It's time, isn't it?"

"Is it?" His voice was rough, almost as if he didn't want to end it. But she guessed he would be relieved once it was over. Richard needed more than good sex. She had been slow to catch on, but Richard Kerrigan needed a different kind of woman altogether.

"Yes," she said, scrambling stiffly to her feet. "I'm afraid it is."

Richard reached for her before she could move away, dragging her against him. "Fine," he rasped, sliding his palms up her thighs. "If you're sure that's what you want."

She glanced down at his hands and felt her stomach muscles tighten. "I'm . . . I'm sure," she whispered.

"All right." He let her go, and when she stepped aside, he at once stood up and began to drag on his clothes.

Dolores watched him dress, loving the way he moved and making no attempt to clothe herself. When he was finished, he didn't look at her but made straight for the door.

She held her breath.

In the end he came back and took her in his arms. "You will let me know if . . . anything happens," he said with an urgency that only served to confuse her until she realized that "anything" meant a baby.

He didn't seem to expect an answer, so she didn't give one.

He bent down, touched his lips to her forehead and left.

It was a cold night, clear and crisp, as Vancouver in September often wasn't. As Richard drove home across the Lions Gate Bridge, the lights of the North Shore and the Grouse Mountain chairlift sparkled cleanly against the darkness of the mountains.

He rotated his shoulder blades to ease the tension in his spine. What the hell was the matter with him? He hadn't known precisely what he intended when he went to see Dolores, hadn't even known what he wanted, though she'd made up his mind on that point fast enough—her version of seeing out the old before ringing in the new, he supposed. He gripped the steering wheel and stared unblinkingly at the lights. No, that wasn't fair. He could hardly complain he'd been an unwilling participant lured by the wiles of a wanton woman. That interlude that had started in the rocking chair and ended on the carpet had been as much his doing as hers.

And it had opened his eyes.

Dolores was the most generous, fascinating, giving woman he had ever met—and sometime during the course of the past week he had discovered he didn't want to let her go. He just hadn't been willing to acknowledge it.

Yes, she was a handful, a butterfly who flitted from man to man. But she also wanted children, was perhaps already carrying his child. It was even possible that because of her own unsettled childhood, she would do her best to make sure any child of hers led a normal, stable family life.

Richard took a hand from the wheel and wiped a thin film of moisture off his forehead. So she thought she'd get bored with him, did she? That was too bad, because it was a lead pipe cinch he'd never get bored with her. Furious, yes. Exasperated, enchanted and amused—but never bored.

As he swung the Corvette off Marine Drive, it occurred to Richard that he had a problem on his hands more challenging than any he had faced in the offices of Kerrigan and Fletcher—or even while indulging his fondness for risk-taking sports.

When a sign featuring an anemic-looking dragon and the

words *White Dragon Inn* caught his eye, on an impulse he pulled the Corvette into the lot and went inside.

"Kerrigan!" exclaimed a voice from somewhere in the depths of an interior lit only by a few orange-shaded lamps.

Richard narrowed his eyes until his gaze settled on a lone figure seated close to a flickering gas fire that gave no warmth.

"Nick Malahide," he said. "What brings you here?"

"Food and drink," Nick replied. He waved at a chair and waited until Richard sat down. "How's Dolores?"

"Impossible. But better. How's Tamsin?"

"The same. Impossible." Nick peered lugubriously into his beer. "Would you believe I used to think women were easy to figure out? What are you drinking, by the way?"

Richard ordered a beer and said he knew exactly what Nick meant about women.

After that the two of them spent a companionable evening agreeing with Sophocles that, of all the calamities that befall mortal man, nothing is worse, or ever will be worse, than woman.

By the time they came to that agreeable conclusion, they had both drunk rather more than was wise and, as a result, were obliged to leave their vehicles in the parking lot and take taxis home rather than risk a confrontation with the law.

They blamed that on women too.

"Doro, you didn't break up with Richard! Not again. I thought you were getting on so well."

Dolores, who was lying on the sofa glaring at the inoffensive rocking chair, said, "Yes, I did. And you thought wrong."

"Oh." Tamsin lowered herself into the rocker, which

made Dolores frown. "And you had the nerve to talk about me and Nick?"

"That's different. He's crazy about you."

"He's crazy about getting his own way, that's all. It's Richard who's different. He spent nearly a week looking after you because you needed him, and you told me he didn't even touch you."

Dolores moved her head restlessly on the arm of the sofa, then sat up. "That wasn't strictly true. He did once. Touch me, I mean. The . . . the morning after Mom and Dad died." She fidgeted with the hem of her wrinkled satin skirt. "It just sort of . . . happened. And then he felt guilty and wouldn't come near me again. Until today."

Dolores wasn't sure if Tamsin's frown was because she hadn't admitted the truth to her before, or because she disapproved of what had sort of happened.

Eventually Tamsin said, "But that's no reason to dump him. That means he respects you."

Dolores guessed her laugh sounded more like a snort. "Don't be naive, Tammy. It means he's a man, and he likes my body a lot better than he likes me."

"You don't know that." Tamsin extended a foot and began to rock herself slowly back and forth.

"I do know that. And for Pete's sake, stop rocking."

As soon as the words were out of her mouth, Dolores regretted them. It wasn't Tammy's fault that the rocker had become a symbol of everything she'd lost.

Tamsin stopped at once, seeming to understand that more had gone on while she was at the movies than her roommate was choosing to explain. "Do you want him back?" she asked.

Dolores gripped her head with both hands. "Lord, I don't know. What's the point, when he doesn't really want me? He's still in love with his sainted Elizabeth."

"But if he did want you?" Tamsin persisted.

Damn Tammy anyway. It was a good question. *Did* she want him back? She had certainly never felt this way about any other man. The others had all been for laughter and dancing and fun, not for any kind of future. Whereas Richard. . . .

Richard wasn't like that. The thought of not seeing him again was . . . Oh, no, she couldn't bear the thought of not seeing him again.

"All right," Dolores said. "All right, I guess I do want him back. But I might as well forget it." She attempted a gallant smile that made her face hurt. "It's been a lousy week, hasn't it? For both of us."

"Mine wasn't so bad. Yours was terrible." Tamsin started to rock again, until Dolores caught her eye and made her stop.

Tammy was right. It had been terrible. So terrible she still felt a little drugged. She hoped the feeling wouldn't wear off any time soon.

"I'll survive," she said. "I always do, you know." Tamsin's smile was sweet and encouraging, and she added severely, "As for you, Tammy, it's time you stopped worrying about me and started worrying about how to make the most of your gorgeous boss. Will he be in the office tomorrow?"

"Oh, he'll be in," Tamsin replied in a voice so filled with gloom it made Dolores laugh.

Thank heaven for dear, funny, solemn Tammy. How had she ever managed to live this long without a friend?

Impulsively she jumped to her feet, pulled Tamsin out of the rocker and began to swing her in a wild dance around the room.

When Dolores let out a whoop as the two of them crashed into the coffee table, Mrs. Sawchuk pounded on the ceiling with a broom.

Chapter Twelve

"Good morning, Ms. Brown."

Tamsin looked up from her computer. *Ms. Brown?* Nick only called her that when he wanted to remind her who was boss. She had wondered how things would be after that peculiarly dreamlike interlude in Victoria. Now she knew.

"Good morning, Mr. Malahide." She kept her face as poker-straight as his.

Nick nodded and vanished into his office.

To Tamsin's relief he remained secluded there until lunch time, when he emerged only to say, "Back at two, Ms. Brown," before disappearing down the stairs.

At two o'clock the performance was repeated. At five o'clock he said, "Good night, Ms. Brown. I'll see you in the morning," and stepped smartly into the hall.

Tamsin had to admit he was giving her exactly what she'd asked for. A return to "the way it used to be" but with even more formality than before.

There was one other difference.

Over the next three days Nick didn't once ask her to search for a file, didn't once forget an appointment and need reminding, and didn't once raise his voice to demand where the devil she'd put "that damned portfolio" or "those purchase orders the workshop wanted signed."

Knowing this silent standoff couldn't last, Tamsin waited, dreading the inevitable confrontation.

It came on the Friday, just after Nick returned from lunch.

Tamsin was bent over the fax machine installing a new supply of paper, and she didn't realize he was there until he cleared his throat.

She straightened at once. "Yes, Mr. Malahide?"

He gestured at the machine. "Get on with what you were doing."

Tamsin got on and waited for the sound of his door closing. When it didn't come, she knew he was still in her office, presumably inspecting the view as she adjusted the paper.

Heat flooded her face, and she swung around so fast that she knocked the fax sideways on its stand. "What are you staring at?" she asked, rubbing damp palms down her skirt.

"Nothing at the moment. I *was* admiring the only part of you that was visible. Why are you wearing beige again, Tamsin?"

"Because I don't want you . . . admiring that part of me."

A muscle twitched on his aggressively jutting jaw. "I'll try to bear that in mind. In the meantime, would you be good enough to fetch me the Staines portfolio, the new bookshelf designs from the workshop and, when you have a moment, I'd like you to run off twenty copies of these figures." He parked his briefcase on her desk, opened it, and pulled out a slim file of papers. "Oh, and two cups of coffee please. I'm expecting Jack Lee from the Lee-Chen Corporation."

Tamsin counted to ten. Nick never asked her to play waitress. He had a coffee-maker in his office and always made his own—his one concession to progressive office practice. So what point was he making by changing the rules on her now?

"Certainly, Mr. Malahide." She took the papers from

him and turned away without batting an eyelid. Two could play that game. Nick might be in a foul mood—probably because for once in his life a woman hadn't fallen gratefully into his bed—but if he hoped to provoke her into losing *her* temper, he was in for a very long wait.

By the end of the afternoon she hadn't lost her temper, but Nick's nonstop demands on her time had forced her into doing some serious thinking.

She had been a fool to imagine they could step back in time. Too much had happened since the day Nick had first taken her in his arms and dried her tears. He would never be able to look at her again without resenting her as the one that got away. And she—she couldn't look at him either without thinking of what might have been, of the joy that might have been theirs, if only Nick had been capable of love.

Tamsin sank into her chair and closed her eyes. It wasn't his fault. He had been brought up to think of love as a delusion and sex as an end in itself.

She couldn't, *wouldn't,* settle for that.

It had taken her a long time to see what was happening, but she knew now that some time over the course of the last eventful months, she had made the oldest mistake in the world.

She had fallen in love with her boss.

Resting both elbows on her desk, Tamsin pressed her fingers to her temples to stem the throbbing in her head. It didn't help. The throbbing continued. And after half an hour she came to a decision.

When Nick stalked through her office fifteen minutes later, she called after him, "Just a moment, please, Nick. I have something to tell you."

He stopped in the doorway. "Yes? I hope it won't take long. I'm in a hurry."

To meet some new woman, no doubt. Tamsin took a

long breath and willed her voice not to fail her.

"It won't take long," she said. "I'm giving you a month's notice. You'll need to start looking for my replacement."

"I'll what?" His fingers tightened around the handle of his briefcase, turning his knuckles bone white as he swung back into the office and stopped in the center of the floor. "I'll *what?*"

Tamsin said, "I think you heard me. I said you'll need to start looking for a new assistant."

"Don't be absurd." Nick's voice cracked like ice in boiling water.

Tamsin, stunned by the force of his reaction, laid her hands flat on her desk and sat up very straight. "I *beg* your pardon?" she said. "Perhaps you didn't understand—"

"Let me rephrase that," Nick interrupted. "Don't even think of resigning."

Tamsin made herself hold his gaze. "I'm serious, Nick. I am leaving Malahide's."

"Because I gave you a bit of extra work?"

"No. Because I can't continue to work for a man who insists on prowling through the office like Dracula deprived of his nightly dose of blood."

Nick, who had been standing with his shoulders squared as if braced for an attack, raised a hand and raked it through his hair. "Good grief!" he said, slanting her a look that didn't remotely remind her of Dracula. "I'm not that bad."

"You are." She sighed. "But that's not the only reason I can't stay."

He slung his briefcase onto her credenza and perched himself beside it. "I didn't think it was."

Tamsin twisted a button on her jacket. "It isn't working, is it?"

"What isn't?"

229

"We can't go back to being the way we were."

He shrugged. "Of course we can't. I wondered how long it would take you to figure that out."

Tamsin resisted an urge to jump up and shake him. Lounging there on her credenza in his perfectly tailored steel gray suit with a small smile lifting the corners of his lips, he looked so unfairly desirable she could barely trust herself to be in the same room with him.

"Since we *can't* go back," she said, gripping the arms of her chair, "you must see that I have no choice except to leave."

"Why not go forward instead?" His smile was coaxing, the familiar killer smile that had been her undoing from the start.

"What do you mean?"

"Accept the offer I made you on the Island. It's not your blood I'm after, Tamsin darlin'."

"I know what you're after. And I've told you I'm not a temporary kind of woman."

"Then we wouldn't *be* temporary. You've suited me as my assistant for almost five years. I see no reason why you won't suit me equally well in a . . ." He hesitated. "Shall we say in a more *intimate* capacity."

"You're talking like a Regency rake," Tamsin snapped. "And I don't want to suit you in an 'intimate capacity.' " Hearing the note of near panic in her voice, she turned to grovel in a drawer for her purse. She had to get out of here. Fast.

"You," Nick said, abandoning his perch on the credenza and advancing toward her, "are a first class liar, Ms. Brown. Allow me to prove it to you."

"No." Tamsin dropped the purse, stumbled to her feet and backed against the desk.

Nick kept on advancing.

"Don't," she said when he stopped in front of her and rubbed his knuckles lightly over her chin.

"Why not? Don't you like it?"

"No," she whispered.

He opened his hand and cupped it around her cheek. "You're lying again," he said softly.

He was right. She was lying through her teeth. "Please," she begged. "Can't you just accept my notice and be done with it?"

"Certainly not. I don't *want* you to leave, Tamsin." He moved his hand to the back of her neck.

Tamsin stifled a groan. He was so close she could smell his clean, minty breath, feel it lifting the hair on her forehead. She couldn't think, couldn't breathe, couldn't move . . .

Yet she must.

"Nick, you can't *make* me stay," she finally managed to gasp.

"No, but maybe I can persuade you." Before Tamsin could grasp what he was up to, he had settled onto a corner of her desk, put his hands on her hips and pulled her between his knees. "There. That's better. Now kiss me."

It was no use. She couldn't help herself. As his hands moved down, massaging and tantalizing her rear, she lowered her head to touch her mouth to his.

At once he hauled her closer. "See what you do to me?" he growled.

Tamsin didn't see, but she felt.

For the next few minutes all she could do was feel, as Nick's arms closed around her, and his lips claimed hers in a kiss so intimate it made her forget every resolution she had ever made about leaving him. Behind her back, his fingers continued to perform their seductive magic, and she knew that if he didn't stop soon *she* would be the one begging him to stay, to finish what he'd started before he drove her mad.

Afterwards, she often wondered how the day would have ended if Sally's cheerful voice hadn't called up from the showroom, "Hey, you still up there, Tammy? I'm just about to close up shop."

Nick slackened his grip slightly. Tamsin groaned and wrenched herself out of his arms. "Yes," she called back, summoning all the breath she had left. "Yes, I'm still here. I'll put the alarm on when I leave."

"You all right?" Sally asked. "You sound weird."

"I'm fine. You go on home."

"Okay. See you Monday." The front door slammed.

Tamsin swallowed hard and made herself look Nick in the eye.

"Alone at last," he murmured, with a villainous leer that on any other occasion would have made her laugh.

"No." She edged backwards in the general direction of the door. "Nick, you're not being fair."

He grinned, a piratical grin that did nothing to lessen her uneasiness. "I have no intention of being fair. Where do you think you're going?"

"Home—if you'll move so I can get at my purse."

"Not until you promise to stay at Malahide's."

"I can't promise that." She unfastened the top button of her suit jacket, then did it up again. "In the circumstances, I don't even know why you'd want me to stay."

His eyes, which had been bright with an aggravating mockery, turned unrevealing as one-way glass. "The circumstances being my abortive attempt to get you to abandon your maidenly chastity?"

"You're being a Regency rake again. But, yes. Exactly."

"I see." Nick straightened his tie and stood up. "To be honest, I'm not sure why I want to keep you. Habit, I suppose."

The words cut with a sharp edge she guessed was meant to hurt.

It did. Deeply.

"Habits can be broken," she said.

"So they can."

Nick turned away and stood with his arms crossed, scowling at her computer. Tamsin decided it was time to leave, but the moment she moved, he raised his head and said, "Some habits are better broken gradually."

"I suppose so." What was he getting at? Did he expect her to leave Malahide's a bit at a time?

Apparently he did.

"I suggest you take your vacation instead of quitting outright," he said. "That will give us both time to decide how to handle this situation."

Tamsin took another step backward. "I already know how to handle it," she said.

Outside in the street, the brakes of a truck gave a protesting whine, and a man's voice shouted a string of colorful obscenities.

Nick's jaw set, and he strode across the room to shut the window with a bang. "As I was saying," he said, "about your vacation—"

"I'm not taking a vacation," Tamsin interrupted. "I'm sorry, but I've given you my notice."

"Which I don't accept. Not yet."

"Nick. . . ." She held up a hand. "Nick, it isn't a matter of what *you* accept, of what suits *you*. This is *my* decision."

"No." He sat on the windowsill, his palms spread flat on

his thighs. "This has to be *our* decision. One that suits us both. Which I don't believe your leaving Malahide's does."

Tamsin reached up to pull her coat off its hanger. What was the use in arguing? He wouldn't listen whatever she said.

As she struggled with the coat, Nick abandoned his post by the window and came to hold it for her.

"I'll drive you home," he said, resting his hands on her shoulders. "We'll talk on the way."

"Thank you, but there's no need—"

"There is a need."

Tamsin shrugged him off and started down the stairs toward the showroom.

"Wrong way." Nick yanked her purse from the drawer and came after her.

The next moment she was being hustled bodily down the back stairs. He had moved with such speed and precision that they were standing in the parking lot before she found her voice.

"I told Sally I'd put the alarm on," she reminded him with a mildness she didn't feel.

Nick swore and went to unlock the Lincoln. "All right. I'll fix it."

Tamsin stood under a stunted and almost leafless birch tree growing in a corner of the lot and watched him stride back into the building like a one-man assault team on a roll.

She shivered, and not entirely from the cold of a typically raw October day. If she hurried, she could be at the bus stop before he came back.

She banished the thought almost at once. Nick wasn't the type to climb tamely into his car and drive away once he found her gone, and she didn't relish a scene at the bus stop.

Reluctantly she opened the door of the Lincoln and sat down.

When he reappeared, Nick said, "It's much too cold to think of taking the bus."

Did he guess she'd been tempted to flee? "I've been taking it for five years," she pointed out. "It never seemed to bother you before."

"It didn't. But then, *you* never bothered me before."

Tamsin didn't know what to say to that, so she said nothing.

The inside of the Lincoln was warm, comfortable, its leathery smell an agreeable contrast to the dampness outside. If Nick hadn't been seated beside her with his thigh just inches from her own, she might even have fallen asleep.

It had been an unusually busy day.

To her relief Nick didn't, after all, say a word about her resignation but drove in silence until they reached their destination.

"Thank you," Tamsin said, reaching for the door handle.

"Not so fast." He extended an arm along the seat behind her back. "We have unfinished business, remember."

"It's not unfinished."

"Oh, yes, it is. Be your sensible self, Tamsin. Give yourself time to think things over. If you still feel the same after a vacation, you can hand in your notice then."

He sounded so calm, so eminently reasonable. Could he possibly be right?

"And you'll accept it? Without any more objections?" she asked.

"Of course."

She suspected there was no of course about it. Nick, as usual, expected to get his own way.

Yet she had to admit that the idea of taking time off to consider her options wasn't entirely without merit. She couldn't think clearly when Nick was around, breathing down her neck, distracting her . . . inspiring dreams that could never be fulfilled. Not that a vacation was likely to change any of that, but if she did as he asked, at least they would both know she'd tried.

Or was she fooling herself, prolonging the agony because she couldn't bear the thought of losing him completely? Of never seeing his much-loved face again?

"If I agree," she said, frowning at an untidy pile of leaves on the front porch, "do you *promise* you'll accept my resignation when I give it?" She wished he would put his arm back where it belonged.

"*If* you give it," Nick corrected her.

Tamsin sighed. "Do you promise?"

To her relief he at last moved his arm from behind her back. "I promise," he said.

"Good. Then, yes, all right. I'll take my month's vacation."

"A *month?* You never take more than two weeks. What am I supposed to do without you for a month?"

"The same thing you do when I go for two weeks. Hire a temp."

Nick fixed a morose eye on a teenage boy and girl wound in an octopus-like embrace against a street lamp. "The last temp we had was no older than that child over there. All she did was giggle on the phone to her boyfriend."

"And you let her?"

"No. I told her to cut it out if she didn't want to find herself out on her ear without a reference. She turned on the waterworks at once—they always do—but we didn't have a problem after that."

"Oh. I'll get you someone older this time."

"Not just older. I want married, over fifty, and preferably with buck teeth and a squint."

"I'll do my best," Tamsin said demurely.

On any other occasion the suspicious look he threw her way would have made her laugh. She didn't feel much like laughing today.

Neither, apparently, did Nick.

Three days later, while Nick was out of the office, Tamsin hired a temp. Ms. Antoinette Ducharmes had neither buck teeth nor a squint, and she didn't look a day over twenty-five. She was also raven-haired, gorgeous and came with a long list of references. Nick wouldn't miss his soon-to-be ex-assistant for long.

In the late afternoon of the day before Antoinette was due to start, Nick rose from his desk and stalked into the boardroom. He couldn't stand the sound of Tamsin's preparations for departure any longer. As he passed her desk, she emptied a tray of chewed pencils into her wastepaper basket. Funny, now that he thought of it, she hadn't chewed pencils since her first year in the office. She'd been such a meek, scared little thing. . . .

Unexpectedly Nick's throat closed up. As he stared out the window contemplating the approaching storm clouds, a voice behind him said, "Nick, I'm off now. I'm sure Antoinette will take good care of you."

Nick swung around, wishing he was at liberty to lose his temper. Unfortunately, since he still anticipated Tamsin's return, he would have to refrain from delivering the summary retribution he itched to mete out. He contented himself with snapping, "I can blow my own nose, thank you. I don't need your Antoinette to do it for me."

"I'm sure you don't," Tamsin responded in a soothing voice that did nothing to dispel his ill-humor.

She was holding on to the back of one of the rosewood chairs, gazing up at him with that deceptively dutiful expression he'd come to know too well. Her soft mouth was slightly open, and he could just see her small white teeth.

He wanted to shout at her, to tell her she had no business disrupting his life on a whim. Instead he heard himself saying, "I'll miss you, Tamsin. Heaven help me."

She stared at him, and he saw her knuckles tighten on the chair.

Now why had he said that? He was annoyed with her for making him insist on this unnecessary vacation, but missing her had been the last thing on his mind. She was efficient, he was used to having her around—that was all. Wasn't it?

Well, yes, maybe. Except that, just at this moment, he wanted to kiss her. Badly.

"Come here, field mouse." He beckoned her with the little finger on his right hand.

She took a step forward, then stopped.

"Oh, for Pete's sake, I don't eat field mice," he exclaimed before rounding the table in long strides to pull her into his arms.

He kissed her good-bye then, and she responded with an intensity that nearly knocked him off his feet. Lord, she tasted good. Sweet, warm, tender. Not like Gloria. Not like any woman he'd ever known.

And she was going away because he wanted more than she'd been willing to give. Much more.

Only a massive exercise of will stopped him from locking the door, tumbling her onto the table and proving to her how much she wanted it too.

He didn't try to carry out his fantasy. He would never forgive himself if he hurt Tamsin.

He dropped one last kiss on her parted lips and another on her nose before he held her away. "Enjoy your vacation, field mouse," he murmured, and went to the drinks cabinet to pour himself a brandy.

He had his back to the door when he heard it close.

"Daddy, why is that lady crying?" asked a little boy with ice cream framing his mouth.

His father glanced at the pale young woman who had just joined the crowd at the bus stop. "I don't know," he said. "I expect she's got something in her eye."

Chapter Thirteen

Richard swore as the intercom to his apartment buzzed insistently. He seemed to swear a lot these days.

"Yes? Who's there?" he snapped.

"It's me. And who put vinegar in *your* Wheaties?" his sister's obnoxiously cheerful voice demanded.

"Janet? What are you doing here?"

"Waiting to get out of the rain. Do you plan on letting me in?"

He pressed the button to admit her, after which blessed silence descended until Janet's impatient knock sounded on his door.

When he opened it, she took one look at his face and said, "You'd better marry her. Dolores, isn't it? The bimbo?"

Richard resisted his immediate inclination, which was to throttle his sister and toss her over the balcony railing. "Her name is Dolores, yes. She's not a bimbo. And you may be right. I ought to marry her—if only to stop her from breaking any more unsuspecting hearts."

"You figure marriage would stop her?" Janet picked up her small suitcase and shoved it at him. "Here, put this on my bed, will you? I'm staying the night."

Richard jerked the case out of her hand, thought of pointing out that she didn't have a permanent bed in his apartment, and decided to save his breath. "Yes," he said. "Trust me, it would stop her. There's just one snag."

Janet studied his expression briefly, nodded and said, "Okay, what's the snag?"

240

"The lady doesn't want to marry me. She says I'm boring."

To Richard's chagrin, his sister burst out laughing. "I can't wait to meet her," she said.

"Oh, yes, you can," he replied. "I've enough on my hands without you stirring the pot." He pulled her inside and shut the door with a bang that blew half the papers on his desk onto the floor.

Nick slammed the phone back into its cradle with such force that Ms. Antoinette Ducharmes came dashing into his office to ask if everything was all right.

"No," he said. "Everything is not all right. Tamsin had her pain-in-the-butt friend, Dolores, phone to tell me she isn't coming back."

"Not coming back from her vacation?" Antoinette widened her seductive brown eyes.

"Not coming back to Malahide's," he snapped.

"Oh." Antoinette flipped back her hair in a gesture he suspected was calculated to display her sweater-clad bosom to maximum effect. "Don't worry, Mr. Malahide. *I* won't leave you in the lurch."

"I wasn't worrying." Nick waved a dismissive hand and turned back to the figures on his computer. "That'll be all. Thank you, Antoinette."

Several seconds later he became aware that the overpowering scent of cheap perfume still lingered in his nose. Antoinette had not left the room.

"I said that will be all," he repeated.

"I know. But Mr. Malahide. . . ." Her husky voice trailed off reproachfully.

"Yes?" Irritated, Nick removed his fingers from the keyboard and looked up.

Good grief. The woman was bent halfway across his desk and actually batting her long eyelashes at him. Surely women weren't supposed to do that any more—unless, of course, they were members of a certain profession. . . .

"Antoinette," he said. "Is something the matter with your eyes? Because if there isn't, I'd be obliged if you'd get back to work." He managed to ignore the very visible cleft between her breasts.

"Oh!" His new assistant tossed her head and turned her back, offering him an excellent view of her nicely rounded backside. "I only wanted to help." She rubbed a knuckle over her eyes and sniffed pointedly.

Nick held his breath and counted to fifty. Did the wretched woman think that going all weepy on him was likely to improve her chances of taking Tamsin's place in what had once been his well-ordered life?

Briefly, the thought gave him pause. Antoinette was an attractive woman, he was currently unattached—and a month or so ago he wouldn't have hesitated to accept the goods he was so blatantly being offered. Yet now he found himself totally indifferent to her charms? More than indifferent. The truth of the matter was that he found her flagrant sexuality annoying—and certainly unattractive.

"I don't need any help," he said as soon as he was able to control the urge to shout. "But thank you. I appreciate your concern."

Antoinette straightened, slid her hands down her hips and said in a voice quivering with reproach, "Yes, Mr. Malahide. I understand." She stalked out of his office with her nose at an angle that would have made him laugh if she'd been Tamsin.

The point was, she wasn't Tamsin, who had just handed in her notice for what, Dolores assured him, was the last time.

Nick lifted a fist and smashed it down on his desk. Dear heaven, how could he have been so obtuse? How could he have failed to recognize the priceless jewel he had once held in his hands?

It wasn't Ms. Brown, office drone, whom he wanted back, but sweet, funny Tamsin Brown who had walked away with his heart when he wasn't looking.

And through sheer, blind stupidity, he had almost let her go.

No. Surely it wasn't too late. He wouldn't allow it to be too late.

Smiling now, a little grimly but filled with a sense of power and purpose, Nick picked up the phone to dial her number.

By the fourth ring, purpose had become impatience. By the seventh he was prowling the floor, ready to hurl the damned phone at the wall. On the ninth ring he came to a halt.

"Hello?" drawled a sultry woman's voice. "Who is it?"

"Dolores? Is that you? Where the hell have you been?"

"And good evening to you, too. I've been out, if it's any concern of yours."

Nick tried not to grind his teeth and failed. "This is Nick Malahide."

"Tammy's not here."

"When will she be back?" Not for the first time, Nick wondered what it was about Tamsin's roommate that so often got under his skin—even when she was trying to be helpful, which today she obviously wasn't.

Dolores took so long to answer he began to wonder if she'd hung up, but eventually she said guardedly, "Not for a while. She's away."

"Visiting her parents?"

When no answer was forthcoming, Nick snapped, "Never mind. It's none of my business. But she must have said when she'd be back."

"No, she didn't."

Nick scowled. If Dolores knew more than she was admitting, she certainly didn't mean to share her information with him. "All right. Thank you. I'll call back," he said, and slammed the phone back onto its stand.

If he'd stayed on the line one moment longer, he would have been tempted to tell Dolores, in words too explicit for tender ears, exactly what he thought of roommates who doubled as clams.

"Women," he growled, strumming his fingers on the desk. He thought for a moment, then once again picked up the phone, this time to call his accountant.

He and Richard Kerrigan had a lot more in common than Malahide's mismanaged books.

Tamsin, who was lying on the sofa with a newspaper over her face, heard Dolores hang up the phone and collapse into the rocking chair. She knew it was the rocker from its squeak. She no longer attempted to sit in it herself, because every time she did, Dolores found some way to make her give it up.

"That was Nick," Dolores said. "I told him you were away."

Tamsin sighed. "Thanks. That's why I didn't want to answer it."

"He'll call again, you know."

"I suppose so."

"Why not give the guy a chance? You know you want to."

"No, I don't. I'm not giving him what he wants just so

he can toss me out once he's got it."

Tamsin frowned as she heard her friend's slippered feet padding toward her across the carpet. A second later the newspaper was whisked off her face.

"You look terrible," Dolores pronounced after a cursory examination. "All blotchy and red. Anyway, even if you're right about Nick, does it matter so much if he throws you over? You'll have had a nice fling, and there are lots more fish—"

"Don't start with the cliches, Doro. Besides, that's not what you feel about Richard. I don't believe you ever thought of him as a fish." Tamsin sat up and rubbed her eyes.

Dolores turned away and began to fidget with a glittery rhinestone earring. "Everyone's entitled to make a fool of herself once," she said. "Richard was it for me."

Oh, dear. Tamsin bent down to pick up the newspaper her friend had dropped on the floor. Was Dolores turning back into the woman she had been before Richard? A good-time girl with a generous heart who had never quite understood that men could feel as deeply as women? Some men anyway.

"Right," Tamsin said. "And I guess Nick was it for me."

Dolores abandoned the earring. "He cares for you, Tammy. There's definitely something there—"

"Yes," Tamsin interrupted. "Something involving bedrooms and silk sheets and Nick Malahide getting exactly what he wants—the novelty of playing with a field mouse like me." She attempted to smooth the newspaper's crumpled pages. "Doro, thanks anyway. Thanks for trying to help."

"Sure. What are friends for?"

Tamsin gave up on the newspaper, swung her feet back

onto the sofa and placed a small velvet cushion over her face.

It was true. She was lucky to have a friend like Dolores. Some people had lovers. She had a friend. You could count on friends in a way you could never count on love.

She supposed that was some consolation.

On a cold, wet Saturday toward the end of November, Richard and Nick reached across their table at the *White Dragon* and solemnly shook hands.

"That's it then," Nick said. "We're agreed."

Richard nodded. "Here's to the ladies," he drawled, leaning back and raising his glass. "Who are made to be loved, not understood."

Nick laughed and called for the bill.

Richard raised his right hand, and the two men slapped their palms together in a familiar gesture of masculine solidarity.

"Brr!" Dolores pulled her purple parka up around her ears as she and Tamsin, clutching Styrofoam cups of hot chocolate, stepped out of the arena into an unrelenting wintery drizzle. "It's cold."

"And wet." Tamsin adjusted the collar of her own bulky parka. "I don't know why you insisted on dragging me to the hockey game again. Our guys always lose."

Dolores glanced doubtfully at her friend, who sounded unusually crabby tonight. Her face was very pale beneath the lamplight, and her gray eyes were dark and filled with sadness. She gave her a halfhearted nudge in the ribs. "It's good for you to get out. Let's face it, neither of us is great company these days."

"I guess not." Tamsin didn't seem to care.

"You can still go back to him, you know."

"Haven't we had this conversation before?" Tamsin snapped.

Oh dear, Tammy *was* in a bad mood. "Yes, I know, but you've been so down, I thought—"

Tamsin shook her head. "Don't. Please. It's been more than two weeks since you took that call from Nick, and now that I've been away from him for a while, I can see things even more clearly." Tamsin hugged her arms around her chest, and some of her hot chocolate spilled into a puddle. "The only reason he refused to accept my resignation was because the idea didn't come from him."

"You don't know that—" Dolores broke off as she caught sight of blond hair gleaming under the light just ahead of her. For a moment she thought it was Richard.

"Yes, I do." Tamsin's tired voice brought her back to reality. "I'm a dreamer, Doro. Nick's not. He's used to seeing what he wants and grabbing it. Right now he's probably grabbing Antoinette."

"I thought you told me he wanted a temp over fifty who—"

"He'll forget all about that when she flashes her cleavage."

Dolores tried to stifle a giggle and failed. It wasn't fair to laugh when Tammy was so unhappy. "Is *that* why you hired her?" she asked. "To convince yourself Nick hasn't changed?"

Tamsin took a sip of hot chocolate. "Maybe. I just know I can't go on working for him, dreaming of a home and children and his head on my pillow every morning—"

"Is that what you dream? I know the feeling." Dolores's sympathy was heartfelt. And, oh, she did know the feeling. Richard's head had been on her pillow one memorable morning. She had even, in her lowest moments, hoped a child would come as a result.

It hadn't happened. When she'd known for sure, for a short time she had wanted to cry. Then she'd reminded herself that Richard didn't really want her, that a relationship based on duty and obligation wasn't a relationship worth having.

Later, to prove to herself that she was able to surmount her worst fears, Dolores had gone back to the restaurant in the sky where she and Richard had not eaten, and taken the elevator to the top. She'd stayed there for several minutes before returning to the ground. She hadn't liked it, but she'd survived.

Somehow, in making that gesture, she'd managed to convince herself she would survive Richard too.

She jumped as the arena's doorman slammed the door shut behind them.

The two women began to walk toward the road, and she saw that Tamsin was watching her with a small, perceptive frown creasing her forehead. "Richard?" she asked. "You still feel the same then?"

Dolores sighed. Obviously she wasn't fooling Tammy. "Yes," she admitted. "And don't look at me like that. I'm as surprised as you are. The funny thing is, I keep thinking I see him, but when I look again, he isn't there."

"Really? You, too? I keep seeing Nick. Sometimes I'm sure he's real, and then he disappears. It's hell, isn't it?"

Dolores nodded. It was something like hell, she supposed. She wrapped her gloved hands around her cup, absorbing its warmth as they turned onto the well-lit sidewalk. The relentless drizzle hadn't let up all day, and the pavement beneath their feet was wet and slick.

"What are you going to do, Tammy?" she asked. "Your

vacation will be up in less than a week, and you know Nick will try to make you change your mind."

"Perhaps. Did Richard try to make you change yours?"

"That's not an answer. And, no, he didn't. So tell me what *you* mean to do."

"I don't know. Take another job. I've had a couple of offers already, but I was thinking of something completely different from Malahide's."

"Oh, sure. Completely different from what you're good at." Dolores stopped to look over her shoulder. "Funny, I could have sworn. . . . Never mind. You know what you need? What we both need? A proper vacation. Somewhere it doesn't rain."

"Who's going to pay for it? I'm out of a job, remember?"

"Not for long from the sounds of it. And, anyway, what are savings for?"

"Retirement. Getting old. Feeding the cat." Tamsin sounded so glum that Dolores burst out laughing. She stopped when Tamsin added even more gloomily, "Besides, you can't leave your clinic."

"Of course I can. That's the beauty of a partnership." She wiped a raindrop absently off her nose. "I can take a month off, and Yoko and Anya will cover for me. They'll be glad of the extra business."

Tamsin came to a stop beneath the sheltering boughs of a fir tree growing in a garden close to the sidewalk. She drained the last of her hot chocolate and crushed the cup in one hand.

"I can't, Doro. Really, it's not the right time for me to go away."

But Dolores, now that she had the idea between her teeth, wasn't about to let it go. She felt a lightening of her spirits at last, a stirring of the first genuine excitement she'd experienced since the day her parents died. She had thought she was adjusting, learning to accept what she couldn't change, and yet everything since that terrible day—everything except Richard—had seemed so dreary, so pointless in a way. She had gone to work, chatted cheerfully with her clients, but it had been empty chat, engaged in for business, not pleasure.

In the evenings and on weekends she hadn't wanted to date and had spent most of her time sitting at home with Tamsin.

With more time to think than she was used to, she had also begun to understand, at last, how betrayed some of the men she had been out with must have felt when she brushed them off. It wasn't a good feeling. No wonder Richard had rejected her. In a way, his attitude had taught her something, and for that she supposed she should be grateful.

She wasn't though. She was hurt. How could she be otherwise?

"A complete change is exactly what we *both* need," she said, turning to Tamsin with unexpected urgency. "Come on, let's run the rest of the way home, I want to look at those maps I've been collecting in case they turned out to be useful. What do you think of Hawaii? Or Mazatlan? Or Australia?"

Tamsin didn't get much chance to think of anything, because Dolores seized both their empty cups, flung them into a litter bin on the corner and, grabbing Tamsin's hand, began to run with her along the slippery sidewalk. A carload of teenagers passing by honked a horn and shouted encouragement. Two men in a Lincoln saw them and exchanged glances, and a policewoman in a cruiser eyed them suspiciously but didn't stop.

By the time the two young women staggered up the steps

to their front porch, it had stopped raining, and both of them were laughing hysterically.

Mrs. Sawchuk stuck her head out the window, saw who it was and exhaled a long stream of smoke. "Stupid girls," she muttered, before snapping the window shut.

If she had waited just a few seconds longer, she would have seen two tall figures dressed in black jeans, black leather jackets, black boots and black leather gloves stroll silently up the path and try the door.

Chapter Fourteen

"The damn roof's leaking again." Dolores groaned when she reached the top of the stairs and heard the steady drip of water on wood. "Guess what, Tammy, we're having another flood."

"We shouldn't have gone out," said Tamsin, who hadn't wanted to go to the game in the first place.

"Oh, sure, we ought to stay home every time it rains and wait for the next bit of our apartment to fall off. That's a great idea." Shaking her head, Dolores hurried into the kitchen to fetch a bucket, discovered it was covered in rust and came back brandishing two battered saucepans.

Tamsin pointed at an untidy pile of papers in the corner. "So much for your maps," she said. "They're soaked."

Dolores groaned again and ran to rescue her property. Tamsin grabbed the saucepans from her hand and put one under the nearest leak and the other on Dolores's bed.

It wasn't until she ran into her own bedroom to check for leaks and divest herself of her parka that she came upon the two intruders in black.

One was standing in the center of the floor in a pool of moonlight. The other had one booted foot slung over her windowsill and was easing himself into the room as if it were his standard mode of entrance.

Tamsin screamed.

"Hold it, darlin'. It's only us." Instinctively Nick took a step toward her. The sight of her small, frightened figure huddled in a parka that seemed too big for her filled him with a wash of guilt and tenderness the likes of which he'd never known before. He hadn't meant to scare her, wanted only to look after her. . . .

"Tammy, what is it?" Dolores, clutching an armful of wet paper, charged into the room like a tigress in defense of her cub. "Has—?" She stopped as Nick stepped into the light. "Oh. It's you."

"Yes. Sorry. I wasn't trying to assault her." He jerked his head at the window, through which Richard had now fully emerged. "Delivery for you."

When Dolores let out a gasp that might have been surprise but sounded more like the preliminary to a tirade, Nick moved across the room to take Tamsin in his arms.

At first she resisted his embrace, then gradually, when her body lost its rigidity, he touched a finger to her chin and raised her head.

"Nick," she said. Her voice was low and surprisingly neutral, as if she were neither pleased nor displeased to see him.

"Yes, it's me," he agreed, and would have kissed her right then if Dolores hadn't picked that moment to drop her wet papers onto the carpet and snap, "Out! Both of you, get out. Now. You've no right—"

Nick turned in time to see her raise a fist and aim it at Richard's chest.

Richard caught it and returned it firmly to her side. "That's no way to treat your future husband," he said mildly.

"I don't have a future husband. I don't want one. Besides, I'd be no good at being a wife."

"Oh, I don't know. Seems to me you'd do well at anything you put your mind to. Now if I could just persuade you to put it to loving me. . . ."

"Richard Kerrigan, I told you to get out." Dolores didn't attempt to hit him this time but pointed imperiously at the window. "The way you came in will do just fine."

Richard glanced at the window and then back at her. "As a matter of fact we'd have settled on the door if it hadn't been locked—and if we hadn't been in danger of landing Mrs. Sawchuk in our net."

Nick choked into his fist, and Tamsin took advantage of his distraction to break away.

"Please leave," she said, adding her quiet voice to her friend's.

Nick looked down at her and thought she looked utterly adorable with her hands on her hips and her soft eyes commanding compliance.

Tamsin, gazing up at him, thought he looked virile, expensive and somehow untouchable dressed all in black and with his green eyes darkened by the moonlight. Yet his face seemed thinner, almost gaunt, and he carried himself as if he were about to crack.

Richard, on the other hand, appeared as cool and impassive as ever, apart from a twitching muscle below his left eye.

"Kerrigan," Nick said, "let's get on with it."

As Tamsin gaped up at him, she heard Dolores let out a squawk. The next moment one of Nick's arms was under her hips, the other under her shoulders, and he was carrying her into the living room like a prize captured in battle—or a bridegroom bearing his bride across the threshold.

She was almost disappointed when he set her down.

Seconds later Dolores was deposited without ceremony beside her. It was immediately obvious that disappointment was not her friend's uppermost emotion.

"If you two don't get out this minute, I'll call the police," she announced, starting toward the phone. As she did so, a drop of water landed on her head.

"Better call flood-control first," Richard advised.

Dolores swung around to glare at him, but when a second drop landed on her shoulder, she muttered something Tamsin couldn't hear and went to call the landlord. They heard her tell his machine that the roof was floating away with Mrs. Sawchuk and that, by the way, two masked crooks had just broken into the apartment. On that parting shot, she marched into the kitchen to find another pan.

Behind her, Tamsin heard a snort.

"We're not actually masked," Richard said.

"No, but it makes a better story—and it might just get our landlord to move. He's protective about his property." Dolores came back with the pan, put it under the latest drip and went to stand beside Tamsin. "All right, out with it. What's this all about? I suppose you two won't leave till you've said what you came to say."

"I always knew you were a fast learner," Richard approved.

"She'd better be." Nick glanced at his watch. "Time's running out. That hockey game lasted longer than we expected."

"Then let's not waste any more time. Dolores. . . ." He turned to face the woman who was looking at him as if she were contemplating dumping the nearest pan of water over his head. "Dolores, will you marry me?"

"No," said Dolores.

Nick reached for Tamsin's hand and brought it to his lips. "Tamsin, will you marry me?" he asked.

"No," said Tamsin, though with less conviction than her friend.

"We thought that's what you'd say." Nick nodded at

Richard as if he were pleased to be proved right. "Okay, let's get going."

Dolores said, "What the—" as Tamsin blinked. The next moment she was once again being borne aloft in Nick's arms. When she twisted her head, she saw that Dolores was in a similar situation in Richard's arms.

Then somehow, to the accompaniment of a few muttered grunts from the men as they maneuvered their burdens down the stairs, they were all outside on the porch.

Tamsin, dazed with shock, gazed groggily up at Nick's face. She felt the strength of his arms beneath her rib cage and the warmth of his body penetrating all her layers of clothing.

As they reached the sidewalk, she began to feel something more. At first she wasn't sure what it was, but when the pale rays of a streetlight fell across Nick's shoulders and he shifted her weight to hold her more securely, it dawned on her that what she felt was hope.

Nick had come for her. And the rain had stopped.

In all the lonely weeks without him, when she had tried so hard to convince herself she had been right to turn her back on Malahide's, she had dreamed that one day he would come. Even knowing the grief and heartache that would surely follow, she had dreamed. . . .

Dolores's long hair was hanging over Richard's arm, and she was wriggling furiously, yelling at him in words that carried clearly through the night exactly what she thought of arrogant, impossible men who thought they owned the world.

Richard only laughed. He had a nice laugh, Tamsin thought. Not as nice as Nick's though.

Somewhere behind them a man's voice shouted, "Hang on, ladies, help's coming."

Automatically Tamsin started to call out her thanks. But, to her confusion, Dolores shouted back, "Don't worry. We're fine. It's these gorillas who are going to find out they're in trouble."

"Do you agree with that, darlin'?" Nick asked.

Hearing his beloved voice, deep, teasing and sorely missed, Tamsin found herself suppressing an imprudent and entirely unexpected urge to laugh. "Not altogether," she said. "And you'd better put me down before I tell that man not to listen to Dolores."

"Right." Nick tipped her onto the sidewalk beside the Lincoln which was parked conveniently by the curb. "Anything you say."

Once again Tamsin was speechless. Beside her, Dolores, her face beneath the streetlight a startling shade of furious pink, was for once also bereft of words.

It wasn't until she found herself deposited gently on the passenger seat beside Nick, with Dolores and Richard in the back, that Tamsin came to her senses and reached for the door handle.

Glancing sideways, she saw that Dolores was engaged in a similar maneuver in the back.

Nick leaned over and snapped her seat belt into place. Another snap indicated that Dolores's attempt to escape had met with a similar setback.

Tamsin reached over to unsnap her belt, but flinched when her hand touched Nick's thigh.

His only reaction was to remove her frantically scrabbling fingers from the handle and, with his free hand, turn the key in the ignition. The next moment he had the car in gear and they were speeding down the block.

As Tamsin struggled for words, it occurred to her that Dolores had gone uncharacteristically quiet. She started to speak, then thought better of it.

Something was going on here that she didn't understand. Nick had always been high-handed, but to the best of her knowledge he had never stooped to kidnapping before. And, until now, Richard had struck her as a gentleman in every way that counted.

They had crossed the Oak Street Bridge before it dawned on her that they were heading for the airport.

Tamsin gripped her hands in her lap. "Nick," she gasped. "Where are you taking us? There's nothing out here except the airport."

"Don't worry, Tammy." Dolores, sounding unusually breathless, suddenly found her voice. "These two pirates needn't think they're getting away with this."

"I thought we were gorillas," Richard said. "And I might point out that I just got away with a very nice kiss."

Oh. That explained Dolores's unusual silence.

An indignant exclamation from the back, abruptly curtailed, seemed to indicate that Richard was getting away with rather more.

Nick patted Tamsin's knee. "My turn next," he said.

Tamsin, feeling suddenly warm, wriggled along the seat until her body was pressed up against the door. "What do you mean?" she asked. "Where *are* you taking us?"

"On our honeymoon, darlin'. We figured it was the only way to convince you we meant business, since you were both so sure we were after nothing but bed and breakfast."

"And we didn't want to bore you," Richard added from the back.

Tamsin heard a thumping sound, followed by a grunt and then silence.

"Our honeymoon?" Tamsin eyed Nick's impassive profile with suspicion. "Doro, did you hear that? I think these two have lost their minds."

"Could be," Dolores responded in a choked voice. "Or maybe they're just hoping we've forgotten that the honeymoon comes *after* the wedding."

"Just so you know," Nick said, "we took the precaution of engaging the services of a marriage commissioner. She'll marry us at once if you say the word."

He pulled the car to a stop, and immediately a man Tamsin recognized from Malahide's workshop came up to take the keys Nick handed him.

When Nick and Richard jumped out to open the doors, the two women, having little option, allowed themselves to be helped onto the concrete.

As the Lincoln was driven away, the men gravely shook hands.

Dolores threw them a disgusted look. "What do you think you're celebrating?" she demanded. "Tammy and I haven't said we're going anywhere with you."

"They went to a lot of trouble though, didn't they?" Tamsin said. "We might as well let them tell us what they had in mind."

Dolores cast a dubious eye at the airport terminal building. "All right. I suppose we can't come to too much harm with half the inhabitants of three continents crashing around with luggage in there. If you're sure you want to hear them out, that is."

"Yes, I am." All at once Tamsin was as sure as she'd been of anything in her life. She wanted to hear what Nick had to say.

"Fine," Dolores said. She turned to Richard, who was holding her wrist as if he expected her to make a run for it. "You can let go, Bluebeard. I'm not going anywhere for now."

"Good." Richard grinned, but when Dolores looked closely, she saw thin lines running between his nose and mouth that hadn't been there before. His hair, longer than usual, seemed darker than she remembered it, too.

She looked away, suddenly overcome with a great longing to touch him. She knew she had to resist it.

When she realized that Nick and Tamsin were already heading for the terminal, she hurried to catch up.

Richard was right behind her.

The International Departures level hummed with all the usual airport noises. Tearful good-byes, children crying, baggage wheels squeaking and people talking loudly in a dozen different tongues.

"Not the most private place for a serious discussion," Nick remarked. "But it'll have to do. Our flight leaves in under an hour."

"Serious?" said Dolores, heading for an empty table at the edge of the food court. "You call this crazy situation serious?"

"No, but the reason behind it is." Richard hooked his thumbs into the pockets of his black jeans, fingers splayed explicitly on his thighs.

Dolores unzipped her parka and sat down rather suddenly in the nearest chair. Tamsin took the seat beside her, and the two men lowered themselves into the two remaining seats.

"Are you telling us this farce wasn't just something you and Nick cooked up for a change of pace?" she said. "Some kind of macho love game—or a way to amuse yourselves on a rainy day?"

"We had to do something to get your attention," Nick replied. He pinned a bleak eye on a passing teenager with royal blue hair and a network of studs in his eyebrows.

"You have our attention," Tamsin said drily.

Nick glanced at Richard. "You first," he said.

"Okay." Richard hooked his arms over the back of his seat. "For my part, the object of this exercise was to prove to you, Dolores mine, that I won't be tossed off like a pair of old boots. I'm not sure why you handed me my walking papers—habit, maybe. But, as you can see, I decided not to walk."

"But you did walk," Dolores pointed out.

"Only temporarily. Once I'd cooled down, I realized I needed time to figure out exactly what I wanted. And what to do about it."

"But—I thought you wanted to break off with me. Was—was I wrong?" Barely conscious that she was doing it, oblivious to the fact that she and Richard were speaking in front of an interested audience of two friends and a dozen or so spectators at nearby tables, Dolores crossed her fingers and slid them into her lap.

Richard, also ignoring their audience, caught the motion, saw her eyes darken and heard the tremor of doubt in her voice. In that moment the gnawing ache that had burdened his days and disrupted his nights since the last time he held her in his arms dissolved like darkness with the coming of dawn.

He vowed then that whether Dolores knew it yet or not, she had broken her last heart.

Nick stood up and held out his hand to Tamsin. "Let's give these two some privacy," he said. Then, turning to Richard he added, "You've got fifteen minutes. After that we'll be back."

Tamsin took his hand and rose without a word.

Richard watched them wander off toward the airport's showpiece, native artist, Bill Reid's famous bronze sculpture, *Spirit of Haida Gwaii.* Then he turned back to Dolores.

"Yes," he said, looking into her eyes. "You were wrong. But as I hadn't admitted it to myself at the time, I can hardly blame you for thinking what you did."

When Dolores's beautiful face lit up with a smile that nearly knocked him off his seat, Richard stood up, came around the table and lifted her out of her chair.

"What happened to the man who objected to making love in public?" Dolores asked as he sat down again and pulled her onto his lap.

"He met a woman named Dolores, and after a while he didn't care where he made love." Wasting no further time, Richard bent his head to capture her lips in a kiss that made the four people at the next table abandon their plates of stir-fried vegetables and rice in order to gape.

Some time later, when it became necessary to start breathing again, Richard ran a finger down Dolores's nose and asked, "Do you think we can start again? From the beginning?"

Dolores caught his hand and held it against her heart. "At the beginning you were a battle-scarred body on my massage table. Of course, I knew the moment you walked into the clinic that you were meant to be mine, though I did my best to convince myself that my interest was purely professional."

"Is that a yes? You'll marry me?"

To his consternation, she hesitated, and when she lowered her eyes and murmured, "I'm not a bit like Elizabeth," he wanted to shout his frustration loudly enough to shatter the skylight above their heads.

"I loved Elizabeth," he said in as calm a voice as he could muster. "But that doesn't mean I want you to be like her. It's you I want, Dolores. *You.* Because I love you."

"Oh." Dolores put her arms around his neck and buried her face in the soft black leather stretched across his shoulders. "I didn't know."

She meant it. She honestly meant it. Richard, overwhelmed by tenderness for this beautiful, courageous, confused young woman who was soon to be his wife, wasted no further time on words but wrapped her in his arms and held her tight. He swore then, silently and with passion, and to whatever deity might be listening, that he would love, honor and protect Dolores Rowan, now and for the rest of his life.

He didn't say so out loud, because he had no doubt she would tell him she was quite capable of protecting herself.

Nick and Tamsin stood side by side gazing at the amazing sculpture of the jade canoe and its extraordinary crew. Their hands on the railing around it didn't touch.

"*Haida Gwaii.* Islands of the Haida People," Tamsin murmured. "It's beautiful in its way, isn't it?"

"Yes, if a canoe-load of mythical creatures rowing to nowhere is your conception of beauty." Nick glanced briefly at the stylized raven steering the canoe, then back at Tamsin's solemn face. "We haven't time to discuss art now," he said.

"You keep talking about time." Tamsin pinned her gaze on a jade green wolf biting an eagle. "Time for what, Nick?"

"Time to catch our honeymoon flight."

Tamsin frowned and stepped away from him as if he'd suggested she make love to him on the spot. Nick saw her fists curl around the rail and her soft mouth tighten with indignation.

Hell. He'd raised all her hackles. And still she didn't trust him. With difficulty Nick stifled a groan. Had he done this all wrong? In his imaginings she had turned warm and melting and sweet, ready to fall into his arms. Instead she was defiant, just as she had been the day she left his office.

It was his fault. He shouldn't have forced the issue. But it was too late now. He might as well proceed as he had planned.

"I thought women were supposed to be the romantic ones," he said. "I can't provide candlelight and wine—at least not right now—but I hoped a honeymoon in Hawaii might do the trick."

"What are you talking about?" Although she continued to frown, Tamsin relaxed her grip slightly on the rail.

Nick attempted a smile. "For the second time, I'm asking you to marry me, Tamsin Brown. For better, for worse and even at the airport, if you like. Does that make me crazy?"

Tamsin turned to face him, and he met her gaze steadily, attempting to transmit the message his flippant proposal might not have conveyed.

"No," she said, her eyes so filled with doubt that he wanted to take her in his arms and promise her the stars. "I don't think you're crazy. Why do you want to marry me, Nick?"

She looked so sad and lost in her big blue parka that Nick felt an unexpected pain in his chest, as if his heart had turned turtle and was helplessly waiting for her to right it.

He said, "Because I can't go through the rest of my life without you, that's why."

"And?" Tamsin urged.

Nick pushed his fingers through his hair, not caring if it looked like a haystack. He took a deep breath. "And I love you. Is that what you've been waiting for me to say?"

Tamsin closed her eyes. "Only if you mean it. All those

years, all those women . . . don't misunderstand me, Nick, but I didn't think you knew how to love."

Nick braced himself against the railing. There wasn't much left to misunderstand. Not that he blamed her for doubting him. It was true he hadn't believed in any kind of love meant to last. Now, because of her, his little beige field mouse, he did.

"All those women?" he said. "There weren't nearly as many as you think. And they meant nothing. Because I didn't know that what I wanted, what I *needed,* was right under my nose in the next office. There's never been anyone for me but you, my darlin' field mouse."

He waited, holding his breath. When she didn't answer, he felt as if the earth had collapsed beneath his feet. Without Tamsin he was rudderless, lost, without a reason for being.

"Am I too late then?" He was unable to keep the roughness from his voice. "Or is there any chance you might feel the same?"

All at once Tamsin's unnatural stillness shattered like ice with the coming of spring, and her face broke into a smile bright enough to warm a summer day. Even the solemn green faces of the canoe's straining rowers seemed to lighten.

"You're not too late," she whispered, as if she had lost the power to raise her voice. "I love you, Nick. Probably I always have. But I didn't come close to knowing it until that day you found me crying behind the curtains."

Nick heard the hiss of his own breath as he released it. He held out his hands. "If I'd known that at the time, I'd probably have left those curtains closed," he admitted ruefully. "I'm glad I didn't."

"So am I." Tamsin caught his outstretched fingers, and

he drew her very gently against his chest. "And to think," she murmured, "that I used to tell Dolores you were just another hopeless male."

"But that's what I am," Nick said. "Hopelessly in love with you." He pulled her head onto his shoulder. "I won't be easy to live with, Tamsin darlin'. I've been doing things my own way for too long to change any time soon. Do you think you'll be able to bear it?"

Tamsin looped her arms around his neck. "I bore it quite nicely for the five years I worked at Malahide's," she reminded him. "Nick. . . . ?"

"Mm?" He ran a hand over her hair. He'd forgotten how soft and sweet-smelling it was.

"If we've just become engaged, and I think we have, do you suppose you could possibly stop talking and kiss me?"

Nick made a growling noise in the back of his throat and wrapped her so closely in his arms that he wasn't sure either of them would ever breathe again. Not that it seemed to matter in this moment of unbelievable relief.

A small crowd of hurrying travelers paused briefly in their dash for the departure lounge. Their smiling glances moved from the couple embracing beside *Haida Gwaii* to the other couple kissing at a table in the food court.

"Cupid's busy today," remarked a cherub-faced man with a white beard. "If I'd known he'd set up shop in Vancouver Airport, I'd have brought my friend, Martha, along. She's been refusing to marry me for years."

The crowd laughed and eventually drifted away.

"Here's Mrs. Mumford with the luggage," Nick said with approval as the four of them approached the check-in counter.

Dolores said, "What luggage? Oh, heavens, we don't have any. Tammy—"

"Keep your shirt on—at least temporarily." Richard grinned. "We're way ahead of you."

"Who's Mrs. Mumford?" Tamsin asked.

"Mrs. Mumford is my new temp," Nick explained. "She's replacing the dreaded Antoinette until the efficient Ms. Brown—or should I say the new Mrs. Malahide?—returns to take her rightful place in my office. Mrs. Mumford also happens to be very good at packing suitcases for ladies who don't have any luggage."

"You thought of everything, didn't you?" Tamsin wasn't sure whether to laugh or hit him, so in the end she decided to kiss him.

"There's one other thing we thought of," Richard said. "That large lady standing over by the tie shop is a marriage commissioner. She's agreed to marry us before we leave. It'll be a bit rushed, but—"

Stunned, Tamsin looked over at Dolores. So Nick had been serious when he'd talked about getting married right away. Funny, it didn't seem urgent any more.

"I always thought if I ever got married it would be in a church," she said uncertainly. "With my mom and dad there. And Susie."

Dolores took one look at her friend's face, and said, "We don't have to do it here, Tammy."

"But the honeymoon. . . ."

"There's no law that says we can't have the honeymoon before the wedding." She looked up at Richard, who was smiling down at her with so much love in his eyes that she couldn't believe she'd ever thought he didn't care. "Not if you trust the man you're going to marry."

Tamsin stared at her, then she, too, began to smile. "I

hadn't thought of that," she admitted. "I guess I've got so used to mistrusting Nick's motives that it never occurred to me—" She broke off when Nick pulled her roughly against his side. "I don't mistrust you any more," she assured him. "Doro, you're right. Why don't we get married in the spring when . . . ?"

She never got to finish her sentence, because the next moment she was practically smothered in Nick's arms.

"Thank you, field mouse," he said in a voice so choked with emotion that at first she wasn't sure she'd heard him right. "We'll be married whenever and wherever you like. Just so long as it's forever."

"I'll second that," Richard said softly. He raised a hand to the grinning marriage commissioner and shook his head.

Minutes later, after checking the luggage collected from a beaming Mrs. Mumford, the four of them made their way toward the plane that would carry them to sunshine and their future.

Epilogue

The limousine containing two brides, four bridesmaids and one father and mother of the bride purred gently up the hill toward the church. "I can't wait to see Nick's face," Tamsin said. "He'll be so surprised."

Dolores adjusted the pale ivory skirt of her wedding dress and consciously repressed any tendency to self pity. "Yes," she agreed. "He will."

Tamsin, attuned to her friend's moods, at once caught the note of restraint. "I'm sorry," she said. "You're missing your family today, aren't you?"

"My parents, yes, of course. I didn't ask the rest of them." She tugged at her veil until it partially covered her face. "They wouldn't have come anyway."

"*We're* here for you." Richard's sisters, Janet and Joanna, chorused in unison from the opposite seat.

"And you've lots of friends," offered Tamsin's plump and kindly cousin, Susie.

Sally, the receptionist from Malahide's, added with youthful lack of tact, "As long as the bridegroom shows up, you're in business."

"Naturally he'll be there." Tamsin's mother, unusually festive in a bottle green suit with gold buttons, frowned reprovingly at Sally.

"Yes, indeed," Mr. Brown echoed dutifully. "Wouldn't want to miss his own wedding."

Nobody argued, and moments later the limo drew up in front of the church to disgorge its passengers in a flurry of ivory silk, yellow roses and primrose-colored lace. As they wound their way up the path toward the turn-of-the-century brick church, the solemn sounds of organ music drifted to greet them across sun-dappled grass.

There wasn't much solemnity, though, about the bustling and shuffling that went on once they reached the vestibule.

Tamsin's father, smiling proudly, took her arm. She gave him a quick nudge, and at once he seized Dolores's arm as well.

Dolores smiled bravely. Kind as it was of Mr. Brown, she would have given a lot to have someone of her own to walk her down the aisle.

Tamsin, understanding, leaned over and whispered, "They're here with you in spirit. I know they are. I can feel them."

"Yes." Dolores nodded. How could she believe otherwise when her friend's earnest gray eyes were so filled with sympathy and affection? Of course her parents were here—in the echoing music, in the rays of soft light shining through the stained glass windows, and always, always in her heart—no longer with pain, but as cherished memories.

The sound of footsteps hurrying up the path pulled her mind back to the present. Why was Tamsin looking at her with that secret little smile curling her lips?

Dolores turned as a new face appeared in the vestibule. A dear, kind face she hadn't seen in years.

"Harry!" she whispered. "Oh, Harry. Is it really you?"

Her favorite cousin, grinning from ear to ear, admitted that it was. "I've come to give you away," he announced. "Margaret and the kids are here, too. And Kitty and Joan and—"

"David and Lorraine," Dolores gasped, for the first time

taking in the beaming collection of cousins gathered on the brides' side of the church. "Oh, Harry, you came. All of you came! I didn't think you would."

"I know. That's what your Richard said. That you wouldn't invite us because you didn't think we'd come. So he invited us—and here we are."

"Oh, Harry," Dolores said again. She rubbed her silk sleeve vigorously across her brimming eyes.

"Hey, hey," Harry said, "we can't have the bride crying on her wedding day."

"Oh, but they're happy tears," she assured him. "Richard's family is here, you see. I didn't think there'd be anyone for me."

She gazed down the aisle to where Richard and Nick stood tall and imposing before the altar. Richard's partner, Mark, and Bill McCrosky, who was Nick's best man, stood stiffly self-conscious beside them.

Richard turned to smile at her then, and when she saw the love and triumph beaming from his eyes, she wanted to run to him and fling herself into his arms right there and then. She contented herself with blowing him a kiss.

His smile turned into a grin, and he blew one back.

Just then someone else pushed through the doorway, and this time when they turned to see who the latecomer was, Tamsin was the one who cried out.

"Oh," she exclaimed. "Dennis! You're so like Nick. I thought for a moment you weren't going to make it in time."

"Plane was late getting in," explained the man who looked like a darker, shorter version of Nick. "You must be Tamsin."

"Yes," she said. "Nick said he couldn't expect his brother to fly halfway around the world for his wedding.

But I knew you would. That's why I asked you. Oh, he *will* be so pleased. And surprised."

"Yeah," Dennis said. "Guess I'm the only family he has left." He paused, cleared his throat and added gruffly, "Until you."

The organist began to play faster and louder, and Tamsin said, "I think he wants us to get started. Dennis, you'd better go and join Nick. Bill knows you're coming. He was so relieved he wouldn't have to be best man and make a speech."

Dennis smiled and, to the accompaniment of puzzled whispers from the congregation, strode down the aisle to join his brother.

At first Tamsin could tell Nick didn't believe it. She watched a little anxiously until she saw the dawning of realization in his eyes. His glorious lips parted then in the smile that had captured her heart so many months before.

While the congregation murmured, Bill slid discreetly into a pew beside his wife, Marriette, who pursed her lips as if she'd just swallowed vinegar.

Briefly, Nick met Tamsin's loving gaze. He shook his head, and she felt a stab of alarm. Hadn't she done the right thing in bringing Dennis? Then he mouthed, "Thank you. I love you," and she knew she had.

The music slowed, then soared into the familiar march announcing the approach of the brides.

Dolores and Tamsin looked at each other and smiled. Then, together, they began the slow walk down the aisle to marry the men they loved.